shades of

white

Dedication.

To my very patient wife - Elaine

who was the

chief proof reader, editor and tea maker.

Preface

My Father, God rest his soul, was a mathematician all of his life and he could see number patterns in everything. Where others saw chaos he could see a set of numbers. As I grew up I never noticed his obsession with numbers and just took his teachings as the type of things all parents give their children. To me it was normal to be doing maths anytime and everywhere. That is probably why at school my only O'level (GCSE in today's currency!) was in Mathematics. Dad must have been so proud of me.

Even during my early adulthood I never appreciated my Father's obsession with numbers. Everyone around him just accepted it as Dad's strange ways. It wasn't until much later in my life that I started to see the patterns that Dad, for the whole of his life, could always see. Most people will see these patterns as just coincidences but to me the more the coincidence happened the more it made me aware of how that particular number affects and interacts with my every day life.

Now in my early 60's I not only look out for MY particular numbers but sometimes make important decisions using my numbers as a reference.

Most people see Friday the 13th as an unlucky day. To me it is one of my favourite and luckiest days of the year.

I was born on Friday the 13th and consequently it helped me decide on the date I wanted to retire on. People have since often asked me if I had inside information as my retirement happened just 10 days before the country shut down for the pandemic. I had actually requested that date six months before the world had even heard of Covid so no; I didn't have inside information, but my numbers helped dictate that date.

Two major numbers in my life are 17 and 27. These are numbers that I just keep seeing everywhere and they confirm to me that

that is the right direction or the right choice for me to make. Both my homes while living in Chester have been at number 17 and although both my homes in Scunthorpe were not at number 17 my family grew up in houses at number 11 and number 6 respectively (you can do your own sums here!!!).

Often these numbers just appear as if by magic. Most of you reading this will laugh and think of this as just superstition or this is something I am just making up. To me nowadays it is so real and my numbers are very important to how I live my life. I think now, just like my Father, I know what MY numbers are and so I regularly and easily recognise them everywhere around me.

I was never an academic and so I left school at the earliest opportunity with my single O'level in Mathematics. I gained an apprenticeship with a National Refrigeration company based in South Wales and worked for them for a total of 17 years. I then secured a position with a Global manufacturer and worked for them for 27 years.

This equates to a working career spanning a total of **44** years. From the very first day that I started my working life until the last day before I retired I had worn every **Shade of** coloured overall you could ever think of. Incredibly, I actually started and finished my working life in **White** overalls!

Book One

Part One - Scunthorpe Steelworks

Part Two - Coming Out

By Terry Freeman

Part One

'Scunthorpe Steelworks'

Part Two

'Coming Out'

Part One

- Scunthorpe Steelworks -

Chapter 1

'In The Beginning'

"WHITE !!!, are you sure they want White"

"You're going on a dirty steelworks to work. Why on earth would they want you to have white overalls?"

This was my mums reaction when I received my offer of employment with a Refrigeration Company at the very start of my working life. I was 16 years old, not yet left school (I still had my one 'O' level in mathematics to take) and I was trying to be a confident, independent adult. I even had my own set of wheels in the form of my "trusty" moped and with my fellow 'bikers' I had managed to travel everywhere around Lincolnshire on it, including job interviews, near and far.

So let me now take you back to 2 weeks earlier when I had attended an interview that would change my life forever..........

On this particular Thursday in May I had been given two job interviews on the same day. One in the morning with a large engineering firm in Gainsborough about 15 miles from my home and the other closer to home in Scunthorpe with a Refrigeration company based on the Scunthorpe Steelworks.

Most people have heard of the steel town of Scunthorpe. This was mainly from being the butt of most jokes including the Mobil's petrol advert from the 1970's based on the Gene Pitney "24 hours from Tulsa" where a driver collecting loyalty points sings that he is "24 toasters from Scunthorpe...". A lot of my friends at the time didn't like the way Scunthorpe was made fun of but I for one was happy the way we were made famous. I've always believed that there is no such thing as bad advertising. If it gets people talking about a product etc. then it has already sunk into their psyche and they are more likely to remember the name than other 'nice' advertisements.

Anyway, I lived in a little village called Messingham about 4 miles to the south of Scunthorpe. Our postal address was always 'Near Scunthorpe' so we all classed ourselves as Scunthopians. Messingham had a great village community spirit but like most villages you needed transport to get anywhere. This is where my trusty little moped was a godsend to me and my friends all felt the same about their mopeds when they became old enough to own motorised transport.

Once I was 16 I was out with my friends riding everywhere. We would spent hours going to the sea side for fish and chips. Then we would just turn around and spend more hours getting home along busy main roads. We would be aware of the very long tailbacks behind us, full of very frustrated and annoyed drivers, all trying to get past us, but we were going as fast as we could. We could only go as fast as the slowest member of our 'gang' and although I was slow I was not the slowest. Only just!!!!

My bright yellow trusty steed was usually quite reliable and got me to where I wanted most of the time. However on this particular rainy Thursday in May 1976 it decided I was not going to get to my interviews unscathed.

My first interview of the day was at Roses engineering works in Gainsborough and was scheduled for 11am that morning. Although it was only 15 miles away, on a moped that is only capable of a top speed of 30mph (downhill with a back wind !!!), I needed to allow plenty of time to get there. Therefore I set off with plenty of time to spare. I wanted enough time to not only get there but find where the interview was. In the days before the internet and Googles own 'street view', you could not explore other towns and cities in the comfort of your own home, all I had was a map book and the instructions in my letter from Roses Engineering.

The rain was gentle but persistent as I set out but it was obvious to everyone but a 16 year old that the rain was never going to help my image for an interview. Wearing a suit on a moped in the rain was never a good idea in the first place. Yes I had my yellow plastic Mac on, which matched the colour of my moped to a T, but being 16 meant I knew it all and no-one could tell me otherwise. No matter how many times my mother offered to take me in the car, I refused to accept assistance. In my mind I was old enough to make my own mind up and wanted to show how independent I could be.

5 miles into my journey and already soaking wet, my moped decided to splutter to a halt. In those days most engines didn't like the damp and my moped decided to follow suit and die a slow wet death at the side of a busy road. I hadn't noticed the big puddle near me when I stopped. I didn't even notice it while I looked closely at the engine trying to get some life back into the little 50 cc engine. I'm sure the large juggernaut going round me didn't even feel the water under its wheels but I certainly felt the cold shower I received as the spray of water drenched me. Great! Now I am not only wet through and my suit was ruined but it was highly unlikely I would be able to get to my interview.

In the days before mobile phones were even a dream in some boffins head, it took me well over an hour in more torrential rainfall to push my moped back home. Thankfully my exploits in the morning just made me more determined to make the interview with the Refrigeration company in the afternoon. After a long soak in the bath with my favourite rubber duck and the smartest "dry" clothes I could find in my 70's wardrobe, I found myself on a bus into Scunthorpe telling a very amused bus conductor of my adventures in the rain. Even I could see the funny side of it by then, and my disastrous morning probably helped me portray an air of confidence and determination to do well in my interview.

Two weeks later I received the letter in the post offering me an apprenticeship with the Refrigeration Company called Kenyon. Based in Pontardawe near Swansea, they had several branches all over the country and the Scunthorpe branch mainly looked after all the air conditioning units around the Scunthorpe Steelworks. In those days there was no such thing as the internet. There was no email, social media or any form of easy, instant or even quick form of communication. You either wrote a letter and sent it on 'snail mail', which is what we called the Royal Mail when the internet came along, or you picked up a landline telephone to talk to someone. All of this means that it can take quite a while to communicate. In our present day of easy communication we forget how job offers would often take several weeks to arrive after an interview. As my job offer arrived only two weeks after my soggy interview I was encouraged to think they were keen to take me on. I was very excited to think I was going to be earning some money and was looking forward to upgrading my moped to something with a bit more power and reliability.

I wrote my acceptance letter and like Harry Potter in Diagon Alley concentrated on my list of necessary purchases I needed before I could attend the Hogwarts of Refrigeration. After all, where do you get a pair of White Overalls from?

When you're 16 and at school you are top of the ladder. All 16 years old know everything, can do anything and often cannot be told otherwise. When you're 16 and starting work, you still have the same thoughts but unknown to you, you are bottom of the ladder.

I was 16, had my own transport (my trusty yellow moped) ready to earn some money and begin to be a confident, and more importantly, independent adult. Exactly 200 years after America's first Independence day (well one day out but please allow me some artistic licence for effect !!) on Monday 5th July 1976, I started my 44 years of working life.

As instructed by my offer of employment letter, I was waiting at the entrance to Scunthorpes Steel Works in my bright white overalls and shiny steel toe capped boots. I had a Tupperware box with some sandwiches lovingly made by my mother the night before strapped to the back of the seat on my trusty yellow moped. I was told to wait for the manager in the lay-by at eight thirty in the morning and he would pick me up to take me to the Kenyon depot somewhere unknown to me on the Scunthorpe Steelworks. This would become my new working home. The start of many years of adventure, misadventure and new experiences. The bright sunshine was beating down on my face and I was feeling very nervous at the unknown but quite proud of myself to be finally working and earning some money.

I enjoyed seeing the trains pulling large torpedoes of molten steel to the casting mills. The lorries laden with steel girders going out the entrance to maybe some far off distant building site. The cars and motorbikes of all different colours and makes taking workers in and out of their usual place of work. I started to imagined myself having one of those motorbikes or even a car in the very near future and that's when I noticed him.

It wasn't that he was any different to anyone else riding a bike to work. It wasn't just the fact that he was riding a shiny new Suzuki moped, the creme de la creme of the moped world in those days!. No, it was the simple fact that he was wearing a bright shiny pair of **white** overalls. It had never occurred to me that there would be anyone other than me starting work. Being 16, my ego had always presumed that I had been the best candidate for the job and that my new found employer would not need anyone other than me.

Mick's long blond hair flowed out from under his crash helmet and he turned through the traffic lights and pulled into the lay-by next to me. Taking off his helmet to talk to me he looked just as apprehensive as myself but still trying to maintain an air of self confidence.

A simple "Kenyon Refrigeration?" from his lips confirmed my suspicions that I was not alone in starting my first employment into the world of refrigeration.

"Yeah, that's right. I think we are both a bit early" was my simple reply.

A short silent pause then followed while I admirably looked over his moped and he sneered at my bright yellow trusty stead.

"Do you know if there is anyone else starting today?" said Mick

"No idea!" I exclaimed "in fact I thought I was the only one. What do you think of these white overalls?"

Mick laughed and agreed "they're stupid aren't they! Fancy having white overalls on a dirty steelworks"

From then on, both Mick and I knew we were going to be good friends.

As we chatted and got to know each other, a Ford Cortina estate car did a very fast and illegal U turn in the road ending up in the lay-by in front of us. Jumping out of the drivers seat was our new boss.

Gareth Phillips was relatively small but a very hyperactive person. He was born and bred in south Wales and although he had been settled in Lincolnshire and living in Scunthorpe for several years now, he still had a strong Welsh accent. To this day I cannot remember ever seeing Gareth in a suit and my very first day of work was to be no exception. He was dressed smart but casual.

"Hello lads" he greeted us "you got here all right then!"

Gareth then looked down at our mopeds and said "I never thought of you both coming on your own transport, but that's all right you can just follow me, OK lads?"

We both nodded our heads in unison as we fastened our crash helmets back on our heads and watch Gareth jump back in his car. Gareth wasted not time in starting his Ford Cortina in motion as we quickly started our bikes. Mick elegantly pressed his starter button as I jumped up and down on the kick start of my moped. Thankfully my trusty stead came to life after only three tries.

As I said earlier, Gareth is naturally hyperactive and his driving reflected this. It was not that he was a particularly skilful driver. On the contrary, over the many years I knew him he had several crashes, scrapes etc and managed to write off several company cars. He always survived his accidents without even a scratch to himself (or others involved thankfully) but each incident simply got brushed aside by him with a shrug of his shoulders as he filled out another form for another new company car. Some people are just born lucky.

There may be a blanket speed limit across the whole of the steelworks but that meant nothing to this mad Welsh man. Unfortunately for me the depot for Kenyon refrigeration was the other side of the steelworks miles away from the entrance. My moped had a top speed of 30mph and even Mick was struggling to keep up with the mad Welshman as his moped could still only manage a respectable 45mph. I lost sight of Gareth within the first half mile. Luckily for me, Mick managed to keep him in view (only just) so all I had to do was try and keep Mick in sight. Junctions and corners slowed Gareth down a bit and I often found myself nearly trying to guess which way they went. By the time I arrived at the finishing line both Gareth and Mick were parked up and stood chatting between each other waiting for me. I don't think Gareth ever understood that mopeds (especially like my trusty stead) were incapable of travelling at the same speed as a Ford Cortina.

Gareth dutifully showed us around explaining that all the engineers were out on site at the minute but this afternoon we would be assigned to an engineer each and would get a taste of what was to come. As Kenyons were essentially contractors on a steelworks their allocated depot was not the grandest of places. There was no large shuttered doorway to allow vans etc access to unload. Just a normal sized door from the walkway that led into a workshop approximately 4 times the size of your average domestic garage. Along the side of the workshop was the largest store of air filters that I have ever seen. Filters imitating pizza boxes comprising of different sizes and colours. Some filters were the size of a 6" deep pan pizzas and others were family size thin crust 24" pizzas. Obviously air conditioning units around a dirty steelworks meant the regular changing of these filters and Kenyon engineers used a lot of these pizza box filters taking them out in a morning like a modern day Deliveroo. Looking at the multitude of filters gave me an insight of how large the steelworks must be and how reliant on air conditioning units these Steelworks must be.

There was only one telephone in the whole of the depot and that was in Gareths office. Well, I say office. With the desk, chair and a filing cabinet in there, there was not enough room left for all three of us to be in there at the same time. To get to the chair you had to squeeze between the desk and the wall and once there you were reluctant to come out as it was such a tight squeeze. Gareth however took pride in it being "his" office and proudly showed it off from the doorway. The most impressive part of his office to me was the fact that they had a telephone answering machine. Wow. How very sophisticated, this was high technology for 1976.

"Lets put the kettle on and make a cup of tea" Gareth suggested. "I'll show you both where we make tea and eat our lunch."

To most employees, in all walks of life, the most important room in the working environment is the mess room. At the Kenyon depot it doubled as locker room, tea room and in fact anything you can think of room. This is where the engineers lived when not out working and would always expect the kettle on when they returned.

Being naive and wet behind the ears I never realised that this was part of a test. Mick had obviously cotton on to the meaning of 'Lets put the Kettle on'. I feel he had been pre warned by his father who worked elsewhere on the steelworks. Me on the other hand just wanted to impress my new boss. I duly grabbed the kettle, filled it up and sorted all the mugs ready for the returning engineers. I even made sure I got the right consistencies of milk and sugar correct for each engineer. In fact even today, after 44 years, I can remember being very pleased with myself that I had made the perfect brew for everyone, even Mick himself thought I had done a good job and congratulated me on winning the best tea maker title.

You see Mick knew. He even had a knowing smile on his face when the very next day he was asked to make a brew. He proceeded to made tea so badly that no-one would drink it. Engineers even spat it out and poured it down the sink before turning to me and designated me THE tea boy for the rest of my apprenticeship.

— — — —

Chapter 2

'Engineering Boss'

Every generation of teenagers are fundamentally the same. We are no different to the generations before us and we will be no different to every generation after us. Teenagers believe they know everything and can do anything. Some have an abundance of self confidence and others have a mediocre amount, but still pretend to be confident to give others the impression they are adults. The truth is that none of us know what we are doing. As teenagers we are barely adults and most of the time we keep making mistakes. This is the important part of life that allows us to learn from our mistakes.

I was one of those that didn't have a clue what I was doing but went with the flow of life. The whole of my four year apprenticeship was a big learning curve. Not just to find out how to become a successful Refrigeration Engineer but how to enjoy life. From the very start of our apprenticeship, both Mick and I were put with qualified engineers to learn the trade. This meant we became very close to our seniors and I found myself getting involved in some of their hobbies and interests.

Gareth - was our boss! or at least he thought he was. Yes, his job title was the manager and yes, he was authorised to tell us what to do, but he was not a powerful authoritative person. Gareth stood only 5 foot 4 even when he was wearing his steel toe capped safety boots. He was born and bred Welsh but could never impose the same stature as Tom Jones. He couldn't sing either!

Some mornings he would enter the mess room with the intention of kicking us all out to do some work but it would always back fire on him.

"Come on guys! Isn't it time you were all heading out to work now?" he would softly say.

Most of us just looked over our papers at him and replied "Yeah sure, we're on our way, give us a minute"

And that would be enough to send him back into his cramped office for another 10 minutes. I suppose it's just human nature to see what you can get away with and so sometimes we used to run a bet to see how many times Gareth would try to get us out to do some work before he got angry. I very rarely saw that side of Gareth, it usually ended with someone simply starting to feel guilty and the rest of us then following suit out onto site.

Gareth was a practical man although most engineers didn't see him as a very proficient one. He had risen through the ranks from an apprentice. He had always worked for Kenyons at their head office in Pontardawe, South Wales and his big break was to come up to Scunthorpe to open up a new depot. He (and his friend Del) had built the depot up from nothing and he worked hard to grow the business but his practical skills were short of a high standard.

One year during my apprenticeship he declared he intended to build himself a kit car. For those of you who don't know, this is where you buy a shell of a sports car and build a fully functioning desirable car from all the parts from a donor car. Gareth's choice of kit car for his project was the Mini Marcos. It was advertised as a project you could complete in a long weekend. For those technical people who had both high standards and were perfectionists I would imagine you could complete the built in a month or two. However Gareth's car took over a year to get onto the road.

One day Gareth agreed to come to work in his pride and joy to show off. We all got the guided tour around the car and the pride in his technical achievement wasn't dinted by the snide remarks from his work colleagues.

I was quite impressed, as to me it was at least in the shape of a sports car. It sounded like a sports car and being low to the ground I imagined it handled well too. Gareth must have noticed my enthusiasm as I was the only one he offered to take for a spin in it. Or was it that I was the only one brave enough to get in a car with this mad Welsh speed king.

One of the engineers held the passenger side door open for me "You're braver than me!" He sneered "it doesn't look too safe to me"

"Oh give over," I happily replied "you're either trying to wind me up or you're jealous"

I lowered myself into the seat as they attempted to shut the door for me.

"It just needs a bit of adjustment" said Gareth "Lift it up then close it!"

The seat belt was one of those 'new' inertia seat belts that we are all familiar with nowadays. However as I pulled it away from the door pillar it jammed several times like a frisky dog pulling back on its lead.

"It just needs a bit of adjustment" said Gareth "Pull it slowly!"

It took several attempts to wrap the belt around myself but I eventually sat comfortably in my bucket seat feeling relatively safe and secure.

Gareth climbed into the drivers seat with the same lifting of his door, and slow pulling routine with his seatbelt, that I had endured. The engine roared into life and Gareth gently reversed out of the parking space.

The Mini Marcos rattled a bit as Gareth negotiated our way out onto the main highway. No I lied there, the car rattled a lot. Everything in the car seemed loose and almost fragile. Sat in a car which was in all tense and purposes brand new, I started to feel uncomfortable as to the security of all the parts. I even started to wonder if my door would stay in place or maybe I should hold onto it in case it fell off, but I was determined to not show any fear so I sat calmly on my seat with my hands on my lap.

We turned the last corner and found ourselves on the main straight highway where Gareth could open the car up and show me what it was made of. He wasted no time in putting his foot to the floor. I felt the G-Force push me into the bucket seat......

.... and found myself in the back of the car!

I had found something else Gareth had not finished properly. He had completely forgotten to bolt the passenger seat down and so when he accelerated, the seat and myself were propelled into the back of the car leaving my 'difficult' seat belt still strapped across the gap where the chair should be.

A good early lesson learnt.   'Never trust a mad Welshman'

As part of my apprenticeship I had to spend a week at the head office to experience all aspects, trades and skills involved in a successful Refrigeration business. As Gareth was originally from that area of Wales he organised for me to stay with him at his mother's house. He arranged it for when he needed to be at the head office for various meetings etc and so having nothing to organise, it was easy for me to just sit back and enjoy the experience.

The drive down at mostly 100+ mph was a real experience but at least the seats were bolted down in his company car. His mother was a lovely gentle woman who made me feel right at home. Scrumptious meals every evening and a soft comfortable bed at night. What more could you want.

On the very last day, it had been organised for me to be with a middle aged Welshman all day who had been 'out on the road' for years and knew his job inside out. I was introduced to Barri as soon as I entered the Service office and we got on like a house on fire from the start. He had more than just the 'gift of the gab' but was so good at compassionately listening too. I felt comfortable to discuss the growing pains and troubles all teenagers have with him and he would be listening enough to offer constructive advice. It may have only been one day that I spent working with Barri but it still stands out in my memories.

We drove up into the Welsh hills for our first point of call at a local golf club. The car park was half full of cars but most of their owners were out on the golf course and the clubs bar would not be open for hours yet. We had a small job to do in the beer cellar which to Barri seemed a simple task. We appeared later in the clubs bar to find the steward to sign our completed paperwork.

"Fancy a drink lads" said the Steward "the usual Barri?"

"It's a bit early, but go on then" accepted Barri

Two full pints of beer were placed on the bar. Most teenagers think they can drink for England but I tried to smile as I hid my shock at trying to down a pint early in the morning in the time it takes to get a signature on our work sheet. Barri simply poured it straight down his throat.

The next job was a good thirty minutes drive away and so it gave me chance to absorb the quickly downed alcohol. However our second job of the day was a nightclub in the city centre.

"The usual Barri?" says the nightclub owner as we emerge from his beer cellar after changing some fan blades.

"Why not" smiles Barri before he downs his second pint of the day.

By this time I had realised two things.

1- everyone in Wales is very obliging and friendly   and
2- Barri could drink!!!!!!!

We went to a total of 4 hostelries that morning and so at about 2 o' clock that afternoon I was very relieved to hear Barri announce

"I think we better have some lunch, young lad. What do you say?"

"I'm famished" was my quick but slurred reply

I imagined a nice little coffee shop nestled in some pretty Welsh village or maybe a spectacular fish and chip shop near the coast overlooking the sea. Wherever we go I was desperate for a substantial meal to soak up some of my intake of alcohol.

Barri had a particular place in mind and drove with determination around the scenic Welsh hills. We sailed through tree lined narrow roads, around winding mountain roads with spectacular views across the valleys. It took all of my concentration to hold in the effects of my intoxication and I never really noticed the breathtaking countryside that surrounded me. I was struggling to keep my breath as it was!!!

After what seemed like an eternity we arrived at Barri's choice for our lunch date. When I raised my head to look out of the windscreen I noticed we were pulling into a car park next to a beautiful white house in a remote village somewhere in the magnificent Welsh hills. The sign hanging above the door had what looked to me like a jumble of mainly consonant letters. This was the Welsh name of Barri's regular public house!!!!!

"I thought we'd have a liquid lunch!" Barri declared.

At the end of the day I was to meet up with my boss Gareth and the plan was to drive the 270 mile journey home that evening. Fortunately for me I wasn't able to share the driving with Gareth and so at least I could try and sleep off the effects of all the beer that day. I was barely old enough to consume the amount of alcohol Barri thought I could handle but to the mad, alcoholic Welshman, it was just another day.

Barri pulled into the factory car park to drop me off and unload all his paperwork. As I struggled to get out of the van and walk across the factory yard to the office Barri turned to me and said

"If anyone asks why you smell of beer tell them we've been to a lot of pubs and clubs all day"

— — — —

Chapter 3

'Mobile Disco'

Peter was only in his early 20s and ran a mobile disco in his spare time. To us he was a trendy young man who knew how to woo the ladies.

He was passionate about his music and had a very extensive record collection. Nowadays DJs keep all their music digitally, in a laptop, memory device or even streamed from the internet. Not so in the 1970s.

Pete had two large suitcases with every vinyl single you could think of. We carried this prized collection from gig to gig like we were Delboy and Rodney going from market to market. They were heavy and Pete cared about these suitcases as if they were his new born child.

Pete had a company van which he could use for personal use but he had been told explicitly that he was not insured to use it for his mobile disco business. This didn't stop him, but he was careful what he said at work in front of the boss. As I was his official roadie he was always trying to get me to keep my big mouth shut. As a wet behind the ears teenager who was trying to project a cloak of self confidence it was difficult for me to not boast about our various antics in the evenings.

Poor Pete often got called into the office for a 'word' because of me.

I couldn't dance, had no sense of rhythm but was good at lugging heavy suitcases and disco equipment around. I was like Rodney from Only Fools and Horses helping DelBoy but with a dodgy mobile disco instead of a successful market trader.

Once the stage was set up and we had done our sound and light checks I usually spent the evening at the bar or behind the stage searching for rare records that someone had requested. I was happy with my disco life. I felt I was being useful and hoped that Pete's magnetism for ladies may eventually rub off on me. — I'm still waiting!!!

Then one fateful night Pete decided it was my turn to have a go at being a DJ. He persuaded me I was ready for the spotlight and that it could prove to be my big break into the entertainment business. He was very good at portraying this, so called, golden opportunity for me.

He described how it could be the start of a lucrative career, maybe eventually becoming world famous on radio and television. The stars started to sparkle in my eyes. Maybe this was how I would obtain some of Pete's magnetism for the ladies!

I myself was quite content with my position at the bar, learning how to drink beer. I was quite happy lugging the big DelBoy suitcases around. I was happy with my lot. However he could be very persuasive, and being a teenager, I eventually agreed to step out of my comfort zone and to do a slot on the decks.

I was very nervous as it was the first time ever that I would be alone on the stage. Pete had even persuaded me that it was best for him to disappear for a while to leave me to it. Little did I realise he had an ulterior motive. He just wanted time away from the stage to chat up some particular girls he had taken a shine too.

Pete had done most of the preparation for me. He had written a list of the records I would play and pointed out the ones that had been specifically requested by some of the audience. Pete had spent the first hour of the evening building up the music to entice everyone onto the dance floor. Pete put his last record on the deck and cued it up.

"and now we have a treat for you all as we have a new DJ who has flown in especially for this gig" he professionally announced.

"Tango Terry will be running the show for the next hour after John and Olivia tell us 'You're the one that I want' " and with that Pete jumps off the stage leaving me to it. John Travolta's dulcet tones ring out around the gig. I was on my own!!!!

You can always tell a good DJ by the number of people on the dance floor. A good DJ knows his audience and knows how to build up a good floor full of dancers. Pete had done a good job so far and all I needed to do was cue the records up and play the records Pete had chosen. I selected my very first record, placed it onto the turntable and, using the headphones, cued the record up so as soon as I pressed the play button the music would start. Danny and Sandy were singing their last chorus and I was ready. Here was my big moment.

Now some of you who know me, are aware that my vocal cords are not at the normal pitch as most people. In fact if ever I need to shout they go up an octave or two. This shouldn't be a problem with a top quality microphone, the finest amplifier money could buy and some large 1970's style speakers. Maybe it was just my nerves, or maybe my teenage self confidence, or I like to think it was more likely down to the record Pete had put at the top of my list. I believe in actual fact, he had set me up good and proper!

Speaking into the microphone at supersonic speed and at a pitch that only dogs and cats could understand....

" that was Danny and Sandy from Grease, now we have the Wurzels with Combine Harvester".

It was a simple statement and to me it sounded perfect. However a couple of enthusiastic dancers just in front of the stage suddenly stopped and shouted to each other..

"What did he say?"

"Not sure, but it sounded like a cat got stuck in the combine harvester"

With that they walked off the dance floor along with the majority of the other dancers.

For the next 30 minutes I never used the microphone once and simply put record after record on. Even when I dismissed Pete's list and started putting some better records on I never managed to get the crowds back onto the floor. I realised I didn't have the type of Tony Blackburn voice people wanted and I was better with the technical side of disco music.

'What a plonker!' I thought - 'I'd best stick with my roadie job!'

— — — —

Chapter 4

'Electric Canine'

During our apprenticeship Mick and I were often left on our own to complete simple jobs around the Scunthorpe Steelworks. We would be ceremoniously dropped off at a job site with the appropriate tools and usually the engineer dropping us off would describe what work was required in great detail. Being headstrong teenagers we obviously never listened to them but at least we were told what to do. Invariable things would go wrong or we just never completed the task required as instructed. This would usually annoy the engineer when he returned and he would then have to help us do the job properly.

One day I was dropped off at one of the Bloom and Billet Mills' main computer rooms.

The Bloom and Billet mill on the Scunthorpe steelworks was a state of the art rolling mill (well it was state of the art in the late 70s!) that rolled steel ingots down to a billet dimensions that then could be sent to other mills to manufacture wire, rail lines, sections etc. This mill in its day was one of the longest in the country and was nearly one mile long from start to finish. To control the precise movements of each ingot as it was rolled down in size along the mill they had powerful computers that in those days filled large rooms. These computers generated an enormous amount of heat and required whole plant rooms full of air conditioning equipment to remove the heat. This was my workplace for the day.

My engineer, Mike, gave me a tour around the plant room and showed me in great detail the fresh air mixing ductwork that had an automated roll filter on it. This filter could automatically detect itself getting dirty and move the roll on to a new, clean section of the filter cloth. To prevent the roll running out and therefore allowing dust and fumes into the system a detector could see the end of roll and stop the motor from winding it on. It would then raise an alarm to indicate the roll needed changing. and raise the alarm.

My job today was to change the detector that had broken. Mike showed me exactly what I needed to do and left me the appropriate tools needed to complete my task.

"Now you know what needs doing Terry?" said Mike as he placed the tools on top of the ductwork in front of me.

"Yes!" I replied in that teenage know-it-all tone.

"You simply have to disconnect those wires carefully noting where they go, then replace the detector"

"Yes Mike, I think I can handle that" I assured him with eyes glancing skyward.

"It shouldn't take you long and I will be back in an hour"

"Don't panic Mike, I'll be fine" I said as he turned to go out the plant room door "I'll see you later"

Mike walked out the door and as the door closed behind him I confidently turned towards my little job. I desperately wanted to prove I knew what I was doing and could be trusted to do more work like this on my own.

I surveyed the job once more to ensure nothing could go wrong and made a note of which wires went to which terminals. Picking up the appropriate screwdriver I disconnected the wires from the detector and pulled them out of the way.

10 minutes later I had removed the broken detector and replaced it with the new detector out of the box. Unlike most teenagers (in fact most men really) I had actually glanced at the installation instructions that came in the box to ensure I fitted it correctly and that I was sure I knew how to calibrate it properly. After all, I wanted to make sure I did a good job.

The wires were a bit frayed and so I took my time stripping the wires back to make a neat job. All I had left to do now was to reconnect the wires.

Just as I went to pick up the screwdriver which was sat on top of the ductwork.......   I was given an almighty bear hug from behind.

"What the bloody hell !!!!" was my initial reaction

"Get off me! I've nearly finished" I shouted dropping the screwdriver back on the ductwork.

I turned around expecting Mike to have come back early and surprise me but I saw no-one. Spinning around puzzled I looked around for Mike.

"What the......??!!" I exclaimed to myself

I looked at the still closed plant room door and decided Mike must be trying to wind me up. I opened the door to look out into the corridor but could not see anyone at all. I went across the corridor to the computer programmers office.

"Russ, have you seen Mike at all?" I asked

"Yes, I saw him about 20 minutes ago when he came in with you, but not since then" Russ told me "Why? have you got a problem?"

"No, No!" I assured him "I just thought he had come back. Never mind, don't worry about it, I should be finished soon"

Scratching my head I went back to the plant room to complete my task. Still puzzled I went up to the ductwork and picked up the wire ready to connect it to the detector. As I picked up the screwdriver off the metal ductwork I got another bear hug.......

That was probably the first time I had ever had an electric shock. It certainly wasn't the last time but thankfully I quickly learnt to ensure the power was isolated before I started any work on electrical systems. This shock was a relatively low voltage and the current had simply gone from the wire in my left hand across to my right hand as I picked up the screwdriver from the earthed, metal ductwork.

Sometimes it wasn't even my fault......

After an accident on my motorbike I had been put on light duties for a week until my badly scrapped knee had mended itself. I was not in any real pain but my right knee had stiffened making it difficult for me to bend. I could walk up and down stairs alright as long as I took them one step at a time. I walked as though I had a wooden leg.

Around this time one of the computer suites at the Medium Section Mill had been upgraded with a new modern air conditioning system and my boss had decided it would be a nice steady job for me to salvage all the valuable scrap metal from all the old equipment.

Medium Section Mill had a great canteen next to the computer suite so it was decided I had all the amenities I needed to allow me to be dropped off in the morning and left by myself all day. My specific job was to cut and remove all the old redundant pipes & conduits etc. and collect them all up into various boxes that had been left for me.

It was a nice summers day and so I could take my time and keep having as many breaks as I wanted on the roof area in the blazing sunshine.

By lunchtime I had already filled several boxes and was starting to wonder if they were getting a bit heavy. Would someone be able to carry them downstairs at the end of the day? I certainly couldn't. Most of the boxes I had filled up in the morning were full of pure copper pipes. This is the material which is worth the most at the scrap merchants and so they were the boxes I filled first.

After a heavy lunch I came out of the canteen feeling rather full and sleepy but climbed the stairs, one step at a time, with determination to get to the roof for a little snooze. Just then, as I opened the door to the roof space I heard my boss call out behind me...

"How is it going Terry?"

"Oh, hello Gareth" came my reply "I didn't expect to see you here until the end of the day"

"Oh, I was just passing and thought I would check you are all right. How is the knee?" he enquired

"Its fine! Very stiff, takes me ages to get up and down the stairs, but apart from that it's fine" I told him.

Gareth followed me out onto the roof and seemed very happy with the amount of copper I had managed to salvage. I wasn't very happy as my planned little nap would now have to wait until he was gone.

"I'm just going to start on all this conduit now" I told him as I picked up my hacksaw and walked over to the first piece.

"Don't worry too much about that stuff as it's the copper we get the best price for" he reminded me.

I sat down next to the first length of conduit still clamped to the wall and with the sun beating down on my face I started sawing. Gareth stood there with his eyes closed collecting sun rays on his face.

Its the sort of noise your brain ignores as background noise. You never realise its there until it actually stops. The gentle hum of all the new air conditioning units on the roof had all stopped together.

We both look at each other and realise something is wrong.

No air conditioning units would mean the computer suite would overheat. No computer suite would mean the mill would stop. We needed to act fast.

Gareth almost jumped through the roof doorway to investigate why everything had suddenly gone quiet. I could hardly jump, but I did manage to hop along after him through the doorway only to find myself in a dark corridor. There were no lights on at all!!!!

"It must be a power cut!" Gareth concludes "Here you hold this door open so we can get some light in here and I will try to find out what happened"

And with that he was gone.

Here I was with a bad leg, stood in the doorway onto a sunny roof looking down a very dark corridor with puzzled occupants of the office building wondering why everything had gone off. At least I was certain it had nothing to do with me. I was just minding my own business on a nice sunny roof.

It must have been over hour before Gareth came back to me. There had been a complete power cut and he had got involved with helping the site electricians try and find out what went wrong. They had struggled to find the cause but at least now they were gently switching back on the breakers etc. and all the lights etc were coming back on line without a problem.

It was getting near the end of the day by this time so we ensured all the air conditioning units started up all right and called it a day.

It wasn't until the next day when I returned to salvaging all the scrap copper etc that I found the cause for the power cut.

The blade in my hacksaw, which I had accidentally left on the roof, had a big chunk of it missing. I believe what had happened was that one of the cables going through the conduit I was cutting up was still live. As I cut through the cable it earthed across the conduit and took out the power to the new air conditioning plant and the office lights etc.

Luckily for me .... I had some spare hacksaw blades.

At the end of the day one of the engineers came to pick me up and we filled his van up with all the boxes of copper and steel. Rick often had his Labrador dog with him but with his van now full of scrap metal his dog had to sit in the middle of us on the front seat. There really wasn't much room for his dog so although part of him was between Rick and myself most of his dog was on MY knee.

We decided it best to go straight to the local scrap merchant to cash in this salvaged metal. Usually the scrap merchant would put our bag or box of metal on a scale in his shed and simply pay us the going rate on what weight it was. As there was so much of it the scrap merchant told us to drive straight onto the weigh bridge to get weighed.

I watched from the office window as Rick drove onto the weigh bridge and then got out so they could weigh the van with just the metal inside. He then got back in the van as instructed and drove to the back of the yard where the scrap merchant wanted us to unload the scrap metal.

Once unloaded, Rick followed the same procedure and they weighed the van WITHOUT the metal inside.

The scrap merchant then calculated the total weight of the metal we had unloaded and gave us the value in a cash payment. Everyone was happy as we drove back to our depot with Ricks dog now in the back of the van.

"That was a great deal" I said to Rick "Look at all this cash"

"It was better than you think, actually" Rick declared with a smile

"I know what you mean" I said "I think they gave us the rate for copper on all of it even though there was some metal conduit in there"

"We did even better than that" Rick explained....

"They even paid us the weight of my dog!!!!"

— — — —

Chapter 5

'Lockable Cap'

I passed my motorbike driving test at the first attempt. My car driving test was a different matter, that was the second attempt. I wasn't impressed with the driving school I went with before my first test as they only seemed to want my money. They even put me down before my test saying I wasn't ready. So after failing my first driving test I went to an independent driving school who had a totally different approach. They helped build my confidence in my ability to drive.

In the 1970's anyone with a full licence could sit next to a learner driver. This meant that when my friends and I fancied a night out one of my friends with a full driving licence would ride his bike up to my house and sit next to me in my dad's mini for us to go round picking everyone else up. Amazing how many people you can get into a mini clubman when you're on a pub crawl !

Please don't get the wrong idea - although in those days the drink-driving laws were more relaxed than today I would never have got behind the wheel of a car over the limit. I would usually drink non alcoholic beverages if I was the driver but the idea of me going out in my dad's mini regularly was to gain as many hours as possible behind the wheel of a car to gain experience. Even today I would say that this is the best way to pass your test. (The driving bit not the drinking beer bit !!!!!)

When you're a teenager you never stay in. Most week nights we would be out drinking & socialising and the majority of those nights I would be the designated driver. Eventually you get so complacent at being able to drive a car that you forget you have L plates on. In fact when I finally took my driving test I was so confident that I had to keep watching my speed. In my dad's mini the speedometer was a large dial in the middle of the dash board. You couldn't hide it, so obviously the examiner must have seen I was speeding at times but thankfully he gave me my full licence with flying colours.

Having a full licence opens up all sorts of opportunities, at home and at work. No longer was I restricted to just one passenger on the back of my bike but I could take a whole group of friends out and about. At work it meant I could now drive some of the engineers cars and vans.

It instantly made me more useful as an apprentice as I could now go and fetch spares etc for the engineers or run all sorts of errands. One particular 'errand' comes to mind for one of the engineers called Stuart.

Stuart was a smaller than average Yorkshireman. What he lacked in stature he made up for in personality. He had a young family and had only recently joined the company after working directly for the Scunthorpe Steelworks. He had been given an older van than most in the fleet, and like everyone else he had spent time kitting it out with all the mod cons!!

Stuart and I had been working on a problem with one of the cold stores in the Scunthorpe Steelworks Central Kitchens. This was a building specially built on the Anchor side of the site which pre-made ALL the meals served in canteens across the site. Obviously one of those ideas some top manager had come up with to save money but the truth was that none of the meals were as good as the freshly made meals like before. In fact they were pretty crap and people started simply bringing in their own sandwiches and avoiding the canteens altogether. One of those ideas which look good on paper but in reality it failed miserably. Canteens on the steelworks never recovered.

Anyway, one day Stuart and I were working on one of their cold rooms and we eventually diagnosed that one of the compressors was failing and needed replacing. As this particular cold room had a lot of food in it and was critical to the running of the central kitchens, the kitchen management had insisted we get a new compressor asap. Usually with this type of compressor it could take weeks to order and get delivered but the management pleaded with us to rush it through as quickly as possible.

Back at the depot Stuart went straight into the office to phone up the distributors.

"Oh hello! Is that Matt?" asked Stuart into the phone

"I need to make an enquiry about a new compressor, it is rather urgent" Stuart continued to read out all the details of the compressor we had collected from the job.

Stuart put his hand over the mouthpiece and said to me "he's having a look but doesn't think they will have one in stock"

"That's what you thought wasn't it" I replied "surely they will just have to move all the food out to somewhere until we can get one"

"That's right" Stuart continued conversing with me "at least the manager had the sense to start phoning round to rent a refrigerated container. They may even get one before we get the cold store fixed"

"That would take the heat off us" I said with a smile

"Oh Hi - yes, I'm still here" Stuart informed Matt at the other end of the phone.

"Yes"

'Yes!"

"Sure!"

"Oh dear"

"Yes"

"Yes!"

"Oh right, I see." Stuart continued

"I'll have to get back to you."

Stuart concluded "I'll have to see what my boss says - Thanks Matt - I'll give you a ring back in half an hour."

"Well, what did he say" I eagerly enquired.

"As we thought," started Stuart "Matt said they don't stock that model in Hull but he did find one at their Birmingham branch"

"Well that sounds good doesn't it" I said "surely they could get that to us in a couple of days."

"Well yes" said Stuart "but he did say that the quickest way to get it would be for us to go and collect it"

"But that's got to be a couple of hours drive away" I suggested "its gone 3 o'clock now so they may be shut by the time we get there!"

"No you're wrong....." said Stuart with a big grin

Holding one finger up, he said "-A- if they know we are going someone will stay back especially for us....."

Holding the second finger up, he concluded " and -B- its not 'US' but just you!!!!   I need to be home before my wife goes to work"

In the following 30 minutes we had organised my next big adventure. I had all the paperwork, ropes and blocks etc to secure the new compressor and the keys to Stuarts van. Stuart had not only lent me his van (as long as I dropped him off home on my way out) but he had lent me his map book so I could find where I was going to in the middle of Birmingham. In those days there was no such thing as Sat Nav.

By 4:30 I had dropped Stuart off at his house and was heading out of Scunthorpe on my big adventure. It may not sound much of an adventure, but for an 18 year old who had only recently passed his driving test and never been so far away completely under my own steam in a company van, it felt like a big adventure.

I headed down the M1 knowing I needed to look out for junction 28 so I could turn off onto the A38 past Derby. This is the route the other engineers had recommended and although I knew it would send me straight to the notorious (and relatively new)

'Spaghetti Junction' in Birmingham they had all assured me it was easy.

"As long as you know where you want to go just follow the signs and you will sail through" they all told me when we headed out the door.

"Junction 27" I said to myself as I headed down the motorway "next one for me"

I gave a physical sigh of relief as I turned onto the A38 and really started to relax and enjoy myself as I passed Derby. It was only when I was about 20 miles from Birmingham that I noticed the light come on the dashboard.

"Oh bugger me, you didn't tell me you needed petrol Stuart!" I cursed to myself.

"Never mind" I thought "I know he keeps his petrol card in the glove compartment so all I need to do is find a petrol station. All part of the adventure"

Another couple of miles and I pulled into a local garage north of Birmingham with just the two pumps outside. I even remembered which side the filler cap was so was quite happy with myself as I pulled the correct side of the petrol pump. Getting out of the van with the petrol card in my hand I gave a big smile when I confirmed the petrol cap was on the drivers side........

That's when my smile slowly changed to a frown.....

Stuart had bought one of those fancy 'lockable' petrol caps! Most vehicles in those days had simple petrol caps that didn't lock into the vehicle.

I looked at the key ring that Stuart had given me but there was just the one key on it. The ignition key. Maybe he kept the key in the glove compartment like the petrol card. I frantically started looking all over the van. Eventually I gave up.

Without petrol I was struggling to get to Birmingham, let alone get home. So I decided my only option was to ask Stuart where his key was. This is decades before the mobile phone was common place. However it wasn't quite the dark ages so there were plenty of public phones around.

I went into the petrol station kiosk and explained the problem I had to the attendant. She smiled and laughed in a strong Brummie accent and pointed toward the public phone on the wall.

"Hi Stuart, it's me Terry" I said as soon as the phone was answered.

"Are you all right? How's my van?" He said in a panic.

"It's all right Stuart, don't panic" I calmed him down " I'm running out of petrol and need to fill up"

"Oh, is that all" he replied "the petrol card is in the glove compartment"

"I know, I've got that, but do you know where the petrol cap key is?" I asked

"Err yes" came the reply

"Well….. where is it?" I said frustrated at his delay

"Its here" came the reply

"What do you mean it's here?" I asked, not thinking straight.

"Its here in my hand!!!"

Silence…….   …..while it sank in.

"Are you still there Terry?" Stuart enquired

"What the hell am I supposed to do now?" I exclaimed "I'm 100 miles away from you with no petrol and you've got the only key. What bloody good is that to me!!!!"

"Oops, sorry" was the only answer I got before I slammed the receiver down.

"Everything O.K" came the Brummie voice from the kiosk desk.

"Yes thanks" I started heading for the door "I'll be back in a minute"

I had decided to move the van away from the petrol pumps before I had started my search for the lost key and luckily the petrol station was not the busiest. As I started to find a way to remove the lockable petrol cap I did become conscious of other customers giving me worried looks but by then I didn't care.

Thinking back now, it probably didn't look very safe - a teenager with a very big screwdriver and hammer bashing the hell out of the side of a van in the middle of a petrol station. At least I came out of it unscathed which is more than I can say for Stuarts expensive lockable petrol cap (or his van!!!!).

— — — —

Chapter 6

'Need for Speed'

Del was a pure blood Welsh man. He was a tall six foot man with long, straight hair past his shoulders. Del was in his mid twenties when I started working for Kenyons which when your only 16 seems quite old. He was one of those hyperactive people who couldn't sit still and into absolutely everything. He was probably brought up on blue smarties! Del was one of my favourite engineers during my apprenticeship and we got on well together. We all worked for a Welsh based company and Del, who originated from the Swansea area of South wales, had served his apprenticeship at the head office in Pontardawe.

Del's name always intrigued me and often confused others. Delahaye John was often misconstrued as John Delahaye. He hated the confusion people had with his name. Del was always very quick, but in a controlled calm manner, to correct those that got confused with his name. Many people would then look at Del with an awkward pause trying to determine if he was pulling their leg or whether he was actually serious. Occasionally someone would be intrigued and question him further to determine the origins of his unusual name. This would get him annoyed and they often felt his wrath without ever finding the information they requested. To this day I still don't know the origins, apart from once when he told me it was a family name.

Del was a petrol head. He loved his cars and the driveway at his home was often full of some classic sports cars. His main passion, when I knew him, was karting. If you asked him about 'Go-Karting' he would bite your head off.

"Go-Karting is a children's pedal cycle" he would insist, "Karting is a proper motor sport!!!"

This is where Del and I saw eye to eye. I liked motorbikes and so it seemed like a dream come true that I could socialise with a real life racing driver. OK it may not be the international circuit. In fact we only just managed the next county on our travels let alone another country. However, to a teenager in the 1970s it was exciting and thrilling. I became Del's pit crew and most weekends were spent at local racetracks with the smell of Castrol R and burning rubber in the air.

One of our favourite tracks was called Hemswell and this was a Karting track laid out on a disused airfield. That's not to say it took up all of the airfield. On the contrary. Karts are not much more than four foot long so they needed relatively smaller tracks compared to a full size formula one car.

The track at Hemswell was an intricate course with several tight bends and some built up banks to keep runaway Karts from crossing into different sections. Most public Karting tracks simply used lots of tyres to mark out a course and keep everyone on the track. These semi-professional tracks gave the drivers more to think about than just going round and round. Drivers needed to know the track inch by inch to ensure they could get themselves into the correct line. Del was meticulous, he did his homework and he knew the tracks he raced on.

"Usual time on Sunday!" Del tells me one Friday afternoon. We were at the end of the working week and the early summer weather looked promising for a good weekend of racing..

"I'll pick you up about 6am"

"Yeah, no problem" was my reply "I will try to be awake this time!"

Mornings are not my thing. Never have been. There had been times in a morning when I had simply rolled over and gone back to sleep. Never on a working day but Sundays in my subconsciousness were not days to get up early. Days in the working week are acceptable but Sundays should always be days of rest. One time in the past, Del had arrived outside my house when I was still asleep and he managed to wake most people around (including my Dad) by using the musical air horns he had fitted to his van. I had learned the hard way to ensure I was up in time.

"Don't be late" Del insisted "Its an important race on Sunday so I want to get there in plenty of time. Get our favourite pit position."

"I will be up, don't worry"

The race track at Hemswell was no more than 20 minutes away from my home so setting off at 6am was definitely giving us plenty of time to get there. Races rarely started before 10am but the gates to the track were often open for general practice if you got there early enough. Nowadays Health and Safety probably wouldn't allow it before all the Marshalls and First Aid people are up and running, but in those days they allowed a few drivers onto the track to familiarise themselves with the intricacies of the circuit. Del knew the circuit inside out but he wanted to ensure everything on the Kart was running at its optimum for what for him was an important race.

By 7am we were not only at the race track but set up in the pits pole position. We were positioned near the track entrance which not only gave us a full view of all the other competitors arriving behind us but also gave me the best view of the track when Del was racing. We carefully and meticulously unloaded the van and by the time the next few competitors arrived we had Del's speed machine on its stand allowing us to work on it at waist height. The weather was overcast but forecasted to be dry for the day and so I was fitting the "slick" tyres to the Kart as requested by Del.

Slick tyres (for those that don't know) are tyres with no tread at all. They give the maximum amount of grip on the tarmac and everyone used them in those days including F1 professionals. The tread on normal car tyres are to ensure any rain on the surface of the road is dispelled from the rubber touching the tarmac and so allowing grip in all weather. Slick tyres cannot be used in the wet as the water on the surface of the road cannot go anywhere and therefore causes total loss of grip.

This race was important to Del and so we had prayed all week for no rain and the forecast was looking good for us. Del had already set up the engine and gearing to suit the Hemswell circuit and so when the tyres were fitted we lifted the kart down onto the floor and I push started Del off onto the track for him to get a few isolated runs before anyone else got on the race track.

Everything sounded good to me and the kart looked to be running well as Del sped around a lonely track. 20 minutes later Del was back in with a big smile on his face and we sat on our deckchairs at the back of the van watching all the other competitors arrive. The general hustle and bustle of a normal race day unfolded around us as everyone busied themselves around the now crowded pit area.

Shortly before 10am the PA system kicked into life and announced. "Will all competitors for the first race please make their way to the starting grid"

"This is it!" Del exclaimed with great enthusiasm.

The first race went well for Del and he qualified comfortably for the next heat. The second heat went well and he ensured he qualified for the final without putting too much strain on himself and the Kart.

We checked and double checked the Kart was in top condition for Del's last race of the day and wheeled the Kart out to the starting grid. I push started him off to get the engine roaring into action and like all the other competitors Del drove around the circuit to line himself up on the grid. Del is not pole position but in a very good position. The flag is raised by the starter (signifying get ready) and then seconds later he drops the flag and they are off……..

At first I wonder where Del is as all the Karts race off the grid toward the first bend. Then I spot him. The only one on the grid!!!!   The idiot stalled it. Probably got so excited and had stalled the engine. A marshal near him runs up behind him and pushes. The Kart quickly roars into life but Del is now a quarter of the track behind the others.

To this day, I believe if Del could drive like that normally he would have easily been a world champion. Before the end of the first lap he had caught up the back runners. He must have been a man possessed as he was doing everything right on a familiar track to him and every opportunity he had he was overtaking everyone. Even the other pit crew members around me were pointing him out and exclaiming "Look at him go!!"

Second to last lap and Del was now in second position. I couldn't believe how he had managed to pull off the 'race of the day' from such a disastrous beginning. He was inches behind the leader going round the last tight bend before the long straight. This was his moment to take the lead and he had positioned himself in the ideal slipstreamed position.

It probably seemed like slow motion to Del but to me and everyone else it happened very quickly. Del's Kart simply lost grip of the track as he pushed the kart round that last bend and he spun round once before hitting the bank. This propelled Del and Kart into the air where the Kart somersaulted several times with Del still sat in the seat holding on to the steering wheel. He landed on his head and finally came to a stop on the other side of the bank. Most of the Marshalls and first aid people were there by the time Del came to a stand still. He had been knocked unconscious and looked to be in a bad way.

I have great admiration to all professional first aiders. Most of them at these race tracks were there voluntarily but they reacted very quickly and knew exactly what to do. They carefully retrieved Del from his bent and battered Kart and once carefully fixed onto a stretcher he was hauled into the ambulance that had parked along side the scene of the accident. The ambulance sped off leaving me in shock wondering not only where my mate was being taken but what I should do now.

The racing fraternity, although very competitive, are also a close knit community. Especially at a local level. Some of the racing drivers and quite a few of their pit crews (at local level these were usually the drivers relatives helping the aspiring young drivers) helped me collect what was left of Del's Kart.

"Here, you grab that end" instructed one of the track marshalls, "and I'll help you carry it back to your van

" Come on everyone" he said to all the onlookers, "lets help this poor lad get what's left of his drivers Kart"

Everyone scurried round and picked up any bits they could find and carried them all back to the pits. To this day I am not sure if we found everything but Im sure the van contained more parts than we came with.

"Can someone tell me where my mate will have been taken?" I enquired at the marshal tent.

"I think it will be the hospital in Lincoln" said one guy behind the desk

"I don't know" said another marshal standing by the table "It could be Scunthorpe General, I think that one is closer"

"no Lincoln is closest isn't it!!!"

"Yes but Scunthorpe is quicker to get to from here"

"Or it could even be Grimsby couldn't it" another Marshall interjected

"LOOK" I shouted "Can one of you find out for definite for me!!!! My mate has just been rushed off in an ambulance. I have to go and try to tell his wife and so I need to know where he is"

"Sorry son, I'll go find out for you" said the first Marshall as he stood up from the table.

Luckily for me Del always left his valuables with me when racing so I at least had the keys to his van. In those days there were no mobile phones or in fact any easy way of communication, so I had no option but to drive back to Scunthorpe and almost 30 minutes after my argument with the Marshalls I found myself stood outside Del's house explaining what had happened and trying to calm his wife (Linda) down. Thankfully Del had been taken to Scunthorpe General Hospital and so it was relatively easy for me to drive Linda to the A&E to be with her husband.

Del had broken both legs and one leg ended up in plaster right up to his hip. He spent over 3 months in plaster and then several months in physiotherapy strengthening his legs and muscles. During all this time I was given his company van to drive around in under the condition I took Linda shopping every week as Linda didn't drive. This unusual arrangement was due to the fact that Del was a long close friend of our boss Gareth. I was very happy with the arrangement as it meant I not only got the use of a company van and saw my friend on a weekly basis but also that all the shopping was done in company time so I had an afternoon off work every week to socialise with Del & his wife.

When Del finally returned to work I had to hand over his van to him and return to my trusty motorbike.

"Lets have a go on your bike Terry" Said Del one day shortly after his return

"I'm not sure about that Del" was my reply " after all your record on Karts isn't too good this year"

"I know its your pride and joy, but I promise I will be careful. I've never been on a bike before."

"Oh that helps a lot!!!" I exclaimed

"Oh, go on. You've driven my Kart lots of times and even had my van for the past 6 months" Del pleaded

Peer pressure has a lot to answer for. Most bad decisions in my life have been from peers persuading you to go against your own gut feeling. This time was no exception and nearly all the other engineers, and my fellow apprentice Mick, talked me into letting Del sit on my pride and joy outside the workshop.

Our workshop was part of a large building containing several different departments. It was known as Redbourn CEW (Central Engineering Workshop) and had a one way system road all the way round it. This road was only about 300 yards all around it and we had come to a compromise that Del would simply go once round the building and come straight back.

My gut feeling was still telling me this was a mistake as I showed Del where the accelerator and, more importantly, where the brakes were. Yes Del was a true petrol head and knew how to race around a track controlling Karts or even cars at high speeds. He was very skilled in his ability to handle fast cars but he definitely had never ridden a motorbike before.

Revving the engine a bit he got the feeling of the bikes power. I was almost relieved to see him set off nice and smoothly without revving the engine too much. My gut was telling me Del would open up the throttle as soon as he turned the first corner. After all he IS a petrol head so he would want to go fast. Maybe because of his accident, or maybe because he was considering my feelings for the love of my motorbike, but I was happy to hear the gentle sound of a smooth engine getting quieter as he went behind the building. We all looked at each other and then turned around to watch for Del appear round the other side of the building.

"I told you he would be careful" said our Boss Gareth.

"Yes, he knows I love my bike"

"I thought he would scream off at high speed" said Pete

"Oh thanks Pete" I said

"He's certainly taking it easier than I thought" said Dave (another engineer)

"Oh you're as bad as Pete" I exclaimed "You've all ganged up on me haven't you!"

Everyone nodded their heads as they stared at the corner of the building expecting Del to come racing round the corner. However 5 minutes later we still couldn't see or even hear my bike and we all started looking quizzically at each other. Everyone was thinking the same but didn't want to say.

"Do you think he is ok?" Gareth finally broke the silence

"Where the heck has he gone with my bike?" I asked nervously

"He'll have gone for a good burn out up Dawes Lane" Pete teased

"Don't Joke" I said as I hit Pete on the arm

SILENCE.....

We never heard him!!!!!

We just stood there with our mouths open as Del came walking back round the corner struggling to push my bike back to our workshop.

"Are you alright" asked Gareth

"Is my bike alright" I shouted

"What happened?" laughed Mick

As Del finally pushed my bike back onto the footpath and I grabbed hold of it to put it back on its stand he informed us "I fell off"

"You what!!!!"

"I fell off" he repeated

"How can you fall off?" Mick said still laughing "you only went round the block"

"Well" Del explained "I rode round to the junction with the main road and a truck was coming up the road so I braked and stopped!!"

"AND" I said

"Well……. You never told me I had to put my feet down when I stopped!!!!!!!"

— — — —

Chapter 7

'Last Step for Mankind'

Dave, like Del, was also a born and bred Welshman, but he was totally opposite to Del. Dave was a short 5 foot 6 and like most people in the 1970s had lots of hair. He had a full beard, in fact a very full, curly beard that made me wonder if he was keeping a small birds nest hidden in there.

Dave's nickname was 'Chopsy'. It was a nickname no-one repeated to his face. It was always used behind his back and although I am sure Dave knew about his nickname he definitely wasn't very keen on it. He would probably argue for hours about why his nickname was so inappropriate but that was the whole point. He just couldn't stop talking, he could talk for England. Sometimes a conversation with Dave would start off being interesting but then he would just get carried away and go off at such a tangent that the original discussion about the latest pop music hit may end up about whether the moon landings happened or not.

Most of the other engineers at Kenyons found Dave annoying and frustrating to talk to. Don't get me wrong. Dave had lots of friends and plenty of customers who found him interesting, as long as they weren't paying for his time. I was one of the few people at Kenyons that got on well with Dave. I've always been able to listen to others. As a typical teenager I thought I knew everything and believed I could hold a good discussion with Dave. Dave often proved me wrong and I was no match for his enthusiasm to just talk and talk all day. We often didn't get much work done as Dave would want to prove a point in a full conversation. This was good for a crafty teenager that realised that getting your engineer distracted meant you could avoid spending the day in hard labour.

Most of my four year apprenticeship was spent on the British Steelworks at Scunthorpe. Kenyons had a few other contracts that the Scunthorpe division looked after and as most engineers were happy to stay close to home, Dave and I were the choice of partnership to be sent away. One such contract was to maintain the large air conditioning plants located on the construction sites of both the Hartlepool and Heysham Nuclear Power Stations. This type of maintenance contract usually meant we had to stay over for a couple of nights. We would travel up on the first day and do some gentle work on site for 4 or 5 hours before checking into some cheap B&B that evening. We could then work a full 12 hours on the second day to get most of the hard work done (if Dave didn't talk too much!) and finally finish off the work on the third day before travelling home.

Dave was one of the original computer geeks and as I was a teenager when the space invaders phenomenon was just taking off, we usually spent most of our free time away from home in the pub playing computer games. Expenses didn't go very far in those days so even though we often found very cheap B&Bs I often returned home quite skint. This was even more so if we had been sent to Heysham, as this is close to the seaside resort of Morecambe where prices escalated during the summer season.

Dave liked his beer but amazingly never really needed much food to soak it up. I would always have the full fry-up breakfast that these B&Bs offered (some better than others) whereas Dave would sit and wait for me every morning and have nothing more than a cup of tea. Works canteens were usually the best source of large meals and construction site canteens were always the best of the best. For a heavily subsidised fee you could get a full three course meal that would make it almost impossible to stay awake in the afternoon. I would always try my best to eat everything offered but when your working colleague is simply sitting opposite you drinking more tea and eating nothing much more than just a rock bun, it was hard.

Rock buns!!!!! Yes rock buns. Dave loved rock buns. I could never work out where he got them from or even how he ate so many. It didn't matter if the rock bun was nice and fresh or was a few days old and 'rock' hard. He would eat them with great vigour. In fact it was the only food item Dave would enjoy as much as his beer. Any time of day (or even night) he would somehow magically produce a tub of rock buns and devour one or two. Most people eat them with a moist butter, cream, jam or suitable accompaniment like you would a scone. Not Dave. He always ate them as they were, dry! Most people would maybe carry mints or sweets around to satisfy a hunger between meals. Not Dave. His hunger satisfier was a rock bun.

After work on the first two days we would go back to the B&B to wash, shower and change before heading out to the pub. I wouldn't need an early evening meal before the pub as I was usually still very full after my mammoth three course meal at lunchtime. Dave probably just ate another rock bun while I got changed.

As Dave and I would spend several times a year visiting these construction sites we became known to most of the landlords at the pubs we visited in the evenings. We were creatures of habit and so we tended to go to the same pub every evening. It was usually the most local pub to the B&B. It needed to be within crawling distance back to our bed and more importantly, they MUST have a space invader machine. In those days the quality of beer didn't matter as much. I was a teenager, I would drink anything.

Most of my visits to these sites were the same as the last visit and all the preceding visits before that. One memorable visit was in the earlier years of our stay at Heysham Power Station. Although our work was always confined to a temporary plant room attached to the side of the main construction, on this particular occasion we were introduced to the construction within the main building.

We had arrived at lunchtime on our first day and as usual were reporting to the site engineer to obtain all the relevant keys and permits to enable us to carry out our maintenance tasks. Dave as usual was talking non stop and suddenly asked,

"Is there any chance we could see what is at the other end of our air conditioning ductwork?"

He said it in such a natural flow of his usual chatting that it almost caught the engineer off hand.

"Sorry Dave" was the reply "what did you say?"

" I just wondered if we could see where all our cool air goes" said Dave "We've been coming here for ages making sure the air conditioning is working as efficiently as it can but have never been allowed into the construction site that it feeds"

"Oh, I see." exclaimed the engineer "I'd never thought of that. I'll tell you what, leave it with me and I will see what I can do. I'm not promising anything but I will see what I can organise for you"

"Fair enough" said Dave and carried on with his normal constant talk about nothing.

The next day I had completely forgotten about the conversation with the engineer until he appeared at the plant room door. Luckily I was actually working hard trying to change some belts on a compressor so it gave a good impression of how hard we did work.

"Are you guys ready to go where no-man can ever go again?"

"What...?!?!?   Is this the Starship Enterprise or something?" I said

Not understanding what he was talking about I simply shouted "DAVE" to attract his attention over the noise of the machinery.

"Hi there" said Dave as he came round the corner within sight of the engineer. "What's up, can I help?"

"Actually, I'm hoping I can help you guys". The engineer then repeated his question "Are you guys ready to go where no-man can ever go again?"

"What do you mean"

"Well I've managed to not only get you permission to go into the main building but I can show you the inner core" he declared.

"The inner core?" we both queried in unison

"Yes. Look we need to go now as I only have a 30 minute window while all the construction workers are on a break"

Dave and I dropped our tools and quickly followed the engineer out of the plant room.

To gain entry into the main building you need to pass through the decontamination room. This is not what you may think but simply where you change shoes and have to don special overalls to ensure the building is and stays as clean as possible. It is to stop any contamination getting into the building and in this industry, nothing gets out. Most food factories have similar arrangements to keep bacteria etc out of production areas. Here they were at the stage of controlling everything in and out. We emerged the other side of the contamination room in our bright 'White' overalls, clean boots, gloves and hair coverings. Dave looked like he was covered head to toe in a white Burka. His beard was managing to stretch the guard he was force to wear around his face and all we could see was his excited eyes peering out between his hairnet and beard guard.

The massive hall we found ourselves in was strewn with construction equipment but unlike a conventional construction site everything looked sparkling clean. There was a highly polished floor with scaffolding in some places and a few cherry pickers parked up under partly finished lighting booms. It was eerily quiet. This immaculately clean, cavernous hall in the middle of a major construction site seemed so unreal. Construction sites were usually dirty, noisy places and here we were in the middle of a major construction site that was spotlessly clean. It was so quiet you could hear a pin drop and more to the point, there was absolutely no-one around except us 3.

"Come on let's be quick" whispered the engineer in the library quiet atmosphere "we have a bit of a walk"

 Across the hall, dodging tools and equipment sprawled all over our route, down several flights of stairs and along some walkways we headed. All the time the engineer pointing out various parts of the workings of a Nuclear Power Station. Just for once Dave hardly had chance to say anything. Like me he was just in awe at the size and magnitude of the construction. We dutifully followed our leader and listened to every word he spoke. I hoped there was not an exam at the end of our tour as I didn't understand any of it.

Finally we arrived at a solid concrete wall that curved around the inner chamber. Two feet off the floor where we stood was a square hole about 3 feet wide and tall. It had obviously been cut into the thick wall to gain access to the inside.

"Here we are then!" The engineer proudly announced "this is it. Once this is finally sealed off no-one can ever go inside here again"

"What, so this is THE inner core" Dave enthusiastically declared

"Correct. The inner core is where the Uranium Rods will be housed at the centre of the Nuclear Power Station and so once the Rods are fitted this inner core will be so radioactive no-one for centuries will ever be allowed in there."

"Wow...." Was all I could muster. I was just blown away at the thought of where we were

"Go on then. Off you go" the engineer said as he directed us into the hole in the wall.

"No! After you" Dave courteously indicated.

"No, actually I cannot go in." We were scarily informed by our guide "One of us have to stay out here for safety reasons and I am the only trained safety watch amongst us"

Before I knew what was happening I was being physically persuaded to climb through the opening. As the concrete was so thick it was more like crawling through a tunnel than climbing through a hatch. Thankfully the floor on the inside was slightly higher than the outer floor and so as I emerged head first in the inner core chamber I could easily walk the upper part of my body out on my hands and knees. I then stood up and took in my surroundings.

The room I found myself in was well illuminated by very bright construction lamps on tripods. The circular room was a complete mess. Bits of broken concrete, steel and plaster were strewn all over the floor. Tools and equipment were dumped around the ground as if they had been discarded quickly (obviously in the rush to get to a tea break quickly). Cables hung around like unfinished cobwebs all emanating from the entrance hatch I had just crawled through.

Dave's head appeared

"What's it like?" he said as he tried to twist his head up from a downward facing position.

"Oh my God. It's a tip!" he proclaimed as he pulled himself out into the chamber "I cannot believe the state of this room compared to the rest of the construction"

"This is like a proper construction site!"

— — — —

Chapter 8

'Sound Sleeper'

During the construction of the Heysham Power Station (and most of my apprenticeship) it was always Dave and I who regularly carried out the maintenance visits. One of my last visits to Heysham was actually without Dave. He had been sent on another job and couldn't attend our usual 'holiday' on the west coast. I was nearly out of my apprenticeship and so almost qualified as a fully fledged Refrigeration Engineer. As the contract was for two people to attend, my fellow apprentice companion Mick had been assigned to join me. He wanted to drive his newly acquired company vehicle and so I was happy to let him drive us up there in his van. We decided to tell the site engineer that Mick was a newly qualified Refrigeration Engineer and I was to pretend to be his apprentice. Mick seemed happy to take control of the whole job and relished in the idea of being in control and trying to tell me what to do.

Mick picked me up from my house and we had a fairly uneventful journey up to Morecambe on the west coast. It was mid summer so the weather was very favourable and the main holiday season was well under way. Driving along the sea front we could see families enjoying the sea and sand, eating donuts, ice cream and fish & chips. We were very tempted to stop and join them instead of going to work in a hot and sweaty plant room.

Mick rose to the challenge and the site engineer was more than happy to see my familiar face. We carried out our first half day of work and I was surprised when Mick wasn't keen to stop work at 5pm as usual. I eventually persuaded him we needed to finish so we could check in at our B&B. That's when he turned to me and admitted his plans.

"We don't have a B&B tonight."

"What do you mean" I exclaimed."I booked it myself as Dave was not going to be here"

"No, I cancelled it" explained Mick "I thought we could get the work done in two days, work 14 hours tomorrow, head home straight after and have Wednesday off."

Mouth open and speechless I just stood there disbelievingly staring at him. Obviously the idea of him being the Engineer and me his apprentice had made Mick power mad.

"So what about tonight then?" I finally found my tongue

"As it is only one night I thought we could sleep in the van and have the money we save for beer instead." Mick unveiled his plan. "We can get showered and changed here and then spend most of the night in one of the night clubs"

My mouth fell open again.

"I'll sleep in the front seat and you can have the back of the van" he suggested

"Mick, you haven't got a transit van! It's only a flipping Ford Fiesta!!!! There is NO back of the van"

"We'll be all right. Trust me" he said.

I was not happy. Yes I was a teenager and yes I had had my share of late nights in night clubs etc but the thought of trying to get even a bit of sleep in the back of a small Fiesta van was not going to work. I was so **not** keen on his plan that I did try to find somewhere to rent a bed but in holiday season in a popular seaside resort it was impossible. I spent an hour or two wandering aimlessly around Morecambe but everywhere was full except the large expensive hotels.

I eventually met up with Mick in a nightclub along the front and noticed he had somehow managed to find a parking space for the van further down the front. I was still not happy with him but had resigned myself to my fate and decided the only way I would get some sleep was if I got lots of beer down me.

Somehow it worked.

I did manage to find a curled up position around the tools in the back and did actually fall asleep. The next morning at 6am I was standing by the van trying hard to stretch myself out straight when Mick said

"My god you do snore loudly don't you"

"Well its your fault" I defended "I needed all that beer to get to sleep in there"

"I was worried at one point in the night"

"Why?" I queried

"At about 4am a copper was walking by and looked in our direction. I don't think he could see me but he stood there for what seemed like an eternity. Then in all the silence you suddenly started snoring very loudly. I wanted to throw something at you to shut you up but I realised if I moved he would see me."

I laughed "serves you right. Bloody stupid idea of sleeping in the van anyway. Come on, I'll let you buy me breakfast"

The day passed very slowly and it felt like a very long day. We had mutually agreed to do all the rest of the work that day so that we could travel home that night instead of trying to get a room in Morecambe. We were both very tired from lack of sleep but successfully got all the work done before setting off late at night. At least we could have the following day off and recover from our tough working holiday.

We were both keen to get home as quickly as we could and thankfully the roads were relatively quiet due to the lateness of the day. I said I would drive the first half of the journey so Mick could get some sleep and then he would drive the second half. I said I would try to stay awake while he was driving and keep taking to him to help stave off the desire for him to sleep.

I had done well to stay awake and we must have been only 30 or 40 miles from home when it happened. I had started reading an article out loud from the newspaper to Mick to keep the conversation going. The roads were practically empty and I was holding my newspaper in front of me so wasn't really paying any attention to the road. I first felt what seemed like some bumps in the road like you do when you drive over cats eyes. Then they got bumpier which was when I lowered my paper to see what was in the road. I expected to see pot holes or maybe debris in the road. In actual fact I didn't see the road!

Mick had fallen asleep at the wheel and he had drifted into the centre of the motorway and was driving on the rough ground of the central reservation.

BANG

We hit the central reservation barrier and scraped along the side of it.

"MICK, MICK….. wake up you idiot." I shouted

Mick immediately woke up and skilfully steered the van back onto the road. Safely back onto the inside lane he still kept on driving. Mick rubbed his eyes and calmly said.

"Ooops……. Sorry about that!"

"Er… don't you think we should stop and see what damage you've done Mick?"

"Do you really think so?"

After half a mile Mick agreed to pull over onto the hard shoulder and we both got out to survey the damage. Two long indentations ran the whole length of the van mimicking the contours of the central barrier. A lot of the paint in the indentations had been scratched but still maintained the overall impression of white. Mick looked at me….

"Do you think Gareth will notice?"

"What!!!! What do you think !" I exclaimed "Of course he will"

"I think your best option is to just come clean and tell him tomorrow morning at work." I continued

The rest of the journey home was done in silence. Although I kept my eye on Mick I didn't believe he could fall asleep after that. I let him drive us home as it was his van and I wanted nothing to do with the damage he had inflicted.

We both needed our 'free' day off on the Wednesday to recover. I was nicely refreshed and, for once, early to work on the Thursday. I was one of the first in and had my main duty of tea making well under way before anyone arrived.

I was sat in the mess room when Mick arrived. He was the last person to arrive in. I fully expected him to go straight into the office to admit his accident to our boss. Instead he simply waltzed into the mess room and calmly sat down next to me. He poured himself a mug of tea and just smiled at me as if he didn't have a care in the world.

"What did Gareth say" I glared at Mick.

"I haven't told him." Mick casually said "I've parked the van over that side of the car park so you can't see the damage and you can only see the good side from here. Gareth will never notice."

Obviously that subterfuge would never last very long with any boss. Luckily Gareth was a very understanding boss and when Mick finally did come clean about his accident, the only punishment he received was to spend the following year driving a terribly dinted van.

The van never did get repaired !

— — — —

Chapter 9

Lysaghts Steelworks (aka Normanby Park) was one of the oldest steelworks in Scunthorpe and was the other side of Scunthorpe to the main site. Unlike the main site which was home to several steelworks such as Appleby, Frodingham, Redbourn, Anchor etc. Lysaghts was on its own.

Lysaghts was a small steelworks compared to the others in Scunthorpe as it had originally been built in 1912 as a fully integrated Iron & Steel making works. This gave it an advantage over the other sites in Scunthorpe where, in my days in the industry, it could specialise in unique steel which were only needed in smaller batches. The larger steelworks like Anchor were all about volume, making steel in 300ton furnaces but Lysaghts only made steel in 45ton batches which suited the demand for the specialist steel better. Just like Sheffield steelworks that became famous for its creation of Stainless Steel, Lysaghts was famous for its production of 'free-cutting steel' which was very desirable in the manufacturing and engineering industries. The downside was how this special steel was made!

One day my boss, Gareth and I had a job to do on the top of the LD plant on the Lysaghts site which housed the main steel making furnaces. This particular morning we had loaded a lot of equipment into the back of his estate car and as it had been determined as a two man job, I was the apprentice to help Gareth get all of it transported up onto the roof area where the job was located.

Luckily for us there was a service lift to the 7th floor but we would still have to manually carry all the equipment up the remaining 4 flights of stairs to get onto the roof space where the condensing units were housed. Gareth parked his car at the back of the LD plant building right next to the ground floor entrance to the lift and we transferred everything we would need into the service lift. Gareth locked his car and we closed the doors and gates on the lift cage before hitting the no.7 button on the panel.

As the lift clunked and rattled its way up we heard a siren go off and we both looked at each other.

"What does that mean?" I said to Gareth

"Not sure!" He shrugged

"Its not a fire alarm or anything is it? Do we need to evacuate?"

"No! Don't panic. I think its just one of the cranes or something as part of the steelmaking process" he assured me "we'll get all this stuff upstairs and then I will go and find out if it affects us"

Before the lift arrived at its top floor destination we could smell it. I looked anxiously at Gareth but he confidently told me we would be ok. In hindsight we should have just pressed the ground floor button and waited below on the ground floor until the fumes had cleared. In fact nowadays with environmental concerns, as well as health and safety regulations, they wouldn't be allowed to discharge those type of fumes into the atmosphere. They would need more than just a siren to warn people of the imminent sulphur fume discharge and I am sure nowadays HSE regulations wouldn't allow anyone above the steel making furnaces during operational production.

Gareth was the boss and he was in charge. He told me to grab some of the equipment, take a deep breath and his plan was to run up the stairs to the roof top with all the equipment and into the relatively fresh air.

"Sod that for a plan!!!" I thought.

I did grab a toolbox in one hand and I did put a gas bottle in the other as the doors of the service lift opened but as soon as I put a foot outside on the landing I put them down leaving them on the 7th floor before starting my run up the stairs, 3 steps at a time! Staircase 1: then staircase 2: followed by staircase 3: but then I needed to take another breath before the last staircase. It felt like it was cutting into my throat as I tried to take a breath. That deep intake that I needed was never going to happen as it wasn't fresh air that surrounded me. Even my eyes stung as I tried to look through the toxic fog around me.

Unaware that Gareth was directly behind me we both simultaneously smashed through the door out onto the roof space. We never stopped but carried on running along the walkway into the head wind to get to the far end of the building. We both finally lent over the hand rail in the relatively fresh air and coughed our guts up.

A British Steel worker came up to me and patted my back with a sympathetic response.

"Are you guys all right?" came the question "Do you need me to call a first aider?"

Neither of us were capable of a verbal response but both customarily shook our heads.

It did take us quite some time to get our breath back and it took the rest of the day to feel like we had recovered fully. In fact I had a bad taste in my mouth for days afterwards and was not happy with Gareth for putting us both in such a dangerous situation. The Steelworker who comforted us on the roof top told us that everyone should know what the siren was for and that everyone knows to get up-wind if you cannot get away completely.

An hour later we tentatively climbed down the four staircases to collect all the equipment we had left outside the service lift door. We struggled so much with lack of energy that it was impossible to carry every piece up in one go so we took several journeys up and down before we could even start the job we had come to do.

It was a good lesson to learn, although we had learnt it a very hard way. It did mean that I never, ever went near the LD plant building if I knew they were about to make that particular type of sulphur-alloyed steel.

A couple of weeks later I found myself in a similar sort of situation where two of us had been assigned a job on a rooftop that needed a large quantity of heavy equipment to be manually lifted up to the condensing units. Thankfully this was no where near Lysaghts or even above any furnaces. This was on top of a rolling mill on the main Scunthorpe site. This was not just any rolling mill but on top of the Rod & Bar rolling mill which was one of the newest and most modern rolling mills on the Scunthorpe main site. This was going to be a doddle after my Lysaghts experience.

Unfortunately there was NO service lift!! We were going to have to carry everything up the whole way by ourselves. There was so much equipment for this job that it was going to take a couple of journeys each to get everything up there. But never mind, it was a lovely sunny day and we could take our time. Mick and I were just finishing our apprenticeships and we were about to become fully qualified Refrigeration Engineers, we knew what we were doing!

What could possibly go wrong??!!

The first trip up the many staircases went fine. I had decided to carry a heavy gas bottle in one hand and a box of spares under the other arm. Mick had decided he would carry the heaviest item first which was the replacement compressor. He placed both hands around and underneath that one item, lifted it out of the van and immediately started up the first staircase. Once at the top of all the staircases we had to walk along a narrow walkway within the roof space to get to a door leading out to our destination. Both my arms ached, as I am sure Mick's did! but the bravado of youth meant we wouldn't show our discomfort to each other, so we just carried on. We eventually came to the door leading out onto the open roof area and exited into the bright warm sunshine. Both of us were exhausted and our arms were now feeling very heavy and ready to drop off.

We both put down our cargo and looked up at the nice warming sunshine. Although we wouldn't admit it verbally we both knew how hard that climb had been. Neither of us relished the idea of going back down for the rest of the gear but we knew we would have to once we had rested and recovered.

This particular roof area was slightly lower than the rest of the buildings around us creating an area that resembled a sunken Italian garden feel about it. A proper sun trap. One end of the roof area had a brick parapet which stood only three foot high but gave you great panoramic views across Scunthorpe. While I enjoyed the sun on my face trying to get the circulation back into my arms I notice Mick was not only enjoying the view over the parapet but actually leaning over it looking straight down. Mick loved heights and I hated them. I was alright on solid buildings looking at panoramic views but it was not my idea of fun looking straight down a sheer brick wall some 70 or 80 feet up.

"I've got an idea" declared Mick as he turned his head back to me from the parapet.

"Oh dear!! What brainwave have you got now?" I worriedly replied

"I've got a long rope in the back of my van" he started "we could use it to haul the portapak up here"

A portapak was a small gas welding kit that we used out on site. The same type of thing as the oxyacetylene set ups you see in every workshop in the country. This kit was a small version of that, in a framework with two wheels that you could easily wheel around to various locations. Great on flat ground but not so easy to transport up and down several sets of stairs.

"You have got to be joking" I exclaimed

"No. It'll be fine. Trust me"

"That's the problem, I don't trust you. You've always had a reputation for crazy ideas and I think this is your most stupid one so far"

I took a look over the parapet and instantly regretted trying to assess the height we were at.

"We must be at least 70 foot up" I said while taking a step back from the sheer terrifying elevation.

"The rope I've got is easily that long, no problem"

With that Mick walked off back across the roof heading for the door to get down.

We drove Mick's van around the back of the Rod and Bar mill and located it at the bottom of this tall brick wall leading up to our working area on the roof. Out came the Portapak and Mick's long coiled up rope. The rope was a half inch diameter sisal rope which to you and me was known as the hairy type of rope! Mick put the coil of rope over his shoulder and grabbed one of the tool bags from the back of his van.

"Right, I'll go up top and drop the rope over the side" he confidently said "If you tie the Portapak securely to the end I will pull it up. If you make sure the wheels start running up the wall it will be fine."

I was not very happy with this idea but decided that once I had secured the rope I could get well out of the way and slowly make my way up the stairs with the rest of the equipment. I could be oblivious to anything that goes wrong.

10 minutes later I hear the distant sound of Mick's voice shouting down to me from above. I shouted back that I was as ready as I could be and I stood well back out of the way to get a better view of the operation. Mick disappeared back from the parapet and I waited, looking up at the top of the wall expecting the rope to gently be lowered down the side of the building.

All of a sudden the large coil of hairy rope came flying over the parapet followed by a long tail of the rope. It looked very much like a large tadpole had taken a dive over a waterfall into a pond below.

It wasn't until it actually hit the ground, narrowly missing the Portapak and Mick's van, that I noticed the long tail end of the hairy rope had followed the coil of rope all the way to the bottom. The whole of the rope was now sat neatly next to the portapak. I looked up in disbelief to see Mick looking down over the Parapet shaking his hands and blowing on them.

I left the rope where it was and simply picked up the Portapak and my tool bag. I slowly walked up all the stairs lugging up the remaining equipment and walked out onto the rooftop to find Mick sat there still shaking and blowing on his hands.

"What the hell happened? I thought you would lower the rope down bit by bit"

"Its bloody heavy that rope" he declared "I decided it would be easier to throw the coil over the side and I would hold onto the other end. The rope just slipped through my fingers. I couldn't hold onto it. I think I've burnt my hands!" Mike held his hands out to show me.

"Why didn't you tie the end to something?"

Mick looked up at me from his sitting position.

"I never thought of that"

— — — —

Chapter 10

'Hot & Cold Yoghurt'

Like all domestic trades such as electricians, builders, plumbers etc. most of your friends and family saw it as an advantage to know someone with the skills and know-how to get jobs around the house done on the cheap. Ask any electrician how many times they have been asked to fit an outside light for a friend. Or any plumber how many times he has been requested to fit a new bathroom suite for someone they know. All of them will tell you 'loads of times!'

Refrigeration was no exception. Even BEFORE I started work at 16 my Auntie Jean had asked me to look at her Fridge door which was sticking! - Ok, I did actually fix the door handle for her but that was nothing to do with my knowledge of refrigeration (or the lack of it!!) it was simply because unlike Auntie Jeans family, I had always been a very practical person.

In the world of refrigeration it is well known that temperature is a relative thing. Whether you are trying to cool a room down to 20'C, a fridge down to 4'C or a freezer down to -20'C the principle is the same. The equipment removes heat leaving a freezer with less heat than a fridge or even a room it is in.

Nearly all my apprenticeship was spent working on the air conditioning side of refrigeration rather than on the domestic cold storage (such as fridges and freezers) that most people use. In those days only large industry and posh people had become familiar with air conditioning in offices and so my friends and family never asked my opinion on their air conditioning problems. My knowledge of cold storage refrigeration in those days was very limited but my good nature meant that any requests to look at their problems were never refused. Sometimes (like my Auntie Jean) I was successful - and sometimes, I was not......

My girlfriend at the time 'Elaine' (who later became my wife) had an older sister who ran the Red Lion Hotel in a little Lincolnshire village outside Scunthorpe called Redbourne. Tom & Maureen had a very successful business as the hotel was on the main road from Lincoln to Scunthorpe and so had lots of passing trade. The restaurant was well known in the area and people often travelled quite a distance to enjoy sumptuous meals there.

I had easily been accepted into the family and was therefore invited to various celebrations which were always held at Tom & Maureen's hotel. I felt like I was not only part of that family but that I was now friends with a local celebrity. It did my street credibility no end of good! Tom was a very good business man and obviously saw an advantage of having a 'family member' in the refrigeration trade who could maybe save him some money.

Tom was always having trouble with his cold store which was located behind the kitchen area at the hotel. I say cold store ..... but in actual fact it was an old refrigerated container he had got cheap several years before and had it located in the car park behind the hotel.

To get food from the cold store the kitchen staff needed to go out the back of the kitchen and into the refrigerated container located just outside the door. On cold, rainy days it wasn't very good for them and on hot sunny days it wasn't very good for the cold store. Every time the door was opened a rush of warm moist air would enter the cold store and raise the temperature. Not only that but the moist air then freezes on the evaporator (the coldest part of refrigeration) and it then ices up. Everybody knows the problem of ice build up in their freezer, well The Red Lion's cold store had a real big problem with ice build up and there was no easy solution to remove it. Tom and the staff had to regularly scrape the ice off the evaporator plates which then just fell onto the floor or shelving within the container.

Most commercial cold stores tackle the ice problem by quickly warming up the evaporator on a regular basis to melt the ice and then let the water drain away out of the cold store. The Red Lion's cold store had no such defrost system as it was originally designed to keep the door closed all the time. As a container the door would only be opened to fill it or to empty it. If the door is never opened then no moist air can get in and so no build up of ice. The Red Lion's cold store door was often being opened hence the real big problem of ice build up.

"Terry, you're in the fridge trade!" Tom started, while I was having a drink in the bar one night with Elaine and some of our friends.

"That's right Tom." came my instinctive reply.

"I'm having problems with my cold store and wondered if you could take a look" he said

"Well I'm no expert on cold stores Tom but I'll have a look if you want. What's your problem?"

"We get loads and loads of ice build up" he replied "but don't worry I'm not expecting you to work out how to fix it, the company who service it for me has given me a quote on a new evaporator that should fix it. I was wondering if you could get it any cheaper?"

Sigh of relief from me..... "Sure, I can take a look and see what I can do"

Now most of you would think.... That seems simple enough. All I had to do was find out what's been quoted and then price it up with the supplier of refrigeration equipment we use. That would have been the most logical way of doing things. However, I had just completed my college training (as part of my apprenticeship) which had taught me how to calculate and size up various types of cold stores. Therefore I found myself wanting to use this new found knowledge. I mistakenly thought that if I did the complex thermodynamic calculations and I got the right cold store equipment I could impress my girlfriend, friends and colleagues. I could show them I knew what I was doing.

Instead of taking the easy road, I set to and started measuring the container. I noted down the relative location and orientation on the earth to incorporate my solar azimuth calculations. I progressed with the complicated heat load calculations and eventually decided what appropriate equipment was needed. In fact I was quite proud of myself. I successfully used everything I had been taught in college on a real life scenario.

Maybe Tom was impressed with my ingenuity. Maybe he was impressed with all the calculations I had shown him. Maybe he simply trusted me. Or maybe he was impressed with my price. After all, I did manage to quote him a price that was less than his usual contractor.

I believe today it was my price that swung it. Business men always look at the price first. Whatever Tom's reasons were he readily gave me the job.

What on earth was I doing…. I didn't really want the job but I had got so involved in the design stages that I had never considered the fact I may get the complete job. Yes, I had now proven my design skills but now had the task of purchasing and installing the new equipment. I was hardly out of my apprenticeship and I had accidentally landed myself a whole cold store installation.

As I have mentioned earlier in this chapter, a typical office room is around 20'C, a typical fridge (for dairy & cheese etc) is around 4'C and a typical freezer (for ice cream etc.) is around -20'C. With this in mind I made one simple mistake with devastating results.

Tom wanted a freezer cold store to hold all his fish, meat, ice cream etc at -20'C. I misunderstood what he actually wanted and designed something that would run at normal fridge temperatures of 4'C. Therefore once I had spent Tom's money and installed everything the cold store spent the rest of its life running flat out trying to get the temperature down to what Tom wanted and not what I had designed it for. Even now, decades later, I feel embarrassed at how I dramatically failed him.

Poor Tom ended up with a 'Hot' cold store.

Amazingly friends and family never noticed my incompetence with Tom's cold store (or just never mentioned it). They unfortunately still kept asking me to look at their refrigeration problems and my good nature meant I never refused their requests.

Some very dear friends of Tom and Maureen's were John & Janet. They had known each other for many years and John & Janet ran a very successful flower shop in my home village of Messingham. John had originally sold cars but his wife, Janet, ran a successful flower shop which eventually became a more profitable business. So one day John got rid of all his cars and turned his business premises into a large flower shop on the main road through Messingham.

One day, John approached me asking if I could create a cool room for him to preserve some of the bouquets they create.

"If we had somewhere to preserve the flowers then we could get on top of the demand, especially at times like valentines day" John started "Ive got an old freezer and wondered if you could change it to run at a higher temperature"

"That should be no problem" I told him "I should be able to get hold of a fridge thermostat and simply fit that for you. Leave it with me."

It's that word 'Simple'! Every time it looks simple you know things are not going to be that simple.

I obtained the appropriate thermostat. I went round to the shop 'Flowers by Janet', and replaced the existing thermostat on his freezer with my 'fridge' one. It sounds simple doesn't it, and true enough it was a simple job.

However the very next day I got a phone call....

"Hi Terry, it's John here" he started

My heart sank "Hi John, how's it going? Did it work ok?"

"Oh yes" John chuckled "the flowers have definitely been preserved......"

"However, we may need to defrost them before we can actually use them!!!!!"

At least John could laugh about it and he only lost a few flowers. He did say the frozen flowers looked magnificent but he didn't think there was likely to be a market for them.

Oh dear….. another of my failures.

Firstly I build Tom a 'Hot' cold store and then secondly I managed to freeze John's flowers. If I was actually self employed I think I would have gone out of business. To my amazement, all my friends and family still kept asking me to fix their refrigeration problems and, as usual, I was too soft hearted to refuse.

One evening, while I was waiting for Elaine to get ready for our date, her mother came into the lounge where I was sat and looked at me.

"You work in refrigeration don't you?" Ethel asked

"Yes, that's right" I cheerily replied as my heart sank with the thought of previous failures.

"Well the door on my fridge doesn't shut properly" Ethel continued "Could you have a look sometime and see if you can see what's wrong"

"I'll take a quick look now if you want" I cautiously replied "but I'm not promising anything".

So Ethel showed me into their kitchen and pointed to the fridge. My apprehension disappeared as soon as I opened the fridge door as even to a layman it was obvious that the seal around the door had perished.

"There's your problem" I told my future Mother-in-Law "The door seal is broken"

"Is that important?" She asks

'Yes, Ethel. The door seal has a magnet in it to help keep the door shut and make a proper seal around the door to keep all the cold air in"

"Could it be changed?" Came her next question

"Sometimes it's possible but the seal has to be an exact match and you may not be able to get one for this old fridge nowadays" I said trying to ensure I didn't get the job.

"Well I had been thinking of getting a new fridge anyway, so your advice has made my mind up for me. Thank you"

Ethel's words were such a great relief to me, so much so that I almost let out a large sigh of relief.

Two weeks later Ethel had her new fridge installed and Elaine had reported how pleased her Mum was with her new shiny fridge. Ethel had even shown everyone how the light came on and off as the door was opened and closed. Obviously her old fridge didn't have this modern technology and Ethel was enjoying her recent purchase. Finally, I thought, I had successfully given someone the correct advice.

Later that week, I found myself again sat in Ethel's lounge waiting for Elaine to get ready for our date. I then made the mistake of asking.....

"How's the new fridge Ethel?"

"Well the door doesn't shut properly" she replied

"What!!!! Not again, surely!" I exclaimed

"But don't worry" she continued "I intend to call the shop tomorrow and get them to fix it as it surely will still be under warranty"

"I agree Ethel" I said "get them to repair it or even replace it if it's faulty"

Why oh why did I not just have a look myself. Even now after all these years I feel bad at letting my future Mother in law down. If I had just taken a couple of seconds to look at the problem instead of trying my best not to get involved, it may have even broken my string of bad luck when it came to doing jobs on the side for family and friends.

Ethel did contact the shop she bought the fridge from.

They did organise for a refrigeration engineer to visit her and look at the problem.

He did manage to fix the problem, and on the same day too!

Unfortunately, it cost Ethel the price of the call-out!

The engineer found that one of the shelves in the fridge was stopping the door from shutting properly. The cause - a yoghurt pot had fallen down behind the shelf!!!!!!!!

— — — —

Chapter 11

'High Security Levels'

Finishing my apprenticeship was nothing special. There was no party, no big ceremony announcing to the world that there was another skilled engineer on the scene. In fact nothing changed at all. One day a letter arrived in the post that contained my original indentures and apart from opening the letter it was unceremoniously put on the sideboard and forgotten about. Luckily my parents saw the importance of the documents enclosed and filed it safely away for my future reference.

By this time I had been seen as a competent enough engineer to be put onto shifts. Our shift pattern meant that I would work an average of 3 days (8am to 4:30pm) and 2 afternoons (4pm to midnight) every week on a rolling basis to include weekends. There was no night shift (midnight to 8am) but whoever was working the afternoon shift could also be called out on emergencies. During winter months this was easy but during hot summer months the lonely afternoon shift engineer could be running around like a chicken with no head.

Steel making is a hot business all year round but even more so on hot summer days and nights. Hundreds of tons of molten metal being poured into moulds and red hot steel ingots being rolled into bars and wires creates an unbearably hot and dusty atmosphere. A lot of steel workers spend 8 hour shifts in pulpits only feet away from these dangerously hot steel products and it can be vital that they get clean and cool air that our A/C units can provide.

As you can imagine, in the summer months all the A/C units are working overtime and break downs were plentiful. Often the afternoon shift would be 16 hours long as there was no-one to take over at midnight. Sometimes I may have managed to get home late after a busy shift and as I drifted off to the land of nod the phone would ring and I would find myself driving back to work at 3am in the morning, as the rest of the world sleeps.

I regularly asked myself (usually in the middle of the night) if there was an easier way of earning a living.

One Friday afternoon, in late Autumn, I arrived at work just before 4pm ready for what I thought would be a relatively quiet afternoon shift. Work loads had calmed down after the usually busy summer months and the day shift engineer had only handed over a couple of jobs for me to attend to. As he and everyone else left the workshop to start their weekend off he told me it had been a nice and easy day.

As the weather had started to cool down for that time of year I decide to have a Jacket potato for my dinner and dutifully placed my potato in the little Baby Belling oven that was provided for us in the mess room. I usual found that it would be nice and crispy by about 6pm that evening and I would organise my work to ensure I would be back in the mess room for my lonely meal.

My first job was to the Steelworks Security central control office. This was a very secure room within an office block near the main entrance. From this room a security guard would monitor the cameras 24 hours a day, 7 days a week. Big brother was definitely watching even before 1984. I felt it gave the busy steelworkers comfort to think that these security officers were keeping a careful watch on their cars while they worked hard. The state of the art CCTV was placed all over the large steelworks site and kept a careful eye on everything that was going on. Anyone up to no good would be seen by the security officer in this control room and he could then put a call out on the radio to apprehend them.

This control room had a very secure door, which could only be opened from the inside, and a sealed window that could let in natural light but would not open to allow any fresh air in. There was a glass fronted serving hatch into the buildings corridor to allow the occupants to communicate with any visitors. The room was so well sealed up and secure that it was essential to have a good air conditioning unit to keep the occupants and equipment cool and, more importantly, a good supply of fresh air. After all it was built like Fort Knox and so could quickly and easily get very uncomfortable when the air conditioning failed. I often wondered why it was deemed necessary to make the room so secure but I suppose someone must have thought it necessary. I placed it high on my priority of jobs that evening and so went there first.

"Hi there" I said into the serving hatch as I arrived "I'm from Kenyons, come to fix your air conditioning"

"Oh great!" came the enthusiastic reply "you're a life saver as its unbearably hot in here, come on in"

The door buzzed as the security officer pressed the door release button and I walked into the stiflingly hot and sweaty atmosphere.

"Oh My God!!! It's hot in here" I said trying to waft the sweaty smell of hot air from my face

In the centre of the room sat a security officer staring at a bank of monitors mounted into a curved wall in front of him. On the desk in front of him was a line of different coloured telephones, a computer keyboard and a joystick to enable him to move some of the security cameras. He had a complete view of the entire site and could keep an eye on anyone up to no good.

"When did you notice it not working then?" I asked as I tried to catch my breath.

"Well it was definitely working fine this afternoon when I came in at the start of my shift" said the security officer "but then a couple of hours ago it just started to blow nothing but warm air."

"Well I'll see what I can do but it's so hot in here it may take a while to cool you down if I do get it going" I stated

"Do whatever you can for us as we cannot even open a window as you can see" said the security officer

"I was tempted to throw my chair through the window" he joked. "We did try to turn it off but that just made the room even worse with no air movement at all"

"Why does it get so hot so quickly? I queried

" Oh it's all these blooming TV monitors" he answered " They kick out a hell of a lot of heat"

I turned to the air conditioning wall unit and started dismantling the front panel to start my diagnosis.

Now for all refrigeration to work, whether it's for air conditioning or for the freezer in your kitchen, you need the basic elements of;

- a cold radiator (called an evaporator) to produce the cold air in the room,

- a hot radiator (called a condenser) to get rid of the heat outside,

and

- a compressor to move all the refrigerant around the system.

I found the evaporator in the wall unit to be warm to the touch and so this indicated to me that the problem was most likely to be with the condensing unit outside.

I told the security officer I needed to check the unit outside and so he pressed the door release button again on his desk and I pulled the heavy steel door to exit the control room.

I walked out the building and around the back to below the control room window. There, below the window, was the condensing unit with a big fan spinning around trying to get rid of the heat. The motor which drives the compressor was also running as it should be but even to an untrained eye it was obvious what the problem was.

I immediately turned around and went straight back to the security serving hatch.

"That was quick!" he exclaimed "fixed it already?"

"Er… No" I said "you're not going to believe this….. but……"

"Someone has stolen your compressor!!!!"

For all the technology they had in that room they couldn't see someone steal something from under their own noses (or their window in this instance).

I sorted them out with some fans and they realised they would have to have the secure door left open until I could order and replace the stolen compressor. Unfortunately for them, that was several weeks later.

My second call that night was to an overhead crane in the Bloom & Billet mill called a V.I.C. This was a Vertical Ingot Crane which picked up cold ingots and placed them into open top ovens. When the ingots were glowing hot enough the V.I.C would then lift them out one at a time and place them on rollers to send it down the 1 mile long Bloom and Billet mill. As these cranes would be working directly above ovens at over 1000'C they needed very powerful air conditioning units to keep the operators cool. The intense strain on these units meant that we were regularly being called out to them.

When the cranes were not being used they could park them up at one end of the mill out of the way to cool down. The ground in this area resembled a scrap yard, it was all rough stones and boulders with scrap steel and debris littered all around. The lower sections of the walls were none existent but this helped bring in cool air from outside and created a nice draft up through the steelwork of the crane to help cool it down naturally.

I parked my van near the steps leading directly up to the crane in question and gathered all my usual tools that I thought I would need to repair the air conditioning. I had learnt (the hard way) that these cranes got so hot that you didn't simply start climbing up the access ladders on them. When you started climbing a ladder you needed to have thick gloves and be sure you can make it to the top without a rest. All the rungs and steelwork could be very hot and tonight was no exception. Although I had a heavy tool bag over my shoulder and a gas bottle in one hand I successfully climbed the hot ladder in a well practiced jerking movement using just one gloved hand.

The sweat was pouring off me before I even started any repairs. I could feel the heat seeping through my thick boots as I stood in front of the main air conditioning unit. Gas leaks on these particular units were a very common problem and I am sad to say that before the introduction of CFC free refrigeration gases I probably contributed greatly to global warming. I would never just top it up without thought of where the gas had escaped, but the intense working conditions these cranes would be under meant that they would often break pipes and dislodge parts. This time was no exception and I spent over 20 minutes of searching in the very hot conditions before finding a broken connector. Once I had ensured the system was again sealed and air tight I gave myself a pat on the back for my insight to bring the gas bottle with me to refill the system.

The relevant gas pressures around the air conditioning unit were raising to normal levels and the evaporator was starting to cool down. The condenser on top of the crane was starting to kick out the excess heat (despite the already high surrounding temperatures) and the crane driver's cabin was starting to feel a bit closer to a respectable working temperature. I was still sweating like I was fully dressed in a Turkish bath, but the crane driver was actually starting to put clothes back on, which was a good sign.

Satisfied that the job was complete I started collecting my tools together. I disconnected the gas bottle from the charging point and was looking forward to my well earned tea awaiting me in the baby belling oven back at the depot. Carefully placing my tools into my tool bag, in the correct order, I ensured they were ready for the next call-out, but more importantly ensured that they were secure ready for my one-handed, jerking descent of the access ladder.

As I picked up my charging lines from the top of the air conditioning unit I saw it fall.

My very expensive, specialist socket set must have been sat on the end of my charging hoses and as I moved them they had tipped the socket set off the top of the unit. If it had fallen towards me it would have simply dropped 5 feet onto the platform I was stood on. Oh no, it had to fall the other way and it disappeared off the back of the air conditioning unit into the abyss. I watched in slow motion as the socket set descended the 60 feet of free fall dispensing its contents over a wide area of the rough stones and boulders below. Even the crane driver looked over his newspaper blowing in the cool breeze I had created for him and said calmly,

"Ooo, that was unlucky!"

He was trying hard to hide a smirk on his face but I was stunned. I had spent 6 months paying weekly sums from my pay packet to own that specialist socket set. It was my pride and joy. I was left speechless.

I descended the crane with what remained of my tools and a heavy heart. Loading everything into the back of my van I looked over at the empty socket set box laid on top of some scrap metal. I at least had to recover what I could, so I locked my van up and scrambled over the rough ground as the crane moved away from above to get back to work.

Once started I seemed to get a determination to try and find everything. I may have found most of my socket set but I had completely lost track of time. It wasn't until over an hour later, as I scrambled under some loose rocks to find the last piece, that my stomach rumbled and I suddenly realised how hungry I really was. Putting the now complete socket set in its rightful place in the back of my van I set off back to the workshop wondering how well my baked potato would be after over 4 hours in the little Baby Belling oven.

Opening the main workshop door I could smell it. When I opened the door to our mess room I had to take a step back to avoid the smoke pouring out and hitting me in the face. It must have taken me several minutes opening all doors and windows to clear the smoke. I was so hungry that I was determined to get some nourishment from my disaster. I managed to retrieve my 'lump of coal' from the oven and set it on my plate along side my butter and cheese ready to do battle. A sharp knife in hand and my make shift oven glove in the other I attempted to cut open my potato. All to no avail.

After a scratching of my engineering head I found a solution. Carefully placing the hot jacket potato in the workshop vice my trusty hacksaw successfully opened the tough jacket to reveal an almost empty shell......

I think its time to find a chip shop!!!!!!!!

— — — —

Chapter 12

'Casual Thief'

I've always been one for being organised. When I want something, whether it's a mug to make a cup of tea or a screwdriver to complete a job, I like to know exactly where it is rather than searching for it. Modern Lean Manufacturing techniques in industry run on the main principle of 'A place for everything and everything in it's place' - From early on in my apprenticeship I have spent most of my working life following this principle.

When I became a fully trained service engineer the back of my service van was no exception. I had shelving to contain all the spares, carefully put in order. I had a space reserved for all my toolboxes and each toolbox or bag was set up so I could just grab the appropriate bag and go fix a particular problem.   I would be exaggerating if I told you it was always neat and tidy as sometimes it would be a proper dumping ground due to the summertime rushing from job to job. However, the basic equipment and tools were always put back in the appropriate place.

In those days you could not buy van racking and shelving from the high street. Anyone with a commercial van who wanted to kit out their van would either need to pay a substantial cost to get some specialised vehicle customiser to manufacture some bespoke modification or the engineer would have to make it himself. As refrigeration work was very seasonal for obvious reasons, we were always very busy in the summer months but often found plenty of free time in the winter. This meant that I spent a lot of my free time in winter modifying and manufacturing custom built shelves etc for the back of my van.

Even towards the end of my career I would see a problem, think of a solution and make something to suit. Even if it was a simple cardboard holder to house a pen next to a desk, just to ensure there was always a pen available to fill out the necessary paperwork. When I was an apprentice most of the engineers would share great van modification ideas with each other and so eventually everyone had very similar vans with all the best ideas being duplicated across the fleet. Everyone had their own interpretations and improvements on a particular idea but one very simple, but very efficient, idea we all used was the special rack to hold refrigerant gas bottles.

The two bottles we always carried in the back of our vans could be firmly held in place as the van bounced and rolled about the bumpy steelworks tracks. Obviously the damage a 30lb gas bottle rolling loosely about the back of a van would be bad enough, but the thought of it flying forward into the driver during emergency braking is too deadly to imagine. So yes, it was very important to have these gas bottles firmly secure in the back of your van. I had mine strapped just inside the back door so no matter how much equipment was loaded into my van I could still get the relevant gas bottle out.

This bottle rack was made up of a simple wooden block with two half moon curves cut into it and a strap across to hold each gas bottle in an upright position. This way I could fasten a gas bottle in place like you would buckle a small child in a car seat. We found the best material to use for the gas bottle seat belt was the strapping as used by lorry drivers everywhere to secure their loads on the back of their trailers. Working on a steelworks meant that there was lots of lorries and trailers about and therefore lots of discarded strapping.

Not long out of my time and as a newly appointed engineer trying to kit my new van out I was told the best place to find some spare strapping would be at the despatch end of Medium Section Mill. Here you get a few lorries and their trailers but the rail despatch shed have lots and lots of railway carriages that transport most of the finished steel products made in the mill. I was reliably informed that if I wander around the railway lines there will be plenty of broken strapping just laying on the floor.

After carefully parking my van down a side road I entered the dispatch shed through one of the side doors and found the whole shed empty. There was no sign of any trains or their carriages. This was ideal for me as I imagined it would be easier to wander around an empty shed rather than dodging between stationary carriages waiting to be laden with steel sections.

As I wandered along one of the railway lines I was firstly disappointed at the lack of strapping I could see. As usual there was lots of rubbish strewn around but apart from some very shredded small bits of strapping I was struggling to find a decent length of good strapping that I could use for my latest project.

Then up ahead I saw it. A lovely piece of nearly new strapping. Light blue and what looked to be at least eight or nine foot long. Shredded at one end where it had obviously broken but apart from that it looked perfect. I had enough for me and anyone else who may need some. I walked up to it and carefully bent down to pick it up………

The sirens went off!!!!!

Whoop, Whoop, Whoop!

It sounded like all hell had been let loose.

Whoop, Whoop, Whoop! - The sirens continued.

"Oh My God!" I thought "Maybe someone has seen me picking up something that doesn't belong to me???!!!!"

I guiltily stood up with the offending item in my hand expecting to see people rushing toward me ready to arrest me. Carefully and slowly I rolled the strapping up into a more manageable coil and continued to look toward the control room to see if anyone was coming to question my intent.

"Surely it's just a bit of waste strapping that had been thrown away" was my intended reply to any accusations.

Whoop, Whoop, Whoop! - The sirens continued.

HOOOONK, HOOOONK, HOOOONK!!! Came a different sign.

"What the hell is that" I said out loud as I turned around.

Coming toward me, very slowly on the same railway I was stood on, was a locomotive pulling several empty carriages into the despatch shed. The Honking noise was the locomotive telling me to get out the way and the original siren was simply an alarm to warn people of a train coming in.

Thankfully I didn't feel guilty anymore.

— — — —

Chapter 13

'Excess gas'

On a steelworks there are very few places that don't need air conditioning. Computers were in their infancy in the 1970s and took up whole rooms kicking out lots and lots of heat, so they were the obvious customers of industrial scale air conditioning. Overhead cranes that lifted and poured out molten metal needed very efficient air conditioning to ensure the cab drivers could concentrate on doing their job and not blinded by sweat pouring down their forehead.

Kenyon refrigeration had a very good reputation for building industrial air conditioning. The KenCold units could not only deliver an exceptionally high volume of very cold air but were built so strong that they could withstand the rigours of the steel industries cranes. When an overhead crane is picking up 300 tons of molten steel it tends to rattle and shakes a lot. Most cheaper air conditioning units I came across, that were probably intended for office use, would struggle to survive.

KenCold units were custom built to withstand whatever environment they were to end up in. One particular environment I always hated was on a coke oven. Scunthorpe steelworks had several coke ovens and the largest and 'best' of these was the Dawes Lane coke ovens. It was the most modern and the largest one on the Scunthorpe steelworks.

A coke oven operates as the name suggests. They put coal into an oven, cook it, then take it out (while still alight) and then pour water over it to put the fire out. Very similar to most of the cooking I do in my kitchen oven!

The Dawes Lane coke ovens were not within a building but outside and exposed to all the elements. The main ovens resembled a large rectangular brick the size of a 4 storey building. Actually more like a row of terraced houses rather than one single building. Each oven was no more than a metre wide, but over 9 metres tall and had a length of about 20 metres. At Dawes Lane there were 75 ovens that were all stacked next to each other to form this large rectangular brick sat in the middle of all the pipework and equipment running them.

On each side of each oven was a tall thin door that could be removed by either the 'Pusher' on one side or the 'Guide' on the other side. When an oven was ready to be emptied, both doors would be removed and the 'Pusher' would simply push all the burning coke out of the other side of the oven while the 'Guide' ensured it fell out into an awaiting train carriage. The train would then drive the still burning coal to a position under a water cooling tower that would extinguish the fire giving off great plumes of steam.

The Dawes Lane coke ovens were the most up to date in the country (when it was built in the 1970's). Most of the gases that the ovens gave off in the burning process were collected and cleaned before being released to the atmosphere. Older coke ovens simply let all the fumes and gases out into the atmosphere. Dawes Lane had obviously spent a lot of time and thought into how to collect all the dangerous fumes and so compared to other, older coke ovens I felt safer at Dawes Lane but it was still not a nice place to work. Any time of year, any weather, the top of the coke ovens was the hottest hell on earth you could imagine.

The first time I was shown a coke ovens was when I was called to an air conditioning fault on the 'Loading Car' which sits on top of the Dawes Lane coke ovens. This machine loads the raw coal into the top of each oven after the doors on the side are closed and sealed.

I had reported to the site engineer who took me through the standard access procedure before I was allowed onto site. This involved the usual paperwork, such as Work Permits etc which are prevalent in any industrial environment. When the paperwork was complete he picked up his radio,

"Engineer to Loading Car, come in Jim!"

Silence……

"Jim, are you there?" the engineer asked

"Yeah, keep your hat on!" came the reply "of course I'm here, where else would I be!!"

"Hi Jim, I just wanted to tell you we have the Kenyon guy here for you" the engineer informed him

"Oh brilliant, I'm sweating cobs up here" Jim said enthusiastically "send him straight up before I waste away"

"He's a new young 'un" the engineer said into the radio "so I'll bring him up myself, just make sure you behave yourself and be careful with him"

My eyebrows went up and I looked straight into the smiling eyes of the engineer.

"Don't worry!" he said to me "I'll look after you"

"We should be there in 20 minutes" the engineer told Jim "we are on our way now"

"20 minutes!!!!" I thought, then said it out loud "How far away is this Loading Car?"

"Oh, it's only next door" the engineer said with an even larger, knowing grin on his face.

"Now you've got all your permits etc, you better follow me" he said as he stood up from his desk.

We walked out his office and across the car park into the welfare building. This was a brick building with wash rooms, toilets and a canteen with large windows looking out onto the magnificent view of the main part of the coke ovens. Just inside the main entrance was a serving hatch with a large sign above telling us 'Safety was your Responsibility'.

"Hi John" the engineer addressed the man behind the counter "This young lad needs to go on top of the coke ovens so can you kit him out with all the gear?"

"Sure thing" said John and turned to face me

"What size are you?"

""What size what am I?" I queried

John and the engineer looked me up and down and said in unison "Skinny medium!" With a smirk on their faces.

John disappeared into the back of his store room while the engineer disappeared into the locker rooms telling me he would be back in a minute.

Resembling a scene from an army movie where the new recruit gets his standard army issue uniform, John reappeared with a pile of clothes and placed them on the counter.

"What's all this?" I enquired

"This is your protective gear, lad" answered John and then proceeded to name and describe each item in the pile.

"These are your pure wool overalls" showing me a set of very thick green woollen overalls "these are flame and heat proof"

"These are your clog boots" John continued "which have wooden soles to protect you on top of the ovens. Those boots you're wearing are no good, the soles would start to melt once you're on top of the ovens!!"

"and this is your airstream to keep all the nasty fumes out of your lungs!"

I looked in dismay at the pile of equipment John had just offered me and I started to worry about where I was about to go.

The woollen overalls were easy to put on, as were the clog boots, but the airstream helmet was an unyielding hard hat with a full screen across the front. It resembled a motorcycle full face helmet but had a section at the back which housed a motor and fan to supply the wearer with relatively clean air across the front of the helmet. Attached out the back of the helmet was a thick cable with a plug on the end.

"What the heck do I plug this thing into" I said holding the plug up.

"Just take one of those batteries out of the rack over there" John pointed across the hallway I was stood in "and when you come back give me everything including the battery so I can recharge it"

As I was not allowed access to the locker rooms (us contractors were seen as the lowest of the low) I had to change into all my safety gear in the hallway. John took my usual safety boots to store safely in his store room.

The engineer returned fully clad in all his 'personal' safety gear and helped me make sure the airstream fitted snugly around my face. I grabbed the tool bag I had been carrying around with me and we set off out the building towards the actual coke ovens.

Over the following years I managed to acquire my own green woollen overalls and clog boots and this made it a lot quicker and easier to attend jobs like this. I eventually got used to how restrictive, cumbersome and how unbelievably hot you get wearing all this safety gear. On that very first day at Dawes Lane coke ovens I was actually sweating like a pig before we even got close to the ovens.

It had started raining as we left the welfare building but the engineer strangely assured me that it wouldn't be raining on top of the ovens. I thought he was just winding me up at the time but I did learn that most rain seemed to simply evaporate before it landed on top of the coke ovens. A strange but understandable phenomena.

We ascended a series of metal staircases until we came out onto a flat roof which was the actual tops of all the ovens. Each of these ovens had 4 round man-hole covers set into the floor we were stood on. These, I was told, is where the raw coal is loaded into each oven. Each man-hole cover was in perfect alignment with its neighbour and they all lined up like soldiers in a parade ground but flush with the floor. Along each side of the roof, in line with each oven, were 75 chimneys which stood 15 feet above us. Each chimney had a hinged plate on the top which sloped inwards towards the working area. The smell of burning coal hung in the air. Smoke and steam bellowed around us as I tried to take in this vision of Hell on Earth. A movement of air from the storm above cleared the smoke slightly and I saw the first glimpse of my target. At the far end of the working area was the 'Loading Car'.

The loading car was a two storey machine that ran on two rails along the working area. It had the slightest hint of being blue in colour once, but like everything else on a coke ovens, it was black, covered with coal dust. The loading car had a cabin that ran only inches from the floor where the driver would sit and workers could easily step into and out of when it was in position. The upper level of this machine housed large hoppers containing the raw coal and a plant room where the air conditioning was housed.

The engineer paused a moment as we stepped out into this working area and he watched my expression of unbelievability. I had not seen or experienced anything like this before and I never realised there were such places like this on this earth.

"Right" the engineer snapped me out of my open mouthed daze "lets get to work"

"Now just a word of warning" he continued "Whatever you do, do NOT step on one of those manhole covers"

"Why?" I asked innocently "will they melt my shoes?"

"No" he answered with all severity "they simply open up into the oven and you may fall inside one"

My mouth fell open to the floor as he walked off toward the loading car.

I gingerly followed along looking down very carefully at each floor plate. I made sure I never went anywhere near any of the man hole covers. Each step I took was carefully placed on the floor making sure it was solid before I put my whole weight on it. Every third step I looked up to check I was going in the right direction. Just as I placed my weight on another of my tentative steps, a mighty woosh followed by a loud bang sounded out above my head. This made me physically jump into the air and take my gaze from the man hole search to see a flame 20 foot high burning out of one of the chimneys above my head.

"What the F@@K!" I shrieked, jumping back in fear and still carefully trying not to step on a man hole cover.

"Don't worry" said the engineer "that's just excess gas from the ovens. If we didn't let it out the whole oven would blow up"

"…and that's supposed to reassure me!" I thought.

I continued on, trying to follow the engineer across this scene from hell on earth. I felt I really could do with the comfort of holding someone's hand but the thought of destroying my street cred in one fell swoop, kept my brave streak going. I successfully carried on avoided the man hole covers below my feet and dodging the searing heat of the burning chimneys above my head. I was very glad to get to the relatively safe haven of the coal dust covered loading car machine. I stood there in my very sweaty woollen overalls very thankful for my relatively fresh air supplied by the airstream helmet.

"Hi Jim" said the engineer as we entered the cabin "Finally got here"

With a beaming smile on his face, Jim acknowledge the engineer and said "I see you told him about the man hole covers then"

"Oh yes, of course!" laughed the engineer "you were watching then?"

I looked puzzled at them both and angrily asked "was that one of your wind ups then?"

"Oh no, he always tells the newbies that" said Jim "It is true that they do lead straight into the ovens"

Jim and the engineer both laughed out loud.

"However, like most people" Jim continued "you failed to notice that they are only 10 inches across. Even a skinny little runt like you wouldn't fit through the hole. Just don't drop anything in there"

— — — —

Chapter 14

In the winter time, when the work was relatively quiet, I often found myself spending time with some of the British Steels own instrument technicians in their workshops. This was mainly because Kenyons on-site workshop was in the same building but also our contract was managed by their boss. We had a close working relationship and often helped each other out on jobs. They sometimes would have to repair electronic equipment which would be housed in a room that we kept cool with our air conditioning. They would usually blame us for the room being too hot for their delicate instruments and we would blame them for their equipment overheating and warming the room up.

This was during the 1980's when home personal computers were becoming very popular. Computers such as the ZX Spectrum and Commodore 64's were very popular and we all had one or the other.

During the quiet night shifts we would take our computers to work to pass the time between 'call-outs'. Looking back now it was probably no different to the young workers today who put their phones in their hands during quiet working moments to either play 'Candy Crush' or catch up on their social media.

To us it was definitely not something you wanted your boss to know about. However our 'Computer Club' eventually attracted up to half a dozen skilled technicians and engineers that were on our shift and we would all meet in Pete's workshop at the main C.E.W (Central Engineering Workshops). The CEW itself was a large engineering building but the instrument department had a much smaller workshop on the side of the building which housed all their delicate instrumentation equipment. The main building, including the offices, became very quiet after 6pm each day as nearly all but the instrument department, worked Monday to Friday 9 to 5.

Most evenings someone would have something new to show us whether it was a new game that would be pushing the boundaries of technology or some new equipment. Some evenings I would turn up and find several benches covered in portable TV's, computers and cables everywhere. Just like a proper nerdy computer club in the local village hall. Most bosses would freak out at such a sight but looking back now I can see and appreciate how much experience and knowledge I gained that helped me throughout my working life. This is where I started learning how computers worked and it has stood me in good stead over the years when it comes to getting software to behave itself.

One of our 'club' members worked in a control room near to Pete's workshop but because of the nature of his work he was unable to leave his post. He had to spend 8 hours a day looking at a whole room full of dials and gauges. It resembled the control room in a power station like Chernobyl but instead of controlling the flow of electricity he controlled the flow of gas across the entire site. I feel sure nowadays it's probably all done on one laptop computer on someones desk, but in those days it needed someone to sit there on a 24/7 basis to keep monitoring and adjusting all the instruments etc.

Ken, who was the gas controller on our shift, had been doing the job for years and knew his job inside out. Therefore he would often have everything running very smoothly and he would occasionally nip into the computer club but never for more than 20 minutes at a time. If he returned to find he had missed a phone call etc. he would tell them that he had had a desperate call of nature. He had an undeserved reputation with management of having a very weak bladder. So much so that he would force himself to go on several calls of nature during the day when management were around to keep up the pretence.

I got on particularly well with Ken as I would sometimes set up my computer in his control room so we could have longer that the 10 or 20 minutes he acquired for us to play a game. People phoning him up would be a real nuisance as we would have to suddenly pause or mute a game and it would inevitably always be at a crucial time in the game.

"Don't these people realise we have got aliens to destroy" Ken would often joke as he picked up the phone.

Ken was a very friendly and outspoken person. He told it as it was and never held back. He was never embarrassed by anything he told you but would often embarrass others.

One evening he was telling me about a video he had recently acquired from someone in his local pub. The seller had told him it was a home made porn movie of very good quality. Ken went on to tell me how he and his wife had settled down one evening to watch this video and they had even set themselves up with drinks, turned the lights down low and took the phone off the hook to ensure they were not going to be disturbed.

"I pressed play on the video player" Ken told me "and we both snuggled down together on the sofa."

"Well I could not believe it" Ken continued "we'd only watched a couple of minutes of the video and I found myself jumping over the coffee table to press stop". (NOTE: in those days there were no remote controls for the video players)

"Good grief Ken" I said "I never thought of you as being a bit of a prude! How come you were so shocked at it?"

"Was it violent….?"

"Was it obscene…?"

"What was so disgusting about it that meant you couldn't watch it???"

"No, no, no" came Ken's reply "It was nothing like that"

"When the wife and I started watching we both instantly recognised the stars of the video.

"It was our next door neighbours!!!! - I've not been able to look them in the eye since."

— — — —

Chapter 15

'Paradise behind the dashboard light'

Before I left school at 16 I had a Saturday morning job at our local garage in the village where I lived. Most of my duties were simply to clear up after the mechanics and sweep the floor. However I was used more and more as the weeks passed, to help the mechanics in their duties and because of this I learnt a lot about cars in general. They even taught me how to drive when I was only 15 which meant I could help them park up vehicles at the end of the day. Unfortunately, revealing this information to my boss at Kenyons meant I was somehow seen as an expert when it came to automotive equipment.

Nowadays everyone enjoys the luxury of good air conditioning in their cars but in the 1980's there were very few cars on the road with air conditioning. It was only the very expensive ones like Rolls Royce and Bentleys etc. and in the Scunthorpe area, there weren't many of those about.

Kenyons contract was with the Scunthorpe Steelworks but the idea was always to expand out into the area. After all, Kenyons was a national company and could provide many services. As local companies got to know us a few jobs outside the steelworks started coming in.

One day, when our boss, Gareth, was on his annual leave, I overheard Mike (second in command) tell a customer on the phone....

"Of course sir, I have just the engineer who can sort that for you. He was originally a car mechanic and then retrained in refrigeration so he will have no problem sorting you out"

My open mouthed expression said it all.

"Let me just take some details" Mike continued waving with his hand for me to come in and sit down "and I will get him to you this afternoon"

"Whoa Mike! What the hell are you letting me in for here?" I burst out as soon as the phone was put down.

"Don't panic" he smirked "from what it sounds like it will be a simple re gas"

"They're never going to believe I've been a fully trained car mechanic and a refrigeration engineer. For that I would have to be an old guy like you, well into in my 30's!!!!"

"Look" Mike tried to comfort my unease "Go have a look, if its not simple you can always give me a ring and we will try to work something out"

"We are requested to try and expand this department" Mike continued "and this is a good opportunity. I genuinely think you are the best guy for the challenge as you will at least know how to open the bonnet of a Porsche 911"

"A Porsche!!!!! Bloody hell, drop me in at the deep end why don't you" I exclaimed "besides, the engines in the boot not the bonnet!"

"See, I knew you were the right guy!"

As I drove out to Brigg that afternoon it dawned on me that I had been conned good and proper. I think Mike knew the engine was in the back of a Porsche anyway but just wanted to trick me into a bit of self confidence. These old guys can be quite cunning at times.

Brigg is a lovely old market town less than 10 miles from the centre of Scunthorpe and so 20 minutes after setting off I was at the reception desk of the Smith Parkinsons Garage in the town centre. This was the main Ford dealer for Brigg but they obviously had some influential people who trusted them with their expensive cars.

The receptionist rang through to the garage and announced my arrival. As I took a seat in the showroom, to await the arrival of the service manager, I had already braced myself ready for his disbelief at such an experienced young expert. Thankfully he showed true relief at having such a highly recommended expert to look at his important customer's car.

"Who's car is it? Anyone famous?" I enquired

"Oh No. No-one famous. It's just our managing directors" he unsuccessfully tried to assure me.

"No pressure then!!"

Trying to sound professional I asked him some details about the car and the problems they were having. Finally he told me the car was in one of the small private garage spaces round the back that they reserved for cars of VIPs, and managing directors. He gave me instructions of how to get round there with my service van and then we parted company.

Great, I thought, at least now I can work in private on the car instead of being in a big garage space with all the other mechanics watching me, as I had imagined. I drove around the back of the garage and found the service manager waiting for me outside a set of three individual garages all with lovely old solid wooden doors across the front of each one. I pulled my van across the front as directed by the service manager as he ensured I was not blocking access to the rest of the yard.

"Right, here are the keys and I'll leave you to it, if that's all right with you. I have a lot of work on but I will pop back later to see how you're getting on. If you need anything" said the service manager pointing across the yard "just ask in the main garage"

And with that he was gone.

There I was with the keys to a very expensive car in my hands. I had rarely seen a car like this before let alone sat in one and I now had the keys and the challenge to try and fix it.

I excitedly but tentatively opened the solid wooden doors as wide as I could and was so relieved to find that the car had been driven in forwards. Not only did this mean that when I started the car all the exhaust gases would be exhaled straight out of the garage into the atmosphere but also, if you remember, the engine is in the back of a Porsche. The air conditioning compressor will be attached to the engine.

Although I would have loved to have taken it for a spin the thought of trying to gently manoeuvre the car out of such a narrow garage filled me with dread. Especially when I thought of what was riding on my successful outcome.

I hoped no-one was watching me as I felt like I had stood there for ages in complete awe at the beautiful machine I had just uncovered. It was a fantastic light metallic blue colour and although it was not brand new it shone greater than any of the Fords in their showroom out front.

I shook myself out of my daze and with renewed confidence decided I better start the car up and check out the problem. Although I was fairly certain what the problem was from the service managers description I always like to ensure the problem is as described.

This was the moment when my heart sank as I realise these little garages didn't give the driver much space to get in and out of the car. As I peered at the space between the right hand side of the car and the internal wall I wondered how the managing director had got out of the car. In my experience most managing directors are over fed and overweight so surely, I thought, a skinny 27 year old can squeeze in that gap.

Two seater sports cars always have longer doors than four door cars so you get even less gap to squeeze through. It wasn't too difficult getting in but when you are trying your hardest to hold round the door to stop it scrapping on the wall I felt like an escape artist in reverse.

With great relief I sat in the plush leather seat and took in the exquisite interior. This car had buttons and dials all over and seemed to have everything you could ever want in a car..... except, to my initial horror, no steering wheel!!!!

"Oh Dammit" I thought "Its left hand drive"

I eventually, with great difficulty and in such a confined space, managed to scramble over to the left hand seat and again was thankful I was in my own little garage with no prying eyes to laugh at my mistake.

"Right take a deep breath" I said out loud to myself "lets see if we can start the engine"

Now in those days, well before modern keyless systems etc, ALL cars would have an ignition switch on the right hand side of the steering column where you put in the key and turn until the engine started. No matter how hard I looked and scratched at my head there was no sign of where the key went.

"This could be embarrassing" I thought "Not only trying to get out of the car again but having to ask someone how to start a beautiful car like this cannot look very good for me"

My confidence sank deeply

Another deep breath to think clearly and luckily I found the ignition switch was unusually on the dashboard to the 'Left' of the steering wheel.

What a great sense of achievement I received as the engine struck up. It doesn't matter if you are a petrol head or not but when you are in control of such a sophisticated and technically advanced piece of engineering the sound of the engine was like sweet music. I realised I had to be careful how many times I got the engine to crackle as I flipped the accelerator but felt my excuse was the need to warm the engine up. I was sure I had attracted some attention but in my mind it was probably more the Porsches fault rather than mine.

To my great relief, enjoyment and a sure confidence booster for me; the rest of the job went as planned.

As I was now sat in the actual drivers seat I found it much easier to get in and out of the car. The owner obviously parks it closer to the right hand side of the garage leaving more room on the drivers side to open the door.!!!

The air conditioning did just simply need re gassing and it was a very simple and quick job to do. Not that I did the work very quickly as I was enjoying myself. So much so that when the service manager returned I had the interior of the car so cold you could have used it as a fridge.

I just hope the managing director had enough petrol to get home that day!

The following week Mike called me into the office.

"You did a great job there last week in Brigg, young Terry"

"Why thanks Mike, I appreciate the confidence boost"

"Yes, the owner of the Porsche....."

"He was the blooming Managing Director" I interrupted.

"Sorry, yes I knew about that before you went" Mike admitted "anyway, he was so impressed with your work he happily recommended Kenyons to the Scunthorpe Ford dealership as well, so thanks to you we now have two car dealerships with us in mind for any future work"

My suggestion of a bonus just received a smile and no reply so I started to turn to leave the office.

"Whoa, wait a minute" exclaims Mike "I've got another job for you"

"But I've got my maintenance down at the BOS plant this morning" I replied

"No this is for tomorrow morning"

"Stop messing about Mike, I'm on afternoon shift tomorrow and you know it" I insisted, while feeling another con coming my way.

"Don't worry, I've already spoken to Del and he will do your afternoons so you are free for this special job" Mike smirked

"Not another car job already!!" I exclaimed

"Well you are the recommended expert"

How could I refuse!

Hartford Motors, Scunthorpe's Main Ford dealership, had organised for me to work with one of their car mechanics on one of their customer's (yes, this time it was a customer!) top of the range Ford Granada. The customer had repeatedly reported water leaking into the passenger footwell and Hartford motors had already determined it was the air conditioning causing the leak. As I was already known to be an ex car mechanic !!!!!!!! They had requested I help one of their car mechanics to remove the dashboard to get at the problem. Removing the dashboard was known to be a two man job and could take over two hours just to get it out.

"8 o'clock sharp" said Mike with one of his biggest smirks ever "and take your time as they promise to pay you for all day."

I was there in plenty of time and as they were expecting me I was shown straight into the main garage area to look at the car. My co-worker mechanic had not yet arrived but that gave me a chance to look at the problem and decide what my challenges ahead were. I needed to try and work out how I was going to look like I knew anything about a dashboard removal.

With my head under the dashboard, laid on my back with my feet out the passenger door, I heard a voice......

"Hi there. I'm John, your mechanic for the day" said John holding his hand out.

He probably was holding his hand out as a gesture of greeting but it was very useful to help me get out of the very awkward position I had found myself in.

"Hi John, my name's Terry" I replied as I stood up on my feet still holding his hand

"Wow, you're younger than I was expecting" he exclaimed

"That's all right cause you're a lot older than I was expecting" I quickly deflected his query

"You're very keen" John said "don't fix it too quickly as we've been given all day to get this right. The customer is furious we still haven't solved the problem after it's third time in with us."

"Three times!! Crikey. No wonder he's unhappy"

"That's why your here, I've heard good things about you"

This started to look harder and harder for me to bluff my way through this. I can probably get away with pretending I knew what I was doing for a while but the thought of all day with such high expectations was starting to weaken my confidence. I felt I was heading for a big fall. The best way I decided to soften the fall would to be as close to the truth as I could. Do NOT sing your own praises.

"So John, have you ever removed this dashboard before?" I asked

"Well not this one but yes a few of these. They're not difficult, just very time consuming" came John's reassuring reply "we should have it out for you to do your magic by late morning but I never start anything before breakfast"

"Look Terry, I don't really start work until half past and I usually get a sandwich from across the road before I start. I saw your van in the car park so just came in to see if you wanted anything getting"

"Oh no that's all right John, I'm fine" I told him "If you don't mind I'd like to at least carry on taking a look at the problem before we start. You go get your breakfast"

"Fine, no problem" said John as he turned for the exit "I'll be back in 20 minutes"

A great sense of relief came over me as I now had some personal space to re-assess the task ahead.

John kept to his word. Just after half past eight he walked into the main garage still chewing on a bacon butty with a mug of coffee in his hand. As he approached me he stopped in his tracks and his happy smiley face slowly turned to a disbelieving question mark.

I was stood with my bottom leaning against the wing of the car and my arms folded with the biggest smile on my face you could ever imagine. All around me on the floor was a big pool of water.

John nearly dropped his coffee. "What the heck have you done? Terry"

"Don't Panic" I assured him "It's all done, fixed"

"No Way!!!" He exclaimed "where is all the water from?"

"That's what was in the air conditioning drip tray behind the dashboard" I told him

"But, but, but" he stuttered his disbelief

I carefully calmed John down and showed him the reason the water was leaking into the passenger foot well.

All air conditioning units remove water from the air passing through them. The water is then collected by a drip tray under the evaporator. The water in this car's drip tray could not take its usual intended flow through the bulkhead pipework, out under the car and onto the road below, due to a simple blocked filter. This filter (when I found it!!!) was easily removed and cleaned from within the engine compartment. In fact as soon as I did remove the filter there was such a torrent of water flowing out I genuinely thought I had broken something. Luckily no-one was watching me at the time and after what felt like an eternity (and a lot of water) the flow died down to a trickle. I cleaned the filter in the nearby sink and had just refitted it when I saw John returning.

I stayed chatting with John for the next hour and made sure all my paperwork was in order before leaving. As I walked out the garage I swear I thought I heard Meatloaf on the radio sing -

'Paradise **behind** the dashboard light'

— — — —

Chapter 16

'Frozen Assets'

As the Scunthorpe division of Kenyons started to grow we got more and more work outside the confines of the steelworks. Luckily the bosses did start recruiting more and more engineers (and apprentices) to help but at times I could find myself travelling further and further afield on calls at unusual and inconvenient hours.

As technology improved and engineering progressed, new innovations and ideas developed. Up until the eighties most supermarkets selling frozen food would have row after row of individual chest freezers for the customers to select their purchases from. Then someone came up with the bright idea of the 'Pack' system.

Instead of lots of individual freezers warming up the shop with the excess heat they gave off, and all the individual compressors, condenser fans etc making lots of noise in the shop, everything would be in a plant room out the back of the shop. The idea was that all the actual 'reprocessing' side of the refrigeration cycle would be in a noisy, hot plant room away from the customers and all the refrigerant could be piped across the shop above the customers and directly into large freezer cabinets.

The advent of early computer controls and sophisticated sensing equipment meant it was now possible to keep every freezer cabinet on the shop floor happy and controlled centrally. You could easily change cabinets defrosting regimes and temperature set points according to what the manager wanted rather than what each cabinet was designed for.

Sounds like a refrigeration utopia but it took many years of trial and error to get to the reliability it is today.

The first installation of this 'Pack' type of refrigeration that Kenyons installed near Scunthorpe was at a new ASDA supermarket that was being built in a little town called Retford. Retford is about 30 miles south of Scunthorpe so it fell into our area when it needed maintaining, or more often was the case, repairing.

From the day the installation team handed the equipment over the calls started coming in. The whole system leaked more than a Tetley Tea bag. A normal domestic fridge could contain 2 or 3 pounds of CFC refrigerant but if there was a leak at ASDA Retford you could loose the whole 200+ pounds of CFC. I am ashamed to admit it now but because of the industry I worked in in those days I think the biggest hole in the ozone layer is probably over Retford.

We eventually got so complacent with ASDA Retford that on receiving a call out we used to head straight to our Scunthorpe depot just to make sure we had enough refrigerant before setting off. We would fill our vans up with several very heavy, large gas bottles and anything else we thought we might need to fix a leak.

If the call came in during the day (even at weekends) we could usually call on another engineer to collect the gas bottles while one of us raced to stem the leak. But at night time - you were always on your own.

In those day supermarkets didn't open on Sundays let alone be open 24 hours a day. Some of the larger supermarkets employed people to restock shelves during the night but ASDA Retford was a relatively small supermarket and so nobody would be in the store stacking shelves overnight. For about eight hours every night the store would be completely locked up and in darkness.

You may well think that during night time there is no-one to notice a freezer being faulty, but that's what supermarket managers liked about the 'Pack' system. A computer kept monitoring every temperature every minute of every day and if something wasn't right an alarm would notify the security guard to call someone out.

Eric was a loveable, eccentric character. He enjoyed his security job with ASDA and always talked with such enthusiasm about everything. Work, home, his family, his hobbies etc etc. the only thing is you could never shut him up.

One night time I met him at the back door near the main plant room and he let me in. I was thankful it was Eric who met me as I know he was always keen to help if I needed all the van full of gas bottles taking through. Being as complacent about leaks as us he went straight to the back of my van to start unloading the first of the large gas bottles but I stopped him in time saying….

"Wait a minute Eric, let's not be too hasty. I'll check the problem first"

Luckily for me, as soon as I walked in the plant room I could hear it, and actually see it. A small connection had come loose and due to the escaping refrigerant the joint was one big ball of ice.

I dashed back to my van for the right equipment and on return found Eric tapping the ball of ice with his finger.

"That was lucky" he said turning to me "can't you just tighten it up?"

"No Eric and don't touch it. If that liquid gas gets on your hands it could give you frost bite" I told him "You know as well as me Eric, I don't trust any connections that the installation team did on this job. If I just try to tighten it it could split wide open and we loose everything"

While Eric monitored my every move, I carefully shut down that particular section so I could remove the offending pipework and remake a new piece. When I was happy that it was good to go I decided I had had enough of Eric's latest stories of his new mushroom collecting hobby, so I sent him off to my van to bring me just one of the smaller bottles of refrigerant that I always carry in my van.

My idea at the time was to put some gas in this section I had just repaired so I could check for leaks and then open it up to the rest of the system before I topped up the whole system. Maybe I was night time tired or maybe I was just rushing to get ready before Eric returned but unfortunately I made a mistake and it was a big mistake which nearly had devastating consequences.

We used to use Schrader valves a lot in those days. These are very similar to the valves on your car tyres. They have a dust cap on to keep them clean but once removed you can then attach your charging pipework which will open the valve within and allow free flow of refrigerant.

Instead of taking the cap off the Schrader valve I intended to use, I took the cap off another one that was fairly close but on a different part of the system. The removal of the dust cap should not have been a problem as the internal valve will not open until you screw your charging pipework on. However, on this particular occasion, on this particular night, and on this particularly poorly installed equipment it turned out that no-one had ever removed the cap from this particular valve. I was the very first engineer to discover the actual Schrader valve within was missing.

As I unscrewed the dust cap off, the pressure behind it just blew the cap clean out of my hand and started pumping liquid refrigerant all over the floor. My quick, unthinking reactions, made me realise that I needed that cap, and quickly. Instinct told me which way it went and as the plant room started to fog up with the volume of refrigerant pouring out I luckily managed to find it within seconds.

Now comes the hard part! Not fully thinking it through but instinctively knowing what has to be done, I plunged myself into the deepening fog and had to use both hands to push hard and turn the cap by hand back onto the empty Schrader valve casing until the flow of refrigerant stopped.

I cannot have been more than a minute between loosing the cap and getting it back in position but most of the damage to me had been done. I looked down at my frozen hands and saw the little white popsicles where all my fingers were completely frozen. They were in the same position I had had them in tightening the dust cap back on. They would not move and, as I have experienced previously with mild forms of frost bite, I knew the delayed pain would soon be here.

The pain was excruciatingly bad. I tried to stifle a scream but it was no good. I was scared I might hit out in anger and break one of the popsicle fingers clean off.

Eric came rushing in with my little gas bottle and looked around.

"What the hell happened?" he shouted "where the hell are you?"

I was in so much pain that I had forgotten the plant room was still foggy with escaped refrigerant.

"I'm over here Eric"

Eric grabbed me and dragged me out the plant room door.

"What the hell happened?" he repeated

"We sprung another leak" I lied "and this time it got me"

He took one look at my white frozen hands and helped me into the kitchen area opposite the plant room.

Between us we spent the next hour busy trying to defrost my poor hands. We started with cool water and gently kept warming them up in the bowl but it must have took at least twenty minutes before I started to feel any movement at all. My fingers must have instantly frozen with the force and ferocity of the escaping liquid refrigerant.

I don't know what I would have done without Eric that night. He later carried one of the large gas bottles for me and even did most of the work, under my explicit instructions, so we could both finally leave as the sun was rising.

Thankfully, as we loaded the last of the equipment into the back of my van, my hands were starting to come back to life. Still in a lot of pain and restricted movement but I felt comfortable to be able to drive home. I had pins and needles for days afterwards.

Eric locked up and we put his bicycle in the back of the van as the least I could do was to give him a lift home.

I can honestly say that this time I enjoyed his latest, very long story about his mushroom searching. His tales kept going on and on long after we had stopped outside his house.

— — — —

Chapter 17

'Changing Times'

During the 1980's my original boss, Gareth, had moved to Wakefield to try and establish the commercial side of Kenyons along the western side of England. The top man, Mr Kenyon himself, had said he wanted to establish his business across the whole of the UK and his domination of refrigeration in all the British steelworks was a very good 'foot in the door' to expand.

Although during this period we had taken on some commercial refrigeration work it was getting harder and harder to use the on-site workshops. These workshops were provided by the British Steel bosses as part of our contract with them and it was getting riskier for the commercial side of Kenyons to operate from there. I'm sure the bosses at British Steel had started to realise that we were doing more and more commercial refrigeration off site. As we had no other base in the area it was obvious we were using their premises free of charge. It was inevitable that another 'off-site' location would be needed.

Gareth had been requested to find somewhere away from the Scunthorpe steelworks and it was quickly decided that instead of a depot in Scunthorpe itself a depot around the Leeds area would be a more ideal location. Leeds was well connected with the M1 running north & south and the M62 connecting east & west. Gareth found a suitable unit on an industrial estate in Wakefield and had therefore moved his family over to that area to start his new empire.

In the beginning of this venture, Gareth was seen as the area manager. He was in charge of the commercial side (operating from Wakefield) and also the industrial side (operating from Scunthorpe). Gareth set up his office at Wakefield and Mike, our Foreman, moved himself into Gareths old office on the Scunthorpe Steelworks. He decided he was now the industrial 'manager' as he preferred the sound of a manager to the sound of being called a foreman!

The Wakefield depot grew quite well. Gareth had managed to secure many local contracts and there was soon a good regular stream of work servicing supermarkets, school canteens, restaurants etc. across a wide area. Mr Kenyon's vision of a business covering the whole of the UK was becoming a reality.

As the work load grew a problem emerged. Sometimes the commercial engineers, based at Wakefield, had to travel east to carry out work around the Scunthorpe area and some of the industrial engineers, based at Scunthorpe, had to travel west to work in other steelworks, mainly around Sheffield. This was actually wasting time and money and it was eventually realised by the bosses that we needed a 'satellite' depot in Scunthorpe, especially as a lot of the original commercial work we had was in the Scunthorpe area. Several local customers had expressed concern that engineers now had to travel all the way from Wakefield instead of 'just down the road' in Scunthorpe.

A workshop and office was desperately needed off the steelworks site to allow us to do some of the commercial work from Scunthorpe. This would keep the bosses of British Steel happy that we were not using their workshops for anything other than the steelworks contract and keep our local commercial customers happy that we were close by. A small workshop and office was found in Scunthorpe behind the Golden Wonder crisp factory and Mike set himself up in his new empire as the Scunthorpe depot manager.

Alan had already been promoted as the foreman on the Scunthorpe Steelworks and Mike had appointed Dave as the foreman of the Sheffield Steelworks. The main industrial contract we had was for the Scunthorpe Steelworks. This was the larger of the sites and required a permanent workforce of a dozen engineers providing 24/7 shift cover. The Sheffield contract was a lot smaller and required Dave to be foreman of a smaller workforce. A workforce of - one!. Just himself!   He was actually very happy on his own. His workforce would always do as he told them and he never answered himself back!!!! Occasionally we would help him out if any particular work needed two men or the volume of jobs just got too much for him.

Although we all worked for Kenyon Refrigeration I always felt that there was stiff competition between Gareth in Wakefield and Mike in Scunthorpe. Mike expanded his empire over the years and not only took on his own commercial engineers but eventually his own personal secretary and a foreman to manage the commercial side.

As the years progressed and I gained more experience I found myself getting sent to more and more of the work outside the steelworks. I still enjoyed my industrial working life on the steelworks and the companionship I got from working in a regular shift environment. However, the steelworks was a hot and dirty environment and I felt I needed a change.

I started to enjoy the variety of work going from shop to office to restaurant to school kitchen etc and saw the challenges of commercial refrigeration as my desired future. In commercial refrigeration you were on your own, often many miles from home and needed to pull on all your knowledge and experience.

After a particularly demanding few night shifts on the Scunthorpe Steelworks, during a hot and busy summer, I finally made my mind up that I wanted to leave the confines of the steelworks behind me and concentrate on the challenges of being 'Out on the Road'.

Alan, our steelworks foreman, was sorting out some spares in the stock room when I approached him.

"Alan, can I have a word"

"Sure Terry" Alan looked up "What can I do for you?"

"Well, I've had enough of being on shifts" I started "and wondered if I could go out on the road permanently"

"Wow" Alan exclaimed "I didn't see that coming. I thought you enjoyed the shift work"

"Don't get me wrong, Alan, I do enjoy the work at times but I am sick and tired of the hot and dirty conditions and now need a different challenge"

"Its not all a bed of roses out there you know Terry" Alan tried to comfort me. "In fact you could end up being sent anywhere"

"Here on the Steelworks" Alan continued "you can rely on being in one area. Out on the road you may be miles away from the depot and your colleagues, having to work anytime, anyplace, anywhere"

"Isn't that a Martini!!!" I joked

Alan laughed at the reference to the Martini advert.

"What I'm trying to tell you Terry is that in commercial refrigeration you could well work longer hours and be further from home at anytime. You have a young family and I want to make sure you understand that you would be leaving a job with regularly hours where the next shift can take over any breakdowns."

"Out on the road" he continued "you finish the day when you finish the job."

"Thanks Alan" I said "but I have given it a lot of thought. You often send me out on commercial jobs nowadays and I now have a taste for the commercial life. I've had enough of being stuck on one site and I crave a challenge."

"Ok" Alan concedes "I'll have a chat with the boss and see what he says. It may not be for some time as I have no-one to take over your shifts at the minute but leave it with me"

Mike had recruited a few commercially trained engineers (poached from rival companies) to help build up that side of the business. As I had often found, they always needed more engineers when the volume of work increased, especially during the hot summer months.

Considering the amount of times I had helped them out, I felt fairly confident there would be a place out there for me......

Part Two

- Coming Out -

Chapter 18

'Getting away from it all'

The Scunthorpe steelworks had taught me a lot. I had started my working career there as a 16 year old school leaver, in my bright white overalls, desperate to leave the educational establishment that both my parents had carved their working lives in. However, there comes a time in everyones life when they need to change direction, start a new chapter, or in this case start a new book!!

I had found myself wanting to remove myself from the hot and dirty conditions of the steelworks and due to my experience in both industrial and commercial sides of my trade I was being used everywhere. This was the time in my life I stepped out of my comfort zone and took a chance for a better life, I made one of the big directional changes of my career and left the regularity of shift work on the Scunthorpe Steelworks to enter the commercial world of travel and the unknown. I say unknown, as in commercial refrigeration you never know what you are going to. You receive a location and maybe a brief note on the problem the customer is having, but often you don't even know where the job is, let alone what you might find there, until you arrive at the location. Exciting at times but often quite scary. Hopefully in this part of my book you, the reader, will discover that a commercial refrigeration engineer could be sent to all sorts of strange places and be faced with some very strange problems to solve.

"Hi Mike" I said early one Monday morning "reporting for duty"

It was my first official day working from the Scunthorpe depot.

"You won't have that smile on your face for long" Mike joked

"Oh come on Mike! I'm really happy to finally get off that dirty steelworks" I defended "I've done plenty of commercial work for you in the past so I'm just happy to finally get stuck into full time commercial work"

"Fair enough, we're happy to have you on board"

"So, where to first" I ask enthusiastically rubbing my hands together.

"Whoa, whoa, slow down soldier" he said pushing both his hands out to calm me down   "firstly I want to make sure your van is fully kitted out"

"What!?! I've spent years kitting out my van. Surely I have what I need"

"Maybe" Mike started "but I want to make sure you have a van full of the right spares and equipment for commercial work. Some of the equipment you used to use was shared with others. We need to ensure you have all the right gear yourself. You can spend this morning making sure you are ready for any eventuality and I have this list for you to help you load up"

Mike handed me a sheet of paper with a list of items written on both sides. I quickly scanned the long list in my hand and exited the office. After opening the workshop shutter doors I proceeded to reverse my van into the workshop believing it was going to be a nice easy start!!

Along the back wall of the workshop were several shelves containing all the regularly used spares. Each shelf was clearly marked with the category of its contents. Some of the shelves contained neatly stacked boxes of electrical spares and other shelves had blue plastic tubs with mechanical valves, nuts & bolts or even some plumbing parts. Copper pipe in straight lengths were stacked in one corner and they were surrounded by coils of smaller diameter copper pipe. Another corner housed several large bottles of CFC's that we all used to fill up the smaller gas bottles that we carried in our vans. In the centre of the workshop was a small pile of brand new equipment obviously intended for me; a portapak welding set, gas detection apparatus, testing and analysing equipment etc. etc.

A big smile came across my face, not only at the sight of all my new toys but because I was now totally contented with my chosen change in career path.

I had often found myself in the past driving back to the workshop stores to pick up replacement parts in my quest to fix some refrigeration unit. Previously most of my commercial call-out jobs were relatively local. From now on I could find myself many, many miles away from the depot making it more difficult, and impractical, for me to return. This was the main reason that all service engineers out on the road would fill their vans with as many spares and equipment as they could.

Scratching my head as I looked at the list Mike had given me I wondered how I was going to fit all this stuff in my already fairly full van. Obviously some stuff was going to have to go. I opened the back doors of my van and started the decluttering process. Luckily I found a sturdy empty box in the workshop and proceeded with the intention of filling it with all the 'industrially' acquired spares out of my van.

"How are you getting on?" Mike's voice seemed to come from nowhere. He had entered the workshop as I was in the back of my van clearing space for all my new found wealth.

"Yeah, sure, I'm ok Mike" I replied

"I see you found the new equipment I got you" Mike pointed to the shiny new equipment "I thought it best to start you off with all new stuff! so make sure you look after it. Just remember it is up to you to look after it all and I will charge you for anything that gets lost or damaged. The same goes for all the spares on that list, if you use any of the spares it is up to you to ensure it is charged to the correct job and replaced in your van when you're back here."

"It's certainly a big list" I said "I'm just trying to find room for it all in here. I'm dumping all this old steelworks spares into this box and then I will try to get it back to Alan on the steelworks sometime"

A smile grew on Mike's face which I thought at the time was just the recognition of the amount of spares I needed to fill my van. It turned out to be something completely different as he obviously knew something that I didn't.

'Don't be too long as we need you out on a job before lunch. When you're ready come into the office and I will give you all your paperwork" Mike turned to go back to his cosy, warm office.

It took me a couple of hours to gather everything on the list. I found myself squashing equipment into any available space in the back of my van with the intention of sorting it out a bit better, later. In commercial refrigeration that 'later' never really comes and the only time you ever get to sort out your van is usually in your own time.

"Right then" I start, as I walk into the office rubbing my hands in eagerness "I'm all loaded up and raring to go. What exotic job have you got for me as my first assignment? It's a lovely day so how about McDonald's in Scarborough or maybe Icelands in Skegness! I fancy having my lunch by the sea."

"Sheffield" replies Mike with the same smirk he had earlier

"That's alright - no problem. I'm only joking about the sea-side. I'm happy wherever you send me." I say, still with that inner glow of starting my chosen new career.

"Where in Sheffield do you want me?"

"Tinsley" came the reply

"What!!!" I said shaking my head as if to clear my hearing

"Yes, Tinsley" Mike repeated

"I thought Dave looked after Tinsley Steelworks!" I shrieked "I've spent all this time trying to get off the Steelworks and now all you want me to do is go over to Sheffield to work at that Steelworks. So much for commercial work!"

My ego was deflated.

"Sorry Terry, but I do need you there this week" Mike apologised

"But, but, but" I tried to object

"I really am sorry Terry, but the priority at the minute is to help Dave who has got behind on his maintenance" Mike now sounded truly apologetic "I promise this is a one off. Help Dave get on top of his work load this week and I promise to send you to the seaside next week"

I returned to my van with head held low in a sulk. As I sat in the drivers seat I looked over to the A to Z and map books neatly laid out on the passenger seat.

"I won't need those this week" I thought "at least I know my way to the Tinsley Steelworks"

I set off at a steady pace with no intention of rushing and wondered where best to find a nice spot to have my lunch. Getting away from it all to the sea side was out of the question for lunch but I was sure I could think of some nice park between here and Sheffield to sit in quiet reflection.

It wasn't until I got on the motorway heading towards Sheffield that I realised two things were wrong.

- I had extracted all the 'industrial' spares stock from my van - now I would have to rely on Dave having any spares I needed. But also......

- I had got rid of all the clean, but heavily stained, overalls I regularly used on the dirty Steelworks.

It was like going back in time to when I was 16 and starting work all over again. All I had left to wear in the back of my van were some very clean and very bright.....

White Overalls

Chapter 19

'Slow Slow - quick quick - Slow'

Although my original intention of going into commercial refrigeration was to get away from the steelworks I regularly found myself having to support my steelwork colleagues. As the years rolled by and the commercial side grew, I worked less and less on these industrial sites but there was always somewhere that needed my help. One such site quickly became known as 'my' domain. To begin with I hated the idea of this being mine but eventually I began to really appreciate the sanctuary of a regular respite from the ever increasing commercial refrigeration work load.

Dave had always been a very friendly engineer but constantly found himself a 'one man band' as others didn't like working with him. Because I had worked closely with him when I had been an apprentice I had learnt how to tolerate him. Unfortunately my boss realised this and so often I found myself being volunteered to help him out. The steelworks contract at Sheffield was one of Dave's largest domains and he often needed my help to get on top of his commitments there. I eventually got used to the occasional day on the steelworks but never really enjoyed it as this was the type of work I had taken great steps to get away from.

Our manager, Mike, was constantly obtaining new contracts in his endeavours to build a small empire for himself. In the 1980s he was very successful and the contracts were coming in thick and fast. This started putting quite a strain on me and all the other engineers out on the road. Not only were our days getting very busy but we found ourselves working later and later into the evening. In the summer months, where the demand from breakdowns seemed to be never ending, I would rarely get home on time, I often even missed our children's bedtimes.

I remember Mike at one time being very pleased with himself when he had secured our first power station maintenance contract. Mind you, this was not just any power station but at the time it was the largest power station in Britain. So I could understand his self appreciation.

Drax power station was located just south of York and so was less than an hours drive from our base in Scunthorpe. Dave, who had been allocated the contract to fulfil, was not initially happy. Most of 'Dave's Domain' was based around the Sheffield area so for the Drax power station contract he would have to travel north in a morning instead of west! (Oh!! What hardship!!!?!!) - Call outs and breakdowns as usual would be covered by any engineer available at the time but Dave still wasn't happy at having to spent time away from his beloved Sheffield.

Dave as usual was his own worst enemy. I could imagine him boring the site engineer on his arrival with his chatty demeanour. He probably made the engineer late for a meeting or maybe stopped him from doing other work while Dave would talk to him about everything under the sun. Dave had always been one of those people you struggled to get away from. I could also picture him spending ages at the end of his working day explaining in far too much detail what he had and hadn't achieved that day. I had a vision of the site engineer getting hot under the collar before he could finally get rid of Dave. I bet the site engineer was probably late home from work that day!

Even though the rumours I had heard about Dave's first visit to Drax had made me chuckle to myself, it really didn't bother me. After all, it was nothing to do with me.

Then one morning, a month after Dave's one and only site visit, Mike called out to me as I entered the office.

"Terry, I need you to go to Drax this morning?"

"Sure, what's the problem" I replied expecting to hear of some equipment that had broken down.

"It's Dave!"

"What!" I exclaimed "I'm sorry Mike but even I cannot fix Dave."

"No, seriously though" Mike started "I need you to take over Dave's maintenance contract at Drax"

"Where's Dave? can he not make it this week?" I asked as I rolled my eyes skyward.

"That's not the problem" Mike confessed "Dave has been banned from the Drax site!"

"What!!" I shook my head in disbelief "but he hasn't been there long. Surely even Dave cannot wind someone up that quickly!"

"Oh yes he can" said Mike "The site engineer phoned me shortly after his first and only visit. He not only complained about the amount of time Dave spent in his office talking crap but he was equally concerned about the time he took to complete the maintenance."

"Surely that's a good thing isn't it?" I queried

"It is for us but the site engineer now wants a reduction in the cost of the contract. We'd originally quoted for four days work and Dave did it all in just one day!"

I stood there still shaking my head in amazement.

"So you can understand the engineer's frustration" Mike continued "I've so far managed to calm the guy down by promising him my top engineer to attend and do a proper job."

"I presume your top engineer is unavailable so you thought to ask me instead" I replied

We both laughed out loud.

"Look Mike" I continued "I don't mind this once but a really don't want this as a permanent thing. I've worked long and hard to get away from the industrial side of refrigeration."

"OK. I understand what you're saying Terry." Mike promised "I will talk some more with the site engineer and if we end up not getting Dave back onto the Drax site then I will share it out amongst all the engineers"

"Fair enough" I conceded "but I'm still not happy"

I sat down in the only spare chair in the office and waited for the relevant paperwork.

Mike handed me two sheets of paper, one of which contained all the contact details of who I had to report to and the other sheet was a full list of all the air conditioning units I was expected to service. I turned the second sheet over expecting the list to continue overleaf but found it was blank.

"Is this it!" I exclaimed

"I know what you're thinking" Mike defended "but even at four days worth of site visits a month we came in as the most competitive. I really need you to take your time to service all the units on that list"

"No wonder Dave only took one day to do it all, I think I'll struggle to stretch it out to four days!"

Mike eventually had to come to a compromise with the Drax engineer and they mutually agreed to reduce the time scale down by 25%. I only had to stretch the work out over 3 days instead of 4 but it was still very hard.

Mike never managed to get Dave back onto the Drax site and his promise of sharing the contract out between us never materialised either. Although I was angry at first I learnt over the years how useful this 'lazy' 3 day contract every month was to me. Especially during summer months when we could all be running around like chickens with no heads. The Drax engineer always insisted that I had to be on site for the planned 3 days and he never accepted any persuasion that the office came up with to try and drag me away on some other dire emergency elsewhere.

Luckily for me the Drax engineer and I got on very well. It was probably a relief for him after experiencing Dave's gift of the gab. I simply checked in at the start of the day and he wouldn't be bothered by me again until the end of the day.

I kept my head down, did the work requested and tried to keep the peace. Sometimes I even bought two newspapers on the way to work just so that I had enough mental stimulation to stop me going mad. It was hard trying to make one days worth of work last three days but that's what both my boss and the Drax engineer wanted so who was I to argue. Let me explain what a typical day at Drax was actually like for me.....

08:00 - Leave home.   *I never left home before this time as I had successfully persuaded the Drax engineer to accept the travel time was part of the 8 hour day. I didn't want to get there too early!*

09:00 - Arrival on site   *I would check in with the engineer and collect any extra jobs he may have for me.*

09:15 - Breakfast   *I always tried to get a hearty breakfast from their canteen. Great value and I could easily waste an hour eating and digesting it.*

10:15 - Start work!!!   *This is when the bulk of the work would be done although I often stopped for elevenses to read my paper and attempt the crossword.*

13:00 - Lunch time.   *Again the site cafeteria was great value for money but often I couldn't eat too much as I had already had a hearty breakfast.*

14:00 - More Work!!!   *This was usually finishing off the crossword that I could not complete in the morning. The Sun crossword can sometimes be very difficult!!!!*

15:00 - Check out Time.   *I would always try to time this for when the engineer is thinking of home time. That way he was quick to sign my sheets without reading the details.*

15:30 - Leave site.   *Security would log the times I arrived and departed so it was important to time my departure correctly*

16:30 - Home.   *Often in summer I would be heading off to some breakdown call to help the other overstretched engineers rather than heading home. But at least I knew I would get another day of rest at Drax tomorrow.*

Now don't get me wrong. Yes I intensionally wasted time when I was on the Drax site but I would still do all the work asked of me. After Dave's attempt to try and do a good job I was under strict instructions to keep the peace.

I obviously did a good job - probably too good at times.

Drax were happy! They were now receiving 3 days of work for 3 days of pay.

The Drax management were happy! They saw a 25% cost saving from the original contract deal.

The Drax engineer was happy! As long as he kept me as their dedicated site refrigeration engineer. In fact he would sometimes change the planned maintenance days to avoid my holidays. I think that was so he could avoid having Dave again.

Mike was happy! We kept the contract year after year and he could see very few call outs to a site that was almost maintained too much.

Little did they know the truth!!!!

I was eventually happy with my own little domain! Three days a month where I could go slow and somedays even slower. A great respite during the quick and often even quicker hot summer months.

———————————

Chapter 20

'I see dead people'

In the world of commercial refrigeration you can find yourself in some very unusual locations. The sort of places that most people never even have to think about let alone work there. That was probably one of the main attractions I had when I chose to enter this forever surprising world of commercial refrigeration.

I had placed myself in a brave new world. This is where I could be working on a diverse collection of equipment ranging from domestic fridges or freezers in peoples homes, through cold stores in large restaurants and shops, to whole building air conditioning units. However, one of the most unusual locations I ever found myself in during the early days of my 'out on the road' career, was in the local hospital. Now I agree this doesn't sound very unusual, but on this particular day I found myself going to the Scunthorpe General Hospital's - Morgue.

Death touches everyones life but most people never see, or really want to know, what goes on behind these particular closed doors. Everyone realises that when someone passes away in a hospital their body cannot stay on the ward but is transferred down to the morgue for safe keeping until funeral arrangements can be organised.

Just like the food in your own home or in your favourite restaurant a persons body will quickly deteriorate if it is not kept refrigerated. All hospitals have cold storage facilities in their morgues. The larger the hospital, the larger the morgue; the larger the morgue, the larger the cold storage facilities they need. Scunthorpe General Hospital was a reasonably large hospital and they had a smart modern Morgue that had a 12 body fridge and a 3 body freezer. Yes, you read right, a 3 body freezer! Sometimes a body would need long term storage and so the freezers were necessary for those that had maybe died in suspicious circumstances or for some reason could not be laid to rest within the usual time scale.

I think hospitals have always suffered from a lack of parking spaces and in those days Scunthorpe General Hospital were no exception. Instead of clamping or towing the badly, inconsiderately parked vehicles, Scunthorpe General Hospital tried to control the parking problem by using a simple parking sticker. This was no ordinary sticker! No! An ordinary sticker was never going to work as a form of deterrent.

The problem with these particular stickers, was not what was written on them but the type of glue they used. They could not be easily removed. Nowadays they probably wouldn't be allowed to use them as they would often restrict your field of vision for days after being posted. They were invariably placed on the windscreen in front of the driver or sometimes, if you're lucky, on the drivers side window. Even when you successfully managed to get the actual paper part of the sticker removed, the glue remained on the window making your vision of the road ahead all blurry. Washing with soap and water would not improve the situation and apart from industrial strength acid or maybe a military flame thrower I never found an easy way to fully clear the residue.

I'd previously worked in various departments at this hospital such as the canteen, pharmacy, laboratories etc and on a couple of occasions I had obtained one of the dreaded parking stickers. I unfortunately didn't learn my lesson the first time it happened but after spending several days attempting to clear the second sticker I swore never to be blinded by another.

Luckily for me the morgue department was in the basement of the hospital with its own access ramp for private ambulances or funeral directors hearses. This allowed these type of vehicles to gain access to the morgue without putting undue stress on any hospital visitors or even patients within the hospital. Not many people knew about this private access ramp and on this, my first visit to the morgue, I was reliably informed there would be ample parking space at the bottom of the ramp. From that day on I was always happy to visit the morgue but still dreaded going to any other department at the hospital for fear of getting another dreaded sticker.

The morgue was in a relatively new part of the hospital and as I drove down the small ramp I was pleasantly surprised at how unlike a morgue it looked. I'm not sure what I imagined a morgue to look like but this definitely wasn't the doom and gloom I thought it would be.

The entrance to the morgue was more like a hotel lobby. A floor to ceiling glass wall with a matching glass door in the middle. The glass was either tinted or it was relatively dark in the lobby area beyond the glass. I suspected the later. Being slightly underground gave the impression you were under a forecourt canopy. It wasn't totally pitch black as if you were underground but the subdued lighting was probably due to the surrounding shrubbery delicately placed to hide the department from general view.

As promised, there was plenty of parking for the very few vehicles that attended such a place. I parked my van in an empty space opposite the entrance door and collected my usual tool bag from the back of my vehicle. Walking across the tarmac to the entrance I tried to peer through the glass door to see what I could expect within. Like a hotel, I expected to be able to walk straight in to a reception area where a receptionist would be behind a smart desk ready to receive me in. Reaching for the door handle I was surprised to find there was no handle on my side of the door and it felt firmly closed when I tried to push it inwards. Thankfully I did discover an intercom nearby.

I heard the buzzer as I pressed the intercom's button. A short pause and then the speaker announced a reply.

"Hello" came a voice from within

"Hi, there" I said "Its the engineer from Kenyons to look at your fridge"

I was unsure what to call a body fridge but decided just a fridge would suffice.

"Oh yes" came the faceless reply "I've been expecting you. Push the door and just wait in the lobby, I'll be with you in a minute!"

The intercom buzzed once more and I could hear the door unlock. The lights in the lobby came on as I pushed the door inwards and walked in. In these modern 'smart' times we take it for granted the automatic switching on of lights, in those days it was an unexpected surprise and I looked around mystified trying to see who had turned the lights on for me.

The small square lobby was clinically clean. Plain, easily sanitised walls and floor with no furniture to sit down on. Still mystified at the automatic illumination of the lobby I stood there taking in my surroundings. Each door around the lobby had a sign on it indicating what lay behind and the first one on my right said it was the entrance to the office. I slowly rotated my head around the room reading each and every sign on each door finally reading the last door on my left which showed me it was the entrance to the actual 'Morgue'. As I presumed my customer would be in the office I returned my gaze to the door on my right just as a voice boomed out.

"There is no body there!" came the spooky sound from behind me

I turned around to see a tall man stood in the doorway to the morgue.

"Sorry to keep you" he said "I was just working on Mozart and I had to put him away"

I looked at him puzzled, wondering if I had heard him correctly.

"I had to put him away to stop him De-Composing" he said with a big smile on his face.

Still unsure whether to take this guy seriously or not I remained open mouthed and speechless.

"OK" he continues "I'll be Dead serious now, but I'm not usually a Mourning person!"

With that he lets out a little titter of a laugh.

I was hoping he had finally exhausted his vocabulary of morgue jokes but I was wrong. I learnt over the following years to accept that nearly everyone who works in a morgue has a strange sense of humour. It probably helps them to get through their day but I found it quite concerning to be treated in such a way on my first visit to such a place.

He guided me through the door to the morgue and I found myself in a large bright room. I tentatively looked around expecting to see a corpse or two laid out on one of the tables. Although the sight in front of me was just like we had all seen on television or in films there were thankfully no cadavers to be seen.

All along one side of the room were the little fridge doors which obviously housed all the dead bodies. Four columns of three high little doors were grouped together and at the far end of the room were another three doors in a single column. The twelve little doors were the main everyday fridges whereas the three separate doors gave access to the freezer where they could keep a body for a longer period. In the middle of the room were three body length tables fixed to the ground and a couple of similar wheeled tables were neatly lined up along the opposite wall to the fridge doors.

"Excuse my sense of humour" my guide said as he broke my gaze at the room. "It helps me to keep sane"

"That's alright" I lied "So what's the problem?"

"It's this one at the end" he said as he pointed to the nearest column of fridge doors "you cannot hear it much at the minute but when I open the door it is very noisy."

"It keeps them all A Wake" comes another pun from his lips!!!

Even I had to smile at that one.

He goes to open a door and I stop him saying "Hang on a minute, Is there anybody in there?"

"No. Don't panic. I've moved everyone down to the other end. We are actually pretty quiet at the moment so we have plenty of room" he assures me.

He opens the top door and I hear the constant sound of a fan blade catching on its casing.

"Oh yes. That's a nice easy job" I say with a grin on my face "Just how do I get in there?"

"Here you go" he says as he pulls the top drawer out of the fridge "you can get up on here"

"WHAT!!!" I exclaimed "you want me to sit on that"

"No, you'll never manage to SIT on it. You'll have to lay down"

I look at him expecting another joke or pun but he was serious this time. Deadly Serious.

With great hesitation I climbed up onto the top drawer with my tool bag and he then slowly slides me into the fridge. Horrified, I find myself laid on my back facing upwards at the bottom of the evaporative unit. Thankfully for me it was a very simple job that took only a few minutes but I learnt a valuable lesson that day that I would never forget. My guide could see my unhappiness at being laid out in a body fridge in a morgue so I was very thankful he didn't even joke about closing the door behind me. I learnt never to trust the door to stay open even if someone did stand holding the door. From that very first time in a morgue I always made sure it was impossible for the door to close while I was inside the morgue fridges.

When the job was complete I sat in his office warming up with a nice cup of coffee. Despite my original apprehension with the mortician's sense of humour I was beginning to warm to him. I stood up and shook his hand to say goodbye.

"You know your way out don't you?" he said......

"don't forget as you leave, take the Last Rite!"

_____

Chapter 21

'2B or not 2B - Gas is the question'

Large hospital morgues were relatively easy to work on as they were usually very large with a good capacity for bodies. They would have multiple shelves that would allow them to rearrange the bodies within the cold store, giving me a nicer working environment. However, those funeral directors that had the facility to store bodies were often much smaller affairs. I never found a funeral directors with anything larger than a three body chiller.

One day I got a call to a funeral directors in Barnsley. Nothing unusual about the place and it was probably the same as most funeral directors. The front of the building was the usual sombre type of facade that fronted directly onto the street. A driveway down the left hand side led around to a small car park at the back. From the car park there was a wide entrance into their large garage space which securely stored their hearses and limousines. On this particularly nice sunny day when I arrived, a couple of employees had got all the vehicles out of the garage and were washing and polishing them in the rear car park. This made it difficult for me to find room to park my van but easy to make the standard comment we all feel compelled to make when seeing someone washing their car.

"Just give it a wash but don't worry about the polish if you run out of time!"

The car washers stopped and looked quizzically across at me, but all I got for a reply was a smile from both of them. Although they were both dressed in identical grey overalls to wash the vehicles it did make me wonder if they were still wearing their black mourning suits underneath. Probably not!

"Is the boss in?" I enquired as I collected my tool bag from the back of my van.

"Yeah, he's in the office. It's through there on the right!" One said as they both pointed to the entrance next to the large open garage doors.

I entered the back of the building through the door they had indicated and easily found the managers office which was just off the small hallway I had found myself in.

"Hello. Hello" I tentatively said as I knocked on a slightly ajar door.

"Yes" came the reply from a man looking up from his desk "oh.. please, please come in"

The man had a very soft tone of voice. Obviously tuned over the years to portray a sense of calm to the bereaved. He was a middle aged man who characterised a sense of control and was obviously in charge. He waved me in.

"What can I do for you" he enquired

"Well I think it's more like what I can do for you!" I said "I'm from Kenyons Refrigeration. You called us to look at your body chiller!"

"Oh yes, of course" came the recognition "I've been expecting you".

He gently stood up and slowly, but confidently, walked around his desk to lead me across the hallway into the mortuary.

Just like a hospital morgue it was a very bright room with pure white tiles from floor to ceiling. The whole of the floor area was covered in floor tiles that were more of an off white colour. Wether this was their original colour or a sign of years of wear I will never know. However the mortuary not only looked spotlessly clean but also smelt strongly of disinfectant. This was one of the better mortuaries I had visited. In the centre of the room was a body length table (thankfully empty!) which was locked into place by the brakes on its wheels. These type of tables could be raised or lowered by a foot lever which not only allowed the mortician to get the table to a suitable working level but would aid the placing and extraction of bodies from the body chiller.

I had spotted the body chiller at the far end of the wall to my left and it was unlike the body chillers I had encountered in the Scunthorpe Hospital morgue. In the Hospital morgue there had been a door to each shelf within the chilled area. Here there was one big door just like the entrance to a cold store in a large restaurant or butchers. The door stood six foot tall from the floor and was approximately 4 inches thick which helped insulate the contents within. A large pull handle on the right hand side of the door would open the door away from the far wall creating a temporary partition stopping you from actually seeing what was inside. A temperature dial was mounted on the wall to the left of the door and the undertaker looked at it as he tapped it with one finger.

"The temperature never seems to get below 7 or 8 degrees" he said

"Ooh, that's not good" I replied "you should be down below 4 degrees for this type of chiller"

"That's exactly what I thought" he turned to face me "Do you think you can fix it?"

"I'm sure I can do something for you" I assured him "Leave it with me"

With that he turned to leave saying he had a lot of work on, but then I stopped him in his tracks by grabbing his arm.

"Hang on a minute. Is there anyone in there?" I enquired "you do realise I will need to go in there at some point!"

"Oh! I never thought of that" he informed me "is that a problem?"

"Er, yes! I'm afraid it is for me. I do prefer to be alone in there"

"Erm, well, yes! there is actually two people in there at the moment." he said with a quizzical look "Let me have a look at what we can do, but unfortunately as you can see, we have no where else to put them."

With that he opened the door and I instinctively peered around the door. I could see that the body chiller had a body on both the top two levels, but unlike the bodies you see in the Hollywood movies where they are covered with a bright white sheet, these were totally naked. I quickly turned my back to this vision and faced into the empty mortuary.

"Look, let me leave you to sort something out." I said as I started for the exit "I will stand outside until you come and get me"

"Help yourself to a coffee in my office" he said as the door closed behind me.

I took this opportunity to retrieve my very large heavy toolbox from the back of my van and returned to his office to try out his coffee machine. A few minutes later he appeared in the office doorway and told me what he had accomplished.

"I have managed to give you the top shelf to work from by moving them onto the other shelves" he started "but I really do not have anywhere else to put them. Will that be ok for you?"

"I'm not happy but it looks like it will have to do!" I reluctantly agreed "as long as they are all covered up"

Obviously he hadn't thought of that! He gestured for me to stay there and turned around to put that request into operation.

A few minutes later he returned and confirmed everything was as requested.

"Will it be a big job?" He asked looking at the large heavy toolbox I had retrieved from my van.

"Hopefully not" I said following his gaze to the floor "Oh no, no don't panic. That's not what you think! Yes it is a large toolbox and yes it is full of heavy tools but this is actually my paperweight!! Nowadays I always put my heaviest toolbox in the body chiller doorway as I am scared of the door closing behind me. In this particular case I'm doubly afraid of being locked in there with those two"

We both returned to the mortuary and he took great pride in showing me his preparation to make my working conditions acceptable. He assured me he would keep looking in on me but he really needed to get back to his office to carry on with some paperwork.

Using a small step stool, I found I could lean into the body chiller to check the efficiency of the evaporator. I quickly confirmed to myself it was a simple shortage of gas that was the problem. On the way back to my van for a gas bottle and charging leads I asked the two car washers if they knew where the condensing unit was for the body chiller.

"It's actually above the cold store in the corner of the garage" the tallest of the two replied

"..but you can't go in there!" The other lad quickly added

"Why not?" I asked

"Because the garage floor has been painted and its drying" came the reply "that's why we have all the cars out here."

Leaving my gas bottle and charging leads at the entrance to the garage I re-entered the building to disturb the boss. He came out with me to assess the problem and discuss any solution that we could come up with. All four of us stood there for some time scratching our heads in deep thought. Eventually the tall 'car washer' finally came up with a solution.

"How about if we get the long ladders and lay them from the top of the cold store to the floor outside the garage" he suggested "then you could walk up the ladders onto the roof of the cold store"

My first thought was what possible use a funeral directors would normally need such ladders for! but then the most obvious query came to mind and I enquired how they intended to put the ladders in place without walking on the freshly painted floor.

"Leave that to us" he said confidently as they both went off to get the long ladders.

A moment later they appeared with a set of long ladders between them. They then laid them out in the middle of the car park while extending them as far as they would go. The tallest lad then stood at the garage entrance holding one end of the ladder above his head while the other lad held the other end. With great skill and dexterity the tall lad passed the ladder over his head rung by rung while the other lad walked towards him. Although it looked a bit "Dads Army' towards the end of the operation as they struggled to hold the weight of the extended ladders, they did eventually manage to position this long ladder from the top of the cold store containing the bodies to the unpainted floor outside the large garage doors.

Both the undertaker and I were impressed and both the car washers had big smiles on their faces.

Like a tight rope walker I successfully (although wobbly) negotiated the ladder a couple of times to get my gas bottle and all the necessary equipment onto my working platform. The middle of the ladder became very bouncy as I walked over it but I was assured by the tall car washer, as he footed the ladder from outside the garage, that it was fine.

Eventually I managed to re-gas the condensing unit and was happy everything was working as efficiently as it should. I started checking for leaks using my leak detector and was then confident that the condensing unit was leak free. I gathered all my tools and equipment together ready to walk back over the bouncy ladder like Indiana Jones would do over a rope bridge. However, before I stood on my end of the ladder I noticed my 'car washing' assistant was no longer footing the bottom end of the ladder. In fact he was nowhere to be seen.

No matter how much I shouted and tried to attract someones attention it was all to no avail. I had no idea where they all were but I could not see or hear anyone. I was alone!

"Never mind" I thought "the ladder is hardly going to fall over, it's nearly horizontal for heavens sake!"

I was confident I could traverse the garage on the ladder without needing someone to foot the end. So after grabbing as many of my tools and equipment I could carry (to minimise the number of journeys) I set off along the ladder.

Every step I took increased my confidence in my task. Even when I got near the middle of the ladder where the bouncing on every step increased I was getting more and more comfortable with the manoeuvre. Then it happened......

.......When moments like this occur the world seems to slow down to a crawl. Everything goes into a Matrix style slow motion. As I felt the ladder slip, I had all the time in the world to turn around to see the top of the ladder as it came away from the top of the body chiller. I could see the top of the ladder slide down the wall of the body chiller and I felt the sensation of falling for every single inch as I plummeted to the ground.

I was awoken from my slow motion dream state by the clatter of the ladder onto the freshly painted floor and the sound of my tools smacking into the floor below. My gas bottle continued the din by rolling over the floor collecting red paint on its way to the other side of the garage.

By the time the three of them appeared at the garage door to see what had happened I was beginning to stand up and recover from my fall. Although the top of the ladder had been over eight feet in the air when it was on top of the body chiller, the middle of the ladder had probably only been about four feet off the ground. I had not fallen very far and thankfully had only managed to injure my pride.

Their freshly painted garage floor received far worse injury than me. Collecting and retrieving all my tools and equipment spread far and wide across the floor caused even more ruination. There was no question about it, the floor would now need repainting but at least the boss didn't hold me responsible.

I still needed to finish the job in hand and so after putting most of my tools and equipment back into my van I went back inside the mortuary to check for leaks inside the body chiller. Laying myself out on the top shelf of the body chiller to work on the evaporative unit directly above my head I started searching for possible leaks. Finally detecting a small seepage from a flare nut on the side of the unit I got my spanners from my pocket to tighten it. Just then I heard a noise. Usually escaping gas sounds more like a constant whistle but this was more like a fart and stopped almost as soon as it started. As I was laid on my back with my head near the door I looked up above my head expecting to see someone stood in the doorway. There was no-one!

Then I heard it again but this time for a bit longer. It was definitely more like a farting sound. That was the very moment that I realise the sound was not coming from the refrigeration equipment above me but was coming from something below me. It suddenly hit me that the leaking gas was not from the refrigeration unit but from one of the bodies below me - One of them was actually farting!!!!

Time to get out!

Although I had not experienced this phenomenon before I was reliably informed by the funeral director, as I got my paperwork signed, that it is a common occurrence. Any trapped gas within a dead body will eventually come out in the form of a fart or, as he agreed, the even scarier sound of an "Ahh" from the persons mouth. The reason it happened when I was in there was the simple fact that the door was left open. The body chiller temperature had risen and so the bodies were warming up making the gas expand.

Understanding this phenomenon helped me get used to the noises, but under no circumstance would I ever let them shut the door on me! My large, heavy toolbox just got larger and heavier.

———————

Chapter 22

'Rewards in Heaven'

Working in commercial refrigeration has its advantages and rewards. Although the hot summer months meant I was very busy I could often find a nice cold store to walk into when I needed cooling down. In fact I remember one particularly hot summers day when I arrived at the Iceland store in the Crystal Peaks shopping centre near Sheffield. I was dripping with sweat after driving some distance in my 'un-air conditioned' van on the hottest day of the year and simply walked straight into their cold store at -18'C. Usually I should have put on the protective coat etc before entering but I was just so hot I walked straight into the cold store in my T-shirt and shorts.

As I stood in the middle of the cold store cooling down I heard a voice call out to me.

"Hello, Mr Kenyon!!! are you in here?" the very quizzical voice shouted out.

"Hello" I instinctively replied as I peered around a shelf full of frozen food.

"Oh there you are" the manager standing at the entrance door continued "Would you mind coming out here please!"

"Sure, no problem" I replied as I exited the cold store

"I didn't believe Sue when she told me where you were!" exclaimed the manager "You do know you shouldn't be in there without a thermal jacket on don't you!"

"Yes, sorry about that. I was just overheating so needed to cool down quickly"

Thinking back it must have caused quite a conversation. Sue had opened the trade door to let me into the back of the store and I instantly disappeared into their cold store. With two thermal jackets still hanging on the peg outside no-one, including the manager, would believe Sue when she reported that the refrigeration engineer had actually arrived and he was hiding in the cold store.

In those days we only had the contract to look after the air conditioning units in Iceland whereas a rival refrigeration company still had the contract to service all their fridges and freezers. I was there to look at the air conditioning and so the report of me hiding in the cold store must have been very unusual indeed.

Iceland originally used to use lots of individual chest freezers lined up in rows creating the aisles. The biggest problem with this arrangement was that each chest freezer would kick out its own heat energy directly into the store. The stores air conditioning unit would then have the mammoth job (especially on hot summer days) of removing all this heat energy to the outside.

A more modern pack system however, would extract all the heat energy through pipe work to a common plant room and then outside. The stores air conditioning unit would then only have the heat energy of a normal room to cope with.

On this particular day the air conditioning in that shop was going flat out and still couldn't cope with all the heat load. The rival refrigeration company had been called the day before because some of the freezers were struggling to get down to temperature and they had managed to blame it on our air conditioning. I sadly informed the manager that the only way he could get the store temperature down would be to turn off 20% of his freezers and I quickly made a hasty retreat (via the cold store again) knowing full well he was unlikely to carry out my suggested solution.

The following year we got the full contract for Iceland which then made it harder for us to blame anyone else's equipment. We still had the same call-outs in the summer months but at least Iceland eventually understood the problem and they started to invest in the more appropriate 'pack' systems.

Sometimes the advantages for working in the refrigeration trade reaped a more materialistic reward. Showing a little kindness at the right time and in the right place could often produce some surprising rewards.

One afternoon I found myself being called to the Bookers cash & carry wholesalers on the outskirts of Lincoln. Some of these larger stores had their own butchery department and so they had a lot of refrigeration equipment for us to maintain. The butcher on that day was a young man called Phil who I could see was rushed off his feet as I arrived. He somehow stemmed the flow of customers at his counter to show me the problem he had got with one of their largest display freezers.

Very perturbed, Phil told me how it had taken him ages to remove all the contents of this big cabinet into the cold store they had and now he didn't have enough room left for the expected delivery he was expecting tomorrow.

"No problem Phil" I assured him "I will see what I can do."

"I was really hoping to be away by five today" Phil told me as he agitatedly looked at his watch "I'm out on the town tonight with my mates."

"I can see you are busy so don't worry about me. You get back to that queue of customers and I will be as quick as I can"

Phil returned to his counter and I started my investigation. Luckily for Phil, and me, the problem was quite simple and I soon had the temperature in the display cabinet dropping back down to below zero. Phil although still very busy, kept looking in my direction, and at his watch. He was obviously worried about getting away from work on time. I gave him a thumbs up signal to indicate things would be ok which seemed to calmed him down slightly but I could see he was still agitated.

By the time the cabinet had reached its optimum temperature there was still an hour to go before closing time and poor Phil now had an even longer queue of customers in front of him. He undoubtedly couldn't get away from his counter. As this was to be my last job of the day I decided to help Phil by restocking the cabinet with all the food he had piled up in the cold store. I don't think he noticed me to start with but as I was carrying the last load from the cold store I could see him physically calm down and a big smile was growing on his face.

"Oh wow!" Phil said as he finished serving his last customer "thank you so much. I was hoping to get that cabinet refilled but didn't think I would by the end of the day. You have saved my life"

A slight exaggeration there I think but he was obviously very relieved.

"Well I could see you were stressed out so I didn't mind" I handed him my report to sign.

"Here" he said handing me two large steaks wrapped up in white paper "put these in your toolbox as a thank you from me."

I quickly concealed the parcel in my toolbox knowing full well the store manager may not have approved of the butcher handing out free food.

Our steak dinner that evening tasted that much sweeter, not just because the steaks were free but also from the satisfaction I had from doing a random act of kindness.

The following week I was back in Iceland but this time it was in Chesterfield.

Chesterfield Iceland was in the city centre but it had a good service yard which I knew I could park in. Often in those days the service yards would get filled up with lots of cars from those that worked in the shops or even cheeky motorists who thought they could get away with free parking. On this particular day I couldn't find an appropriate space but eventually parked across a couple of cars near the Iceland trade entrance. I believed the cars probably belonged to some of the Iceland staff anyway, but if they belonged to the general public then they deserved to be blocked in!

As I entered the trade door I asked the lady who had opened the door whose cars I had blocked in and she assured me that they were both indeed Iceland staff. She directed me to the managers office where I met a middle aged man looking through reams of paperwork.

"Ah, Mr Kenyon" he said as he looked up from his desk "Just the guy I wanted"

"Reporting for duty sir" I japed

"It's not a serious fault but the main cold store just isn't quite getting down to temperature" he informed me "It is cold in there but the thermometer reads only minus sixteen degrees and I know it should be below twenty degrees!"

"Oh dear" I said "I will take a look but I was told it was one of your freezers so I haven't brought a ladder with me. I do know that the condensing unit for that cold store is on the roof so do you have any ladders here I could borrow?"

"I'm afraid not" he said

"Well, I'll take a quick look and see what I can do but if I do need to get on the roof I'll have to go back to the depot to get some. It may mean me coming back tomorrow."

"See what you can do" he concluded "and in the mean time I will ask our neighbours if they have any ladders we could borrow"

It didn't take me long to realise I couldn't do anything without access to the roof and so I returned to the managers office within minutes of me exiting.

"I really do need to get on that roof" I started "any luck with finding me a ladder?"

"Well the manager at Currys next door says you can borrow their ladders if we are desperate" he happily reported

"Oh! that's brilliant" I said "can you tell him I will nip round to their back door now"

As I arrived at the back door to Currys the roller shutter door was raising and a young guy was stood next to a set of ladders laid out on the floor. I picked them up and he told me to simply leave them outside the roller shutter door when I had finished with them.

'Great' I thought 'at least now I didn't have to do a one hundred mile round trip just to get some ladders'

Thankfully these ladders were of the new type of aluminium construction. Compared to the wooden ladders I possessed at home, they were extremely light and easy to man handle. I happily carried them over to Iceland and laid the ladders out on the floor. The sun was shining and it was getting towards the end of the working day and so I was confident this would be my last job of the day.

Pushing the top section up to its maximum length I then lifted the ladders up against the wall and discovered to my disdain that they were not quite long enough to actually reach the roof. They were close! but not close enough. They were short by about two or three foot.

Our depot ladders would have reached three or four feet above the roof allowing me to easily step off the side of the ladder. However two or three feet below the roof was a real problem.

I stood back and looked around the building trying to judge if any section of the roof may be slightly lower than the section I had chosen. No, it all looked about the same height! Then I noticed a small outlet spout coming out near the top of the wall that I could maybe use to help me climb over the parapet. Was this a possibility OR do I drive one hundred miles (round trip) to get the appropriate ladder?

Luckily for me, my van was positioned in the ideal place below this spout allowing me to position the set of ladders against the wall and then footed against one of my back wheels. This gave me the confidence that the ladder was going no-where. It could not slip down while I was up there and it felt very firm and secure when I tested it at ground level.

I have never been a lover of heights but after convincing myself that this set up was safe I tentatively started climbing with my tool bag over my shoulder. As I neared the top of the ladder I blindly felt for the top of the parapet and became more confident when I gripped the rail along the top. Now all I needed to do was pull myself up over the parapet while using the protruding spout as a foot hold......

As I almost fell over the parapet I heard a crash from below!!!

The protruding spout wasn't as secure as I had expected! Unknown to me, as I had put my weight on it the spout had dislodged and fell to the ground with a crash. I peered over the parapet to the ground below. Fortunately it had missed my van. Unfortunately though, it had landed on one of those two cars I had blocked in.

"Oh S**T!!!" I said out loud

Luckily for me the problem with the condensing unit on the roof was a simple fix and so it wasn't long before I could quickly, but very tentatively, descend the ladders to see what damage I had done. The six inch pipe, that was once a spout, was sat in the middle of the roof of one of the cars. I expected a great deal of damage but to my surprise the bit of pipe was happily sat on the roof without any sign of dint or scratch. I quickly removed the incriminating evidence and tried not to look suspicious as I inspected the car more thoroughly. I really could not find any sign of damage.

I am still not sure to this day, but I believe the spout probably fell all the way to the ground making the crashing sound that I had heard from beyond the parapet and then it must have gently bounced onto the roof of the car.

I returned the ladders to Currys and reappeared in front of the Iceland manager who was still sifting through all his paperwork.

"All done and dusted, just my paperwork to sign" I reported as I handed him my report.

"Great stuff!" he said "How were the Curry ladders then?"

"Yeah! No problem" I lied "saved me coming back tomorrow"

"I'm glad" said the manager "as the Curry's manager didn't think they would reach!!!"

I stifled a sigh.

"Actually, while you're here" the manager continued "I wondered if you could do me a little favour?"

"Erm… What do you need?"

Pulling out a metal box from beside his desk the manager asked "Could you fix this under one of the counters for me? Its a secure money box to keep bank notes in for the till. I think it only needs a couple of screws"

"Sure, why not" I agreed "can you show me where you want it?"

The manager took me to one of the tills at the front of the shop and explained where he wanted it positioning. He gave me the accompanying screws in a clear little bag and showed me the keys which were taped securely inside the drawer.

Ten minutes later I had securely fitted the drawer and was showing the manager my handiwork. He was a very happy man. In fact he was so happy he told me to pick any gateaux I fancied from the store freezers as a reward for a job well done. I picked the largest and most expensive I could find and smiled at the thought of the fruits of my labour as I returned to my van.

Leaving Chesterfield on my way home I turned onto the M1 and was feeling very happy with myself. Not only had I fixed his cold store problem but had the good fortune to NOT damage anyone's car. I looked down on the passenger seat and admired my prize for installing the metal drawer for the manager.

That was when I suddenly realised what I had done! When I showed the manager my handy work I had closed the drawer……

..... leaving the keys locked inside!

———————————

Chapter 23

'Diggers Dig Deep'

"Would you like some overtime this weekend?" Mike, our branch manager, said to me one Friday morning.

"Yeah sure" was my reply "Mind you it depends on where you're sending me!"

"Oh don't worry Terry. It's right up your street!" He said with an almost undetectable smirk on his face. "Its only a vehicle air conditioning about 10 miles north of Wakefield but the customer can only make it available at the weekend"

"That's sounds OK. Go on then, give me the details"

I easily got suckered in. I should have known better! It sounded like an easy bit of overtime. I could picture myself in the comfort of a large heated garage working on some expensive luxury car like a Rolls Royce or maybe a Bentley. Maybe just a quick re gassing of the system.

No, of course not. This 'vehicle' turned out to be a 100 ton, large excavator in the bottom of a stone quarry.

To make matters worse, my wife complained that she had planned for us to go shopping on Saturday, so I was in trouble with her as well.

After a bit of discussion, we decided we could kill two birds with one stone. We could both travel to Wakefield, I could drop Elaine off at the shopping centre and then travel onto the quarry to do the job. Afterwards we could meet up in the food court in Wakefield city centre and have lunch together. As I was not on call that weekend I wouldn't need my pager so Elaine could carry it and I would page her when I had arrived back in Wakefield after the job.

In a world without mobile phones and very limited mobile communications this theory was sound and on the whole the plan worked very well. However the actual job was far from the plan I had in mind.

"When the pager goes off it will mean I am back in Wakefield and I will meet you at the food court" I told Elaine as I dropped her off by the side of the road near Wakefields indoor shopping centre called The Ridings.

"Don't worry about me Terry, I'll be fine" Elaine reassured me "you know how much I love shopping"

I set off for my work place and I watched Elaine in my rear view mirror as she happily walked into The Ridings. I headed north out of the city with my trusty road map laid out on the passenger seat of my van, guiding me to the stone quarry.

Where's your Sat Nav! - I hear you say. What Sat Nav.... In those days Satellite Navigation was a science fiction dream. The only way you navigated was with a road map that you hoped was at least up to date. The night before I had studied the map and had already worked out which roads and turnings I needed. It was a skill all of us service engineers had got quite adept at. How to memorise a route and then drive along with one eye on your passengers seat map.

The journey to the quarry was very uneventful and I was very pleased with myself as I pulled into the car park alongside the site offices. Everything looked closed and empty except for just one Ford Sierra sat alone in the car park. I parked along side the Sierra hoping to see the digger driver sat patiently inside. No, there was no-one to be seen.

'Probably sat in the office' I thought to myself as I proceeded to exit my van.

I walked the short distance to the site office entrance but found it in darkness and locked. As I turned from the door scratching my head in thought of what to do next I heard a noise. From around the back of the offices came a very muddy Land-rover at speed. The Land-rover screeched to a halt directly behind the only two vehicles in the car park and out jumped my digger driver.

"Hi, you must be the engineer from Kenyons?" The driver stated the obvious as he walked towards me with his hand held out ready for a handshake.

"Er, yeah, that's right" I replied

"Great, my name's Jim" he told me enthusiastically "Fantastic timing as we have only just arrived too"

"We??"

"Yeah, it's just me and my son" Jim told me as he turned and pointed towards the 4x4 Land-rover. "Me and my family are actually on holiday at our caravan in Bridlington and so my son said he wanted to come for the ride with me. Hopefully you won't be too long and we can get back to some fishing this afternoon."

"So where is the digger?" I enquired looking around for a maintenance shed.

"Oh didn't they tell you!" said Jim "It's down there I'm afraid" Jim points over the cliff edge indicating the digger was at the bottom of the quarry.

"Oh great!!" I exclaimed "Is it best for me to follow you down in my van?"

"Not a chance" Jim laughs "The 4x4 can struggle at times so your van won't stand a chance. Best thing to do is put everything you may need in the back of the 4x4 and I'll drive us down. Its a bit muddy up here from all the rain this week, but trust me it will be better down in the bottom of the quarry"

Jim's son stayed sat in the middle of the 4x4's bench seat watching Jim and I transfer all my tools, gas bottles and anything I thought may be useful, from the back of my van into the back of the 4x4. Jim was obviously keen to get going as soon as he could and I often had to reprimand him when he literally threw some of my gear into the back of his 4x4.

The engine roared into life and I had hardly managed to shut the passenger door when we sped off out of the car park. Jim was either in a rush or he was simply a fast driver. I think it was a bit of both.

We turned left as we exited the car park and raced behind the offices onto the gravel track along the top of the quarry. Looking out of my side of the 4x4 I could look directly down the cliff side into the quarry. I have never been very keen on heights and I tried my best to put on a brave face as I tried to quickly fasten my seat belt as we bounced along the very muddy gravel track.

Jim had warned me about how much mud the previous weeks rain had made and he was right to tell me my van would not have stood a chance. Even the 4x4 was slipping and sliding a bit. Looking at the very deep tracks in the muddy, gravel track it was obvious these tracks were usually occupied by large quarry trucks and not road legal vans like mine.

We got half way around the top of the quarry before Jim declared we should try a different route.

"The muds just getting too deep now" he said "but don't worry I know a short cut!"

We somehow managed to turn around and head back towards the offices. At least the sheer cliff was on his side of the 4x4 and it meant I didn't have to look directly over the edge.

Suddenly he turns right, as if he is doing a re-enactment of the Thelma & Louise film where they drive over a cliff. This forces me to stop pretending to be cool and instantly grab hold of anything solid within my reach. Jim's son calmly turns to look at me as I have not only gripped the seatbelt anchor point with my left hand but also put both my feet onto the dashboard to brace for impact. Not a cool, collective look at all.

As we thunder downhill on a track cut into the side of the quarry, Jim's son smiles at me and returns his gaze to the track ahead. The track ahead looked less muddy than the one on the top. It was narrower than the top track and there were no more deep tracks that the large quarry trucks usually form as they obviously couldn't come down this way. I still wouldn't say it was smooth.

We still seemed to bounce down the track with most of my equipment in the back rolling about behind us and me wedged into my seat holding on with all my strength.

Ahead, I noticed two diggers parked either side of our track.

"Oh, is one of those diggers yours Jim?" I ask with great relief

"No, no!" Jim replied "they're just track diggers"

"Mine is that big one in the bottom" and he proceeded to turn his gaze over his right shoulder and point down the cliff edge while still driving at break-neck speed towards these two diggers.

Jim's son continues to stare ahead (I think he was enjoying every minute of it), I stare ahead with bulging eyes and Jim also returns his gaze to the track starring ahead.

With my feet still on the dashboard wedging me tightly into my seat, my train of thought is on these two diggers in front of us coming up fast......

Is he going to turn off before them????

No... there doesn't seem to be another 'secret' turning!

Oh, he looks like he is going in between them.....

Is there enough room???

IS THERE enough room????

I HOPE THERE IS ENOUGH ROOM!!!!

OH MY GOD!!!!!!

Instinct kicks in and I release my grip of the seat belt anchor point to put my hands over my eyes. I hear the door mirror clip the left hand digger and feel the G-forces propelling me forward as we grind to a halt. The seat belt retains me in my seat and my hands stay covering my closed eyes.

I hear Jim's son nonchalantly say....."Dad, I think you've scared the fridge man!"

I slowly open my eyes and spread my fingers to see what we had hit. Unfortunately (or maybe fortunately) in front of us was nothing. And I mean, nothing.......

"Oh, bugger" declares Jim "Looks like they've dug the track up now!!"

We had stopped right on the edge of the track end. The two diggers had obviously spent the week removing this so called short cut and in front of us now was just a big void looking directly down to Jim's ginormous excavator in the bottom of the quarry.

Jim slams the 4x4 into reverse as I try to get my breath back.

"Looks like we'll have to go back to plan A." Jim says undeterred.

Thankfully, the rest of the day went better.

We successfully negotiated the deep cut furrows in the original top perimeter track and found what I believed to be a much safer route down to Jim's beloved excavator in the quarry base.

Jim and his son sat for over an hour in the cab of the large 100 ton excavator while I sweated it out in the engine compartment repairing and re-gassing the air conditioning unit. The large engine roaring away only inches from my ears. I did get my own back (a bit) on them by getting the cab so cold that they both had to vacate the comfort of the cab before they froze to death.

A couple of hours later I was parking up in The Ridings Shopping Centre in the middle of Wakefield and found a public telephone to activate the pager Elaine was carrying. We met as arranged for lunch in the food court and she listened in horror at my narrow escape.

Elaine may have spent more money than I had earned that day but I was not concerned. I was just grateful to be away from Jim and his beloved excavator in the bottom of the stone quarry.

I was very grateful to still be alive.

Chapter 24

'Bull in a China Shop'

"Your final job of the day today.." started Barbara "…. is Steven Smiths. It's certainly on your way home" she said laughing slightly.

Barbara was a middle aged, Yorkshire lady who looked after our Wakefield office. She had that down to earth, honest Yorkshire attitude who would often receive a wind up from us but was never fooled easily. She was our area manager's personal assistant, office general secretary, telephonist, work planner and controller all rolled into one. In fact anything needed doing in the office Barbara did it, and she was very efficient too.

Barbara was not lying. Stephen Smiths was a garden centre on the outskirts of Scunthorpe. My home town. It was a large complex selling not only gardening equipment and plants but all the paraphernalia we nowadays associate with this type of garden centre. In those days it was quite a novelty to wander around such a place ending up with a cup of tea and a slice of cake in their cafe. That's where I was heading, the cafe.

Although to the general public the garden centre looked very smart and well laid out, behind the scenes it was run on a shoe string. The boss didn't like to spend money but he enjoyed charging higher than normal prices in his shops. The cafe sold some lovely cakes and produced some lovely meals which attracted lots of customers. However in the actual kitchen the equipment was of the cheaper type. It was always prone to breaking down and we received regular call outs. Not a bad thing for me on this day as it gave me a final job for the day less than 10 minutes away from my home. I may even get to see the kids today before they go to bed!

Stephen Smiths was a trail blazer. They had a one way system where you entered in one door but could not get to the tills and exit until you had walked around most of the displays tempting you to buy more than you came in for. Several main halls displayed everything under the sun for the gardener and anyone else who wandered in. The first of these halls even had smaller shops built along two sides that displayed everything from Christmas decorations (even in summer) to craft goods and artists brushes. As I said they were real trail blazers, most garden centres in the 1980s would simply sell a wide variety of plants with a few gardening tools near the tills. Here at Stephen Smiths they would tempt you with all sorts of goods that you never knew you wanted. Nowadays, this is exactly what we expect from the large nationally owned garden centres. A one stop shop.

As it was an autumnal day, mid week and late in the afternoon I easily managed to park my van in the main car park at the front of the building, even quite close to the entrance. I knew the cafe was right at the back of the store, as this location draws all the customers to walk through the whole store, so reducing my distance from my van to the job was a great advantage for me. It was never my idea of fun carrying heavy gas bottles, tools etc through the maze of delicate displays while trying not to be a 'bull in a china shop'.

I collected my usual tool box of regular tools from the back of the van and headed straight through the store to the cafe. The kitchen staff were always very pleasant there, probably because they saw us so often, and so I was immediately offered a cup of tea as I walked into the food preparation area.

"So what's the problem today" I said to the cafe manager.

"Its the fridge door" she replied "it just won't shut properly"

I instantly had a flashback to my Mother-in-laws fridge door all those years ago when I was an apprentice. I quickly looked to make sure there was no yoghurt pot stuck in there somewhere!

No. Nothing so simple.

"OK, I'll take a look"

"Oh! And before you go the big boss wants a word with you in his office" the manageress added.

"No problem" I said as I accepted my free cup of tea.

It was a very simple 10 minute job that only needed a bit of adjustment to the door hinge. I took my time not just because I wanted to enjoy my free tea but really didn't want Barbara to give me another job. I was less than 10 minutes from my home so if I just stretched this job out until after our office closed, and Barbara went home, I could have a relatively early finish. My perceived diligence to my work was eventually rewarded by a gift of some cake that they couldn't keep until the following day. Arriving at jobs like this at the end of the working day was always very rewarding.

"All done!" I finally declared as I was collecting my tools and filling out the paperwork.

"That's great" accepted the manageress "now don't forget to see the big boss on your way out"

"Oh yes." I exclaimed "I had forgotten. I better take all my tools (& cake!!!) back to the van first though"

"Yes, don't let him see I've given you some free cake" she said "you know what he's like, he'll try and charge you for it!"

I collected all my tools into my toolbox and said my goodbyes.

The big bosses office was right next to the till area and the main exit. I rushed straight through the tills to my van so I didn't get accosted by him with free cake in my hand. The only downfall with this tactic was the fact you cannot go IN the exits. So once I had put my tools and contraband cake safely into the back of my van, I had to enter the building back through the entrance doors and wind my way through all the fancy goods displays to get round to the tills and the big bosses office.

I knocked on the door and entered when requested.

"You wanted to see me before I left" I started

"That's right" he said looking up from his desk "I have a little job for you before you leave"

My heart sank. It was always trouble when people use the 'little job' phrase. It invariably was NOT little.

"Of course sir" my professional work ethic kicks in "What can I do for you?"

"Well, as we are coming to the end of the summer season we need all our hall heaters starting up" he told me

"erm… Its not really my forte" I honestly replied "I'm really the refrigeration engineer more than the heating engineer"

"Your office did say you would be able to sort it out for us. I believe they just need switching on" he said.

Earlier that year our department had taken on an experienced heating engineer on the idea of taking on these sort of contracts. I realised my office had probably told the big boss of Stephen Smiths that someone would be along to sort it out but I wasn't sure they expected me to sort it. However, if it was just a simple case of switching them on I couldn't see any problem and it would save another site visit from Martin, our 'Gorgi Registered' heating engineer. ('Gorgi' in those day was the 'Gas Safe' equivalent today)

"OK" I agreed "I can take a quick look, but if there are any problems I will get Martin to pay you a visit as soon as he is free"

"That's great" the boss said "I'll show you where they are"

I'm sure you (the reader) are like me - I imagined Stephen Smiths warehouse heaters to be free standing boxes in the corner of each hall with ductwork on top, either blowing warm air out of grills or ducting it to a higher level across the space it was intended to heat. This is how most industrial air conditioning units are set up. The main equipment may even be in its own plant room separate to the intended space it is conditioning.

Stephen Smiths heaters were a miss match of different types. Every single one of them heated their intended space differently. Some radiated heat from a long stretch of glowing shields and some units contained fans to circulate the warmed air across the vast halls. All of them had two things in common. They were gas powered and ALL of them were at least 12 feet above the ground. I pointed this out to the big boss and he dutifully showed me where I could obtain a set of steps to gain access.

With a big sigh, I resigned myself to looking at the job in hand and the big boss left me to it, assuring me he would be in his office if I needed anything.

The first couple of radiated heat shield heaters were fairly straight forward to light up and I gained a lot of confidence to see the glowing warmth of the burners go on and off as I tested each thermostat worked as efficiently as they should.

I have never been a lover of heights and so standing on top of a 12 foot step ladder, in the middle of a great hall, above ceramics and all sorts of fancy goods, was very nerve racking for me. My confidence grew with each heater I got going but due to my hatred of heights I thankfully never got confident enough to be complacent. Toward the end of my work I was actually starting to enjoy myself in a strange sort of way. I had started outside my comfort zone but was getting more and more job satisfaction with every heater I struck up.

The extra work had delayed my home going by an hour but now I was coming to the last heater. Through the large glass windows at the front of Stephen Smiths I could see the night drawing in and it was getting dark outside. As the working day came to a close the garden centre became very quiet. This helped me easily position my step ladder to gain access to each heater.

The last heater was a convection heater positioned in the roof space above the Christmas Store that was located within the first hall. Although the access was probably the hardest to get to, when in the roof space I would be able to work from a fixed, sturdy platform which would satisfy my height phobia.

I position the step ladder carefully around the Christmas baubles within the Christmas store and climbed up to remove a roof tile where I was told the access to the platform was. Success! With the roof tile removed I could see the job in hand so I carefully climbed up into the roof space.

Quite happy with myself I sat on the platform with the heater control panel in front of me. Unfortunately, unlike all the others, this one would not fire up after being switched on. I tried the usual switch off and on to reset the controller but all to no avail. I began scratching my head and got myself a little frustrated. However this was the last job (thank goodness!) and I could still be home in time to see the kids before bedtime.

A full 15 minutes of testing and adjustments later I finally heard the burners strike up and the fan started blowing the warm air across the vast hall. A big smile came across my face. I quickly ran through my testing regime to ensure it would work correctly throughout the coming months and collected my tools together ready to go home.

"What the ....!!!" I exclaimed out loud as I looked through the previously removed ceiling tile access space.

Below me was nothing!!!! and I mean nothing!!! Well, there was a table of Christmas baubles but more to the point, there was no step ladder!!!

I shook my head in disbelief, as if that might magically make the step ladder reappear.

"Hello! Is anyone there?" I said into the void below me

"HELLO. HELLO"

No noise at all come back.

I looked at my watch and realised it was nearly closing time. The thought of me being stuck up here all night flashed into my mind.

'Don't be stupid Terry' I thought 'at least the big boss knows I am here. Somewhere!'

'I need to attract someones attention!' My thought pattern continued 'but who the heck is going to come into the Christmas Store in September? and when the garden centre is about to close'

I stood up and realised that although I was in the roof void above one of the sub-shops I could look over the heater out across the first hall toward the tills. Nearly closing time mid week meant that there were very few customers about and apart from the girls starting to close the tills up I could see no-one about to help me.

Then out of the corner of my eye I saw the automatic entrance doors open and a middle aged woman comes rushing in. I realise that unless she is actually in a rush to buy some Christmas baubles the chances of her entering the Christmas sub-store were slim. The only chance I have is to attract her attention as she winds her way through the one way route past the sub-stores.

I climb up onto the heater so I can peer over the edge directly down to the entrance to the Christmas Shop.

"Hello….. excuse me….. hello" I try to sound calm and warming

The lady stops and looks around.

"Hello…. Sorry, but I'm up here"

Her gaze raises but she obviously never considers someone directly above her.

"Hello??" She quizzically replies

"Yes. Hello."I enthusiastically replied "I'm here in the roof"

At this point she looks directly up at me and sees just a head peering out above the heater. Even though it startles her I was grateful she kept her balance and didn't tumble like a bull in a china shop into any of the surrounding ceramics.

"I'm sorry to shock you but I need your help" I plead "Someone has removed my stepladder and I cannot get down."

"Could you get a member of staff to come and help me please"

I'm not sure what the poor lady said to the girls at the till but it certainly made them laugh. Whether it was the realisation that this crazy woman, at the end of their working day, was actually telling the truth about a man in the air or it was the sight of me laid out on top of the heater in the roof space smiling and waving back at them. Whatever made them point and laugh at me also made me a lot happier knowing I was about to be rescued.

I was even happier when I arrived home 20 minutes later and was treated to the sound of my two children.

"Daddy, daddy, daddy!!" they shouted as they ran up to me.

My heart melted. I had made it home before bedtime.

_____

Chapter 25

'The Mulberry Bush'

"You've been found guilty of your crimes and I now sentence you to a day in prison"

"What the heck are you talking about Barbara" I replied, as I stood in the Wakefield office the other side of Barbara's desk.

"I've got a job for you in Wakefield prison today" Barbara declared

"Wow!" I exclaimed "I didn't realise we had a contract with them. I've never been before, is there anything I should know before I go?"

"Yes. It's full of criminals" joked Barbara as she looked up from her desk with a big cheeky grin on her face.

"Oh, very funny" I smiled back "You know what I mean. Wakefield Prison is a high security prison holding some of the worst criminals in the country, a bit like this office….!"

Barbara laughed out loud.

"…. so I'm sure they don't just let anyone in. What do I need to take with me to prove I'm innocent?"

"Oh don't worry about getting in" Barbara answered "The biggest problem you'll have is getting out!"

"Oh thanks very much" I surrendered

"No, don't worry Terry. Just report to the entrance and they will give you full instructions. You may be there for most of the day as it takes a long time to get in and out, but you'll be pleased to know I won't be disturbing you as you cannot take your pager in"

"Peace and quiet at last" I concluded.

HMP Wakefield is in the centre of Wakefield behind some commercial buildings and surrounded by domestic houses. The main (and I believe only) entrance is on Back Lane opposite Parliament Street. I still wonder today if the streets were named because of their location to the prison but as Love Lane runs along the side of the prison it may just be my vivid imagination.

It took less than 10 minutes to travel across the city from the Wakefield office. I pulled up in front of the large wooden doors marked vehicle entrance as there was no obvious indication of where I could park. I was expecting to enter the pedestrian entrance to the left and report in and find out where to park, but before I could kill the engine the tall wooden doors started to slowly open. They were expecting me!

As the doors opened I could see an enclosed space the size of a large tall garage with another door at the far end. The space was long enough for about two cars and was well lit by lighting high up on the ceiling and further fluorescent lighting along the side walls.

A uniformed prison officer waved me in and indicated for me to open my window.

"Please stay in the vehicle unless told otherwise by me and only me" he said "My name is Simon and I will be your escort today"

The large wooden doors behind me closed as I parked in front of the second doors and I turned my engine off under the instruction from my escort.

"Can you first of all confirm your name and company please?" enquired Simon.

Even though my van had 'Kenyon' written in 2 foot high letters along the side of my van I told him the details he wanted to know.

"I just need to search your van before we proceed so can I ask if the back doors are unlocked, Terry"

"Err, no" I answered as I went to get out my van with my keys.

Simon blocked my door from opening and reminded me to stay inside the vehicle. He took the keys from me through the open window and handed them to his colleague.

As Simon went through the checklist on the clipboard in his hand he noticed my CB radio.

"I'm afraid that cannot go into the prison grounds so you will have to remove it" said Simon

Thankfully at this point Simon allowed me to exit my vehicle so I could retrieve the appropriate tools from the back of my van to disconnect and remove my CB radio. He took that and my pager into the office along side the garage tunnel and I could see Simon through a large window as he locked the items in a locker. He handed his completed checklist and clipboard to the officer at the desk and returned back to me.

"Right then Terry" Simon said as he sat in the passenger seat next to me "that's all the checks done."

"Now when the door in front opens I need you to drive through and then stop until the door closes fully behind us" Simon continued

Simon seemed a different person now. Inside the entrance garage he came across as very official and tough. A very serious face that had no smile or frown. He came across as very efficient at his job and was in complete control. Now he was like my best friend. A smile dominated his face and he was eager to find out about me and to tell me about his many years in Wakefield prison. He was now very friendly and chatty. In fact he hardly shut up.

As we drove around the inside of the perimeter wall he gave me some of the history of HMP Wakefield and how they now house some of the most notorious and dangerous criminals in Britain. I started to wonder if he was trying to scare me a bit until he started telling me about the Mulberry Bush that he pointed out in the middle of the exercise yard.

"Surely you know the old Nursery Rhyme?" He looked offended at the smirk on my face

"Well yes, but surely that isn't the 'actual' Mulberry bush?" I defended

"Yes!!" he insisted "that is THE Mulberry Bush! We don't have female prisoners here now but it was reputed to be the song the female prisoners sang as they exercised around the tree."

Simon had worked at HMP Wakefield all his working life and obviously not only enjoyed his working life there but took great pride in where he worked. He seemed very knowledgeable about the history of the prison as well as the history of its inmates. I took his story of the scraggy looking tree with a pinch of salt. I wasn't completely sure he was winding me up, as it did sound plausible, but I definitely didn't fully believe him.

After the slow drive around the inside of the prison walls and the opening and closing of several gates we pulled up next to a relatively new building in the very centre of the prison grounds. The large older buildings towered around us. Row after row of small barred windows ran the length of these buildings. As I stepped out of the van my mind wandered as I took in my surroundings. I could envisaged all the most dangerous criminals in the country living behind these little windows in their tiny cells.

"Now, we need to carry up everything you think you need" Simons voice broke my dream like world.

"But I don't know what the problem is until I look at the fridge" I said

"Well let's take as much as we can carry" Simon suggested "I can help but we must account for everything we take up. It's only one flight of stairs and there is an office up there that is out of bounds for prisoners. We can securely put some stuff in there"

"Hang on!! Prisoners!" I stood with a worried look on my face "I thought I was in the kitchen. Surely I'm not expected to work around actual prisoners!"

Simon just looked at me with his head tilted to one side

"This is a prison, who did you expect to find in here!!!" Simon explained

"..... but don't worry, all the prisoners working in the kitchens are on very good behaviour. We don't let just anyone work in there......"

Simon picks up a gas bottle and my charging leads from the van. As he unlocks and opens the door he turns to me and continues:

".... besides, you're in the butchery department!"

As we entered the unlocked door I discovered we had entered an enclosed staircase. This led directly up to the food preparation area of the kitchen with another locked door at the top of the staircase. Simon unlocked each door in front of us and immediately locked it behind us. We entered the kitchen and I noticed several people preparing meals on long steel tables just like any other kitchen area I had worked in. My worries melted away. To the right was a double door with a 'Butchery Department' sign above it and to the left of that was a set of 4 steps leading up to a glass walled central office. Simon and I entered the central office with all my tools and equipment and were greeted by two other prison guards sat drinking tea watching the prisoners below.

We left most of my equipment in this secure office and Simon led me down into the butchery department to show me the broken down fridge that I had come to repair. The two inmates within the butchery department watched us closely as we walked across the room. Both of them at a central table carving up large joints of meat with large knives and hatchets. I couldn't take my eyes off them as my worries and concerns returned.

"Here we are" said Simon as we stood in front of two standard six foot industrial fridges. "It's this one on the right. Apparently it just won't come down in temperature"

"Ok" I said still worryingly glancing at my fellow occupants of the butchery department "Lets have a look"

Simon helped me climb onto the table next to the fridge so I could look at the condensing unit on the top. Very quickly I ascertained the problem and told Simon it would hopefully take no more than about 40 minutes to fix.

We both returned to the central office to retrieve the gas bottle and charging leads we had thankfully brought up from the van. Simon helped me arrange my tools and equipment on the side table that would become my working platform. I started looking for leaks on top of the fridge. All of this time, Simon had not been more than 2 feet from my side. It was a comfort to know he was there even though he constantly tried to assure me that I was perfectly safe.

"I'm just going to see my mate in the office" Simon suddenly declared "You'll be all right with these two. They're harmless and I will keep an eye on you through the window. Just wave if you need anything and don't leave your tools unattended"

With that Simon is across the room before I can object. The two inmates look up from their work and one of them looks directly at me with a smirk on his face (and a big knife in his hand!!!!). I decide to turn my gaze back to my work and just get the job done as quickly as I can.

"Du yu wan' a coffee?" A deep gruffted voice came across the room.

"Sorry - what?" I instinctively replied, even though I had actually heard the question

"Du yu wan' a coffee?" the inmate repeats

'Well how can I refuse!' I think. He had now come over to the table I am stood on and was looking straight up at me. Thankfully the knife I had seen in his hand earlier was not with him.

"Thanks, great. Milk and one sugar please" I nervously accepted.

The coffee was rather good considering my situation. It was a welcome distraction and helped sooth the dry throat I had acquired from all the stress and worry. Even if the coffee was bad I would have drunk it with great relish as I did not want to offend my server.

"Du yu wan' a nuffer?" Came the same gruffted voice as I lowered my empty mug onto the table.

"Err, thanks" I stupidly accepted as I handed him my mug.

Simon returned as I was tidying away my tools and he checked my work as I completed the paperwork. We gathered all the tools and equipment together, carefully checking that everything we brought into the kitchen was removed with us to my van below.

We finally start our journey out of the prison and as the first of many gates open in front of us Simon turns to me and says "Do you know who that was?"

"Who! - who was who?" I replied imagining him talking about one of his colleagues in the office.

"The guy making you a coffee" he declares

"What the big guy in the butchery department?" I look at him as I drive through the gate.

"Yes.. Do you know who that is?" Simon repeats

"No. Should I?" I ask "Don't tell me he's a notorious criminal."

Simon smiles.

"Is he???" I suddenly believe Simon may be about to reveal a big secret.

"That's 'Bob the Brain'" Simon declares with dramatic pose.

"Well, we call him 'Bob the Brain' but his real name is Robert Maudsley. The notorious serial killer. Surely you've heard of him?"

"Oh wow!!" I fake acknowledgement of the name

"and you let him make me a coffee. Twice!!!"

FOOTNOTE:

At the time of me working in HMP Wakefield there was no such thing as the internet and so I was unable to check up on who served me coffee. Today it is easy to research these facts......

Robert Maudsley was (and still is) seen as one of Britains most notoriously dangerous killers. He got the name 'The Brain Eater' by early reports of him eating a victims brain. The press nicknamed him 'Hannibal the Cannibal'. At the time of writing this book - he still resides in the basement of HMP Wakefield in a purpose built solitary confinement cell due to the callously vicious murders of two other Wakefield inmates. He has a whole life sentence and will never be released.

Thanks to the internet I now know the truth about 'Bob the Brain'.
I now believe Simon was actually trying to wind me up and he knew the notoriety of Robert Maudsley would suffice to scare me. If, at the time, I knew who Simon was referring to it may well have worked.
To this day, the identity of the gruff speaking inmate who made me coffee in the Butchery Department, still remains a mystery.

However (again thanks to the internet) what I believed on the day to be a wind-up by Simon turns out to be the honest truth. In the centre of HMP Wakefield is the origins of a Nursery Rhyme where 19th century women prisoners exercised around ......

The Mulberry Bush

Chapter 26

'The Hand of God'

In those days, before Health and Safety started putting their foot down on working practices, I could often find myself in undesirable situations or even discovering unusual items in unusual places. In those barbaric days businesses were not obliged to maintain their shop equipment or even keep them as hygienically clean as they must do today. Don't get me wrong, most businesses recognised the need to keep things clean and well maintained but it was the minority few that were blinkered and could only see the short term profits. Thankfully most of those businesses ceased trading once customers realised what sort of place they were buying from.

Potato storage is one of those undesirable places I never really liked going to even in the daytime. A large potato storage warehouse just south of Scunthorpe at Hemswell Cliff in Lincolnshire was a regular call out place for us. Their equipment was very old and instead of having several smaller units to keep their warehouse temperature constant they had a couple of large systems each with a single large compressor. Often the call outs to this location were due to one of the compressors failing. This would then equate to half the cooling capability gone in one fell swoop. Not much room for error!

My first ever visit to this potato store, in fact my first visit to any potato store! started with me entering the site managers office. From there he begrudgingly agreed to show me where all the equipment was and, as in his words, he was very busy so he would have really preferred his usual engineer. I grabbed my tool bag out of my van and hurriedly followed him across the forecourt.

"I hope you have a torch in there" he said looking at my tool bag as we marched towards the warehouse building.

"Why? Is it dark in the plant room?" I replied

"No the plant room is fine but you will need it to get there" came the answer.

I looked puzzlingly up into the bright blue sky. It was the middle of the day!!

We walked through the open ended part of the warehouse where the production line workers were sorting potatoes on a conveyor belt before they were funnelled into sacks for distribution. A surprisingly noisy area with some very bored and unhappy workers. We finally came to a small entrance door that was located in a much larger door. The manager opened the little door and hurried through. I followed into the main warehouse as he shouted back instructions to ensure I closed the door after me.

I turned around to close the door behind me and the total blackness suddenly enveloped me. I had never before experienced such darkness. The door in front of me, that I still had hold of simply disappeared from my sight. I could hear the managers footsteps walking further away into the darkness behind me.

I turned around and although I could still hear his footsteps getting further away I could not see him at all. In fact I could not see anything, no matter how much I tried or how much I looked around there was absolutely nothing to see. Eyes open or eyes closed, it was the same experience. I wondered why I could not see him and more to the point, how the heck did he know where he was going without the aid of any light.

His footsteps stopped and I now had complete silence around me. This plunged me into an unexpected experience I imagined to be similar to one of those sensory deprivation tanks. Thankfully the complete silence did not last long as the managers voice echoed across the vastness. He chuntered at me to turn my torch on which prompted me to successfully find it. It was clipped to the side of my bag and when switched on illuminated enough to tell my brain that my eyes were actually open.

The vastness of the warehouse then became clearer to me. The ceiling must have been 30 to 40 feet above me and I had the width of a football pitch to walk across to join the manager who was now at the other side of the warehouse. The amount of illumination from my torch was quite pitiful compared to the vastness of this eternally dark space. The darkness felt like it was absorbing every single candle power my little torch was producing. As I walked in a straight line toward the manager outside the plant room door I could then take in the volume of potatoes this single warehouse contained. Stacked floor to ceiling as far as the eye could see (which wasn't very far with my torch!!) were square wooden crates full to the brim with potatoes.

Thankfully the plant room was, as he had predicted, well illuminated and I could work in relatively easy surroundings to solve his problem. As I happily worked away it never occurred to me, until I finished my work, that I still needed to walk back through the sensory deprivation tank to get out. This time without the guide from the manager who had rapidly returned to his office after showing me the plant room. At least I could turn my torch on before I closed the door this time.

The manager was a lot more friendly as he signed my paperwork. He gladly taught me about potato storage. He told me that potatoes can be stored for a long time as long as they were chilled and kept in complete darkness. They possessed no lighting in the warehouse at all and only allowed the main doors to be opened for short periods when they loaded or unloaded the crates. He was so used to the layout of the warehouse and the darkness in there that he said he could find the plant room blindfolded (not that you needed a blindfold!).

In the 1980's we had a lot of low cost supermarkets. One such company call CostCo used us as their main refrigeration engineers. To save money they didn't actually have a maintenance contract with us so we rarely had chance to maintain any of their equipment. They had a special call-out contract where we were obliged to give them a priority response to any of their calls over any non contracted business.

Most of our contracts were full regular maintenance and those businesses would usually have the highest priority response to any calls 24 hours a day. Companies like McDonald's even had a time limit in which they could expect an engineer on site within 2 hours of their call. This speedy response expectation was often impossible to deliver. If, for example, I was in Newcastle and received an out of hours call to go to the McDonald's in Peterborough then even if I could leave as soon as I received the call it would take me longer that 2 hours to even get to Peterborough. This particular extreme scenario never actually happened to me but it was always difficult to fulfil the contract time limit that some over enthusiastic salesman had originally agreed to.

I never liked going to a CostCo because you knew their equipment would be dirty and poorly looked after. I believe sometimes they would just call with a fictitious fault expecting us to clean their display cabinets for them. No such luck there from me. This was one supermarket chain that I never considered buying anything from, no matter how cheap it was. They had cut their running costs to the bone and I could see behind the facade they gave to their customers.

One day I had been called to a CostCo supermarket in Dewsbury Yorkshire, and the job card message simply said 'not right'. When I queried the office what that meant I received a simple shrug of the shoulders.

Entering the shop through the rear warehouse doors I was met by the manager. He told me that the problem was with his dairy fridge and his explanation of the 'not right' request was that all the contents had a strange smell as if it was all going off.

He took me through to the shop and we both stood in front of the dairy display unit that contained everything from milk and butter to cheese and yoghurts. He picked up a tub of margarine and held it up to me.

"Here, have a smell of that. And we only put it out this morning."

"Oh yes!" I said turning my nose away "that's not very good. Probably best to get this emptied so I can try and find the problem"

"No can do" he quickly replied "There is only me and two assistants today and they are both on the tills."

"Oh great, thanks very much" I exclaimed " so where can I put all this stuff? I will need to empty so much of it anyway to get to the drains that are below that bottom shelf"

I grabbed one of their trollies from the front of the store and loaded it up with everything on the lower levels of the display unit. All the cartons of yoghurts, butter, milk etc I just piled on top of each other until the trolly was full to the brim. Anyone unaware of who I was would think I had gone mad buying all this stuff. I made no intention of stacking it neatly in the trolly as it was not going to be me that had to reload it. Everything I touched had this funny smell to it. Where any reputable supermarket would have shut the unit down completely until it was repaired and would have disposed of the unsaleable goods. I knew CostCo would simply put it back out regardless. I wanted no part in putting these products back out to sell.

I wheeled my trolley full of smelly goods into the warehouse at the back of the store and left it there as suggested by the manager. He had no refrigerated space to keep it and I think he just hoped I would get the display unit repaired before the goods went off. To me they were well past their best anyway.

I returned to the shop display and unbolted the chiller units floor panel that gave me access to the evaporator in the base of the unit. As soon as I took the first panel off I could see the problem and had to turn my head away to avoid the stench that came out. I had often experienced blocked drains where the drip tray under the evaporator had filled up. Even to the extent where it covered the evaporator but that was usually just water. This was a milky colour with bits floating in it and some of those bits had mould growing on it. Luckily for CostCo the fans on this design of display unit were in the back of the unit clear of any liquid. I believe the unit would have blown up days ago if the fans were submerged in this flood of hazardous wastewater.

It was fairly obvious there was a lot more than just the water that usually drips from the evaporator. This was a culmination of leaking milk bottles, spilt yoghurts and any other dairy product that had found its way below decks. A simple lack of regular cleaning had culminated in this foul smelling concoction and it was now up to me to clear it all up.

Whatever it was that was blocking the drain thankfully soon moved with a good prod from the longest screwdriver I could find. To my relief the hazardous fluid started swirling down the discharge pipe. Several buckets of water and a bottle of bleach (which I had removed from one of CostCo's shelves) later, the unit was starting to smell more like a hygienically cleaned display unit.

I did feel sorry for the manager. He was expected to run the store with far too few staff and probably on too little wage as well. However I was never going to put the trolley full of spoilt goods back out on display for them to be sold. As I drove away I was fairly sure the manager would refill the display unit with the trolley load of unsaleable smelly goods, whether it had actually gone off or not. In their eyes, if its cheap enough someone will buy it!!

Sometimes the undesirable situations are a complete shock. In the case of me attending to a fridge in a shop in Ashby I was, at first, quite puzzled at the thought of a fishing tackle shop having a fridge. I presumed it was probably just a domestic fridge for the staff to keep their milk and sandwiches in. How wrong could I be!

Yes the fridge was in the back of the shop but that is where my expectations ended. It was a full height industrial fridge. Shiny steel casing with a solid stainless steel door. Along the top was an air grill which hid the condensing unit and had a temperature display mounted in full view showing 7'C.

Although 7'C is on the warm side for a fridge it was still within the acceptable limits of 4 to 8'C for a normal domestic refrigerator. However the handwritten notice sellotaped to the side of the display warned people the refrigerator must not go above 2'C. I was curious about how low the shop owner really wanted his fridge as I know this temperature would normally start freezing any liquids within.

When the shop owner opened the door to show me the contents I instantly realised why he wanted the relatively low temperature.

In front of me was drawer after drawer full of wriggling maggots. A whole drawer of the usual creamy white maggots. Another drawer crammed with red maggots and another crowded with green maggots. There was even one drawer overflowing with blue maggots. All the maggots were wriggling like mad and producing a strong stench of ammonia.

This was why the shop keeper was concerned. Maggots are best kept at around 0'C to keep them dormant. Too cold and they turn brown and die, too warm and they live their short life before turning into flies. I dreaded to think what would have happened if they had all hatched into flies before we had opened the door. Probably a good idea for one of those Stephen King films.

The most worrying time I experienced was when I attended a call out to a butchers in South Elmsall. A small town south of Pontefract in Yorkshire, South Elmsall had the standard type of High Street (which was actually called Barnsley Road) containing all those lovely family run independent shops such as the Butchers, the Bakers but no candlestick maker, well not in this town anyway.

South Elmsall had a typical sort of market place which was in the centre of the town just off the high street. It was primarily an open air market but instead of the stalls being just tables under canvas canopies, each unit was purpose built of brick and tile. They resembled rows of little terraced houses containing only one room which was the shop.These had the advantage of being securely locked up on non market days allowing the market holders to leave their produce within the unit if they wanted.

The butchers shop I had been called to was located almost directly across from the market place, actually on Barnsley Road. They also possessed one of the stalls within the market place and my job that day was in that market unit. Their cold store apparently was making a loud noise that was scaring their customers away.

I parked in the empty market car park and crossed the road to enter the butchers high street shop.

"Hi there. I'm from Kenyons and I've come to look at your noisy cold store" I said to the butcher behind the counter.

He held his hand up to his ear cupping it as if he was deaf and couldn't hear me! So I repeated my introduction.

"Can't you hear it from here?" He said with a smile on his face

"Oh, I see what you mean" I finally got the joke

"I'm only pulling your leg" he said "but it is very noisy. You wait until we cross the road. Just give me a minute and I will take you over and unlock the place for you. I can't stay but you'll be ok on your own won't you?"

It didn't seem that noisy as we crossed the road or even as we entered the market place but, as we approached the butchers unit at the back of the market place, I could then hear the distinctive rattle of a fan blade catching on its casing. My first impression, as the butcher unlocked his unit and raised the roller shutters, was that the fan blade would just need a bit of adjustment and it would be a quick and simple job.

The shop unit was no bigger than a standard garage. About 10 by 20 foot inside. The door behind the shutters opened into one side of the unit with a display cabinet and work counter down the middle. Across the whole of the back of the unit stood the cold store rattling away to its hearts content. If the noisy fan had been on the evaporator within the cold store it would have been muffled by the cold stores insulation. Therefore this was obviously coming from the condensing unit which sat on top of the cold store behind a simple grill.

"As I said, I cannot stay with you" the butcher told me "not just because its too noisy but I have a busy shop to deal with. I'll pop back later, but if you finish before then just pull the shutter down and come back to the shop. I can come over to lock up later"

And with that he races out the door with his hands on his ears.

'First things first' I thought 'Let's switch the power off to deaden the noise.'

'Ahhh - silence at last! .... '

I knew that as long as I didn't open the cold store door the temperature would stay low for hours, even with the power switched off. I went to my van to obtain my toolbox and a small set of steps that I sometimes carried with me.

"Take your time Terry, this is a nice easy job and I am sure I can stretch it out" I said to myself

Standing on top of my steps I removed the front grill to gain access to the noisy condensing unit behind. My first line of sight was the bent fan blade that had been causing all the problem but before I attempted to remove the fan guard and fix the problem I noticed something else laid in front of me less than 12 inches from my face. I firstly stumbled, shocked at the sight, and then regained my balance. Standing perfectly still on top of my steps with my mouth open wide, I processed what I was looking at.

It was a hand!!!!

.... or at least what was left of a human hand.

It was just the skeleton of a single human hand and it looked, to my untrained eye, like it was complete. A whole skeletal hand from the wrist to the tip of each finger. The bones were completely clean of flesh (thank goodness) and it was laid out in front of me like the Adams Family servant hand -The Thing-.

Had it been trying to crawl out of its prison on top of the cold store? Maybe it had damaged the fan blades to raise awareness to its plight!!!!

Here was my dilemma !

- Do I move the hand so I can complete my work as quick as I can and get the hell out of there.
- Do I report my findings?   But who do I tell?
- Maybe the butcher himself is putting something special into his pies?
- Maybe one of his employees has mysteriously gone missing in the past?
- If this is just the hand then where is the rest of the body?
- Do I contact the police and let them sort it all out??????

Oh dear, what a dilemma !!!

Thankfully I made the right choice and didn't make too much of a fool of myself. I went back to the butchers to report my finding convincing myself that the Butcher was not a bad man. He laughed out loud when I told him what I had found and he admitted to wondering where it had gone.

He came back with me and he proceeded to pick up the hand to show me it in more detail. It was actually a very good plastic hand with all the joints connected with little wire links. The plastic bones were all the right size and colour but you could tell instantly when you held it in your own hand that it was a fake.

Apparently they had used it in a Halloween display one year and when they couldn't find it they believed someone had actually stolen it.

A gave a great sigh of relief at his explanation but I still couldn't quite get to grips with his strange Yorkshire sense of humour. I decided to finish the job as quickly as I could and then get myself out of there.

God only knows what lies **within** the cold store.

———————

Chapter 27

'Secure Melodies'

I remember once coming across a security guy on his patrols around an office block in the dead of night. Whenever I saw him he was usually singing out loud, in fact as loud as he could. I had always presumed it was because he liked to sing and especially when there was nobody around there was obviously no-one around to complain at his atrocious ability.

One night I decided I would question him about his singing. I was expecting him to maybe inform me of some forthcoming amateur production he was practicing for, maybe he was practicing for a local choir he was a member of, or maybe he was a happy, contented guy who just loved to sing out loud. I was amazed at his response.

He smiled at me and looked around as if he was about to reveal a deep secret.

"Truth be told, I'm actually afraid of the dark" he admitted.

"What!" I exclaimed "that's got to be a bit of a disadvantage for a night security guy."

"Actually, I still don't understand why you sing" I continued

"Well" he said "if I walk around these offices singing at the top of my voice and there is someone about they will know I am on my way and hopefully clear off well before I get there!!   - No surprises for either of us!"

I'm not sure that's the idea of a patrol done by a night security officer but it seemed to work for him.

During one of my regular weeks of being on-call, I was travelling back from a job at an Iceland shop in Newark late one night. It was a calm quiet night on the roads which was no surprise to me as it was midweek and just coming up to midnight. Most people at this time of night would be fast asleep either dreaming of future holidays or maybe having a nightmare at the thought of work the following day. Here I was still at work almost 16 hours after starting the day but finally heading home to my family and my bed.

I had managed to drive around Lincoln on the ring road and was within 30 minutes of my home when my pager went off, signifying I had another job to go to. I was on the north side of Lincoln just about to get onto the back roads of Lincolnshire trying to avoid the main A15 roman road. The A15, although a very straight road, can still be busy with large lorries even at this time of night. Like a lot of local people, I found the curvaceous back roads through the little villages to be the quicker and less frustrating route.

The first telephone box I came across was on the village green in Scampton. Village street lights tend to be fewer and less brighter that towns and cities so I found myself pulling up to the side of a very dark and spooky phone box in the centre of this famous Dambuster village. With a sigh of relief I discovered the interior light lit up brightly as I opened the door of the telephone box. In preparation to collect the details of my next job I placed my notebook and pen on the little shelf next to the telephone. The number of our out-of-hours call centre was imbedded in my brain from the many times I needed to call them so I just went into a tired autopilot mode and dialled the number.

"Hi there, it's Terry from Kenyons here. You paged me! Have you got another job for me?"

"Yes sorry Terry, a busy night for you as usual" came the reply "I have a call from the security guy at Asda in Castleford. Do you want his number?"

"Oh bloomin' heck!" I said "please tell me its not John!!"

"Sorry, he didn't give me a name" said the operator "Will you call him back or do you want me to call him?"

"Actually, that would be a big help" I took him up on his offer "Tell him I will be there in about an hour and I'm on my way now"

Already very tired from my 16 hour day of work, I climbed back into my van and set off for the Asda supermarket in Castleford.

Just after one o clock in the morning I pulled into the large supermarket car park. In those days there was no such thing as 24hr shopping and so the car park was empty apart from one other car obviously belonging to the security guy. If I had arrived several hours earlier there may well have been several shelf stackers still in the store but as we were now officially in the middle of the night it was going to be just me and John!!!

I knew it was John on duty that night as soon as I got out of my van. It wasn't that I actually recognised his car or that I knew his shift rota; it was the sound of John that gave it away!

John liked his music. Most people would have a radio, a getto blaster or such device to play in their lonely night time office. No, John liked his music loud, and not just loud but he liked to play his music very loud over the supermarket internal sound system. It was so loud you could distinctly hear it outside in the car park.

I got my hearing protection from the back of the van as I collected my usual bag of tools and proceeded to the main door. This is where the usual problem with John begins. How do you raise his attention with all this racket going on.

Luckily for me this time John had been looking out for me and he appeared at the entrance to unlock and slide the doors open. The sound wave hit me like the heat from opening an oven door. I immediately placed my hearing protection over my ears, much to the amusement of John.

"Sorry" he said with a giggle "I promise to turn it down a bit"

"WHAT DID YOU SAY!!" I jokingly shouted

John let me in and with me in tow, headed off to the main office to turn the volume down. I had learnt from my previous encounters with John, that the best you can hope for is to get him to at least turn the volume down. He never turned it off and turning the volume down never, ever lasted. He would often keep turning the volume back up a little bit at a time until it was again full blast. I'd got used to knowing that any call-out to this particular supermarket in the middle of the night, meant you were best to be as quick as you could to get the job done before you became deaf. It was always advisable to get the job completed before John returned the volume to his favourite, but unbearable, levels again. Sadly you could never get him to turn the music off completely.

Now I have so far called the noise - music!!! and I realise everyone has there own preference to their favourite genre. I pride myself in being tolerant to all types of music. However, I never understood John's type of music and why he loved it so much.

To this day, and it is probably Johns fault!, - I still cannot stand Opera.

Luckily for me that night the problem was quite quick and easy to fix and I was getting my paperwork signed in John's office less than an hour after arriving. The time was now just after 2am in the morning and I was looking forward to going home to bed which was still another hours drive away.

John's phone suddenly rang and we both looked at each other in surprise at the thought of someone calling the store at this hour of the morning. John lowered the volume of Kiri Te Kanawa, which was still blasting out from the sound system, and answered the phone.

"Hello! This is Asda superstore, Castleford" John started "Yes, he's still here. Do you want to speak to him?"

John handed me the phone and I answered with a very puzzled look.

"Hello" I said slowly

"Hi there" the caller started "its the call centre here and I've been trying to page you for over an hour but getting no reply. I've just had a lovely chat with your wife who said she had no idea where you were."

Looking sternly at John I said to the operator "Oh, sorry. I couldn't hear the pager due to ambient noise I'm afraid. Don't tell me you've got another job for me, do you?"

"So sorry" came the genuine concern "I really need you in Scunthorpe now"

'At least I am finally heading back to my home town' I thought as I took down the details.

Finishing my paperwork with John I continued to pat each and every one of my pockets trying to find my pager. I eventually decided that my pager must have been left in the van.

John slid the door closed behind me as I left the supermarket. As I searched my van for the illusive pager I could hear the volume of Kiri Te Kanawa's voice increase as John returned the volume of the internal PA system to its previously ear piercing level. That was the exact moment a vision popped into the forefront of my mind. I could see my pager as clear as day. I just hoped that it was still in the same location that I could now envisage in my mind.

Obviously the reason I could not hear the pager was nothing to do with the security guard, John or even Kiri Te Kanawa at full volume. It was because it was actually 60 miles away from me sat on the little shelf in Scampton's telephone box.

I certainly did a lot of mileage that night. I had to go back to square one! I had to got back to Scampton on my way to the next job.

Thankfully not many people use telephone boxes in the middle of the night and so my pager was still happily sat in the dark on the little shelf in the telephone box on Scampton's village green. As I opened the door, the pager got illuminated by the boxes internal light and then it started to vibrate.......

Oh great!!!! Another sodding job!!!!

Chapter 28

'Disney on Ice'

As the years rolled by I found myself being busier than ever. This was not just because we had more and more contracts but because the CEO of Kenyons was cutting back on the amount of offices we had around the country. I now worked from the Wakefield office which was close to some major motorways, the M1 & M62, giving us quick and easy access to our designated area of responsibility.

However, by this time we were responsible for most of the east side of the country from Newcastle down to Peterborough. Our contract with the fast food restaurant McDonald's meant we had an expected call-out to be less than 2 hours. This meant that any McDonald's manager who phoned us with a problem could expect one of our engineers to be on site within two hours. On paper, this could work. Newcastle is just under two hours away from Wakefield and Peterborough is just over two hours. In real life this never worked.

I was told, when objecting, that the chances of me being in Newcastle when a call to Peterborough came in was very unlikely. In practice, we rarely achieved the two hour call-out rate no matter where we were when the call came in. However, it didn't mean we didn't try and we all tried to answer our pagers as soon as was possible to reduce the delay.

Beep! beep! beep! went my pager just as I was overtaking a lorry on the very busy A1 north road. I was heading out on my first call of the day from Wakefield going to an Icelands in Middlesborough. My brief was that their cold store was just not getting down to temperature. Conscious of our new McDonald's contract demands I decided I really needed to find a phone box quickly rather than calling the office from Middlesborough.

I pulled off at the next exit and made the snap decision to turn left at the first junction as it looked the best way to civilisation. A mile of winding country roads later and I still hadn't found any rural community let alone a telephone box. I took a right turn and then a left turn in my desperation to find any sign of a settlement. In our modern world people forget how difficult it was at times to find your way around. Today we just look at our Sat Nav or maybe consult our mobile phone. In fact if I had a mobile phone in those days I wouldn't even need to look for a phone box.

I eventually opted for a sign telling me a certain village was only two miles down a narrow farm track and hoped it was at least civilised enough to have a phone box. I was so relieved when I came out of a tree lined road and found myself in the prettiest village I had ever seen. A handful of quaint houses surrounded a village duck pond at the side of the road. The sun even started shining as if I had found some fairytale hamlet from Walt Disney's imagination. There in the centre of the village was the instantly recognisable red phone box we all knew and loved.

I parked my van at the side of the road right next to the telephone box and ensured I had my notebook and pen with me as I entered this pristinely clean phone box.

"Hi-ya Mike" I said into the phone "It's Terry here, what have you got for me?"

"Where are you?" Mike said in reply

"No idea! What job have you got for me?"

"I need to know where you are Terry" said Mike

"I'm on my way to Middlesborough, just as you told me to do this morning!" I informed him

"But where exactly are you?" Mikes persistence continued

"I told you I have no idea"

"What do you mean you have no idea"

"Because I really do not know where the hell I am" I was starting to get annoyed with this questioning.

"You must know where you are!" stated Mike crossly

"Look Mike" I lost my patience "You paged me when I was speeding up the A1 to Middlesborough which is where you sent me just over an hour ago. I pulled off the A1 and have been searching this wilderness somewhere in the middle of Yorkshire for a phone box. I think I finally found where Walt Disney lives and Mickey Mouse has just cleaned this phone box ready for me to use. NOW, please tell me where you want me to go and I pray to God it is not a McDonald's in Timbuktu."

"No, no, no. That's alright, calm down. I don't have another job for you. I just wanted to know where you were"

It was lucky I didn't break the phone as I slammed it down into the cradle. I think it's time for a calm down tea break in this surreal village.

Finding your way back to a main road is so much easier than getting lost in the Yorkshire wilderness. Most signs clearly indicate the way to a main road. Motorways have very distinctive blue notices but even lesser roads like the A1 were clearly shown on all road signs for miles around. An hour after finishing my unplanned tea break I was pulling up outside my designated job location in Middlesborough.

I parked my van outside the trade door to Iceland supermarket in the city centre shopping precinct's service yard. I retrieved my tool bag from the back of my van and went to ring the bell on the outside of the entrance door.

"So you're the top engineer!! Are you?" the store manager said sarcastically as he looked over my shoulder.

I turned around to see if he was talking to someone directly behind me. That's when I realised what he was really looking at. Sat in the parking bay behind where I stood was my ageing, rusty van. I must admit, the condition of my dirty, dusty and road weary van didn't give a good impression. I had never given it much thought before but he was right. The condition and first impression my van gave did not depict a good image. This irate store manager in front of me had obviously been calmed down on the phone by a promise of a top engineer. Quickly I had to reply…

"Oh that!!! Yes my Volvo estate is in for a service today so I had to borrow one of the apprentices vans. That's why I am a little bit late I'm afraid. Sorry. Can I come in and you can show me the problem."

The store managers problem was the old story. His store was one of the older stores where they had rows and rows of freezers kicking heat out into the store and the stores air conditioning could not cope with the excess heat load. Obviously he was getting sick and tired of calling us out to the problem but there really wasn't much we could do until his store was upgraded to a better and more efficient system. At times like this it is not a good idea to try and reason with an irate customer.

I went into the plant room where the main air conditioning unit was and made a lot of noise with my hammer making sure the noise would be heard around the store. Banging on the side of large ductwork can make a very impressive noise, along with the occasional dropping of metallic spares within that ductwork.

20 minutes later I was stood at the managers desk wiping my brow from sweat and hoping he would sign my paperwork without much questioning.

"I must admit it does feel a bit better already" the store manager declared.

"Well I've got as much as I can get out of the air conditioning for you" I said with a straight face "it has such a lot of work to do still so it may take a few more hours but by tomorrow morning it should be down to temperature"

"Well I'm not sure what you did but you've done more than any of the others, thank you"

At that very moment my pager went off and as the store manager was now in such a good mood he allowed me to use his desk phone for me to call my office.

"Hi Mike" I said "Where to next?"

"I have a McDonald's for you"

"Oh God, I hope it isn't Peterborough as you do know I'm presently in Middlesborough"

"No, don't panic. that's ok but have you finished there yet?"

"Yes, just finished now. Where do I need to go?"

"Up to Newcastle!! - but be doubly quick as the guy is furiously steaming. His ice maker has packed in and he is loosing his temper"

"Oh thanks very much Mike. That's two of those you've given me today"

Thankfully the Iceland store manager couldn't hear Mike's side of that conversation so he didn't understand my reference to him but I did feel Mike was setting me up with all the exasperated customers today.

I arrived at Newcastle's McDonald's within the contracted 2 hour limit for call-outs. It was a hot summers day and so I could understand the desperate need for ice in everyones drinks but couldn't fully understand why the manager was so upset about it.

"How long will it take to fix?" Came the question as soon as I walked in.

"Woah, hang on a minute. Can I take a look first!" I defended

"We need it working as fast as you can" he shot across me

"Slow down a bit." I tried to comfort him "I will be as quick as I can but it will take at least 30 minutes to produce the first ice cube once I get it going"

The manager held his head in his hands and shook his head in disbelief. Then in calm submission he said "Ok, see what you can do"

Feeling sorry for the guy who was obviously very agitated at the loss of his precious ice maker I went straight to work on repairing the large ice making machine that are common to all McDonald's. These machines can produce a phenomenal amount of ice (when they work!) and have a large skip like container below them where the staff can scoop up all the ice needed into their containers.

It did take over an hour before it was fully working again and the first few ice cubes started dropping into the skip below. Such a magical sound to the manager (and myself) when the first few cubes dropped into the empty skip. Normally you don't hear the cubes dropping onto other cubes but with the skip being totally empty the noise of those first few cubes dropping the full height of the skip and hitting the bottom of that space sounded like a drum gently tapping in the background.

The staff gave out a cheer and the managers eyes lit up so much at the sound of the ice cubes that I thought he was going to give me a kiss!!!!

"I am curious though" I said to the manager as I cleared away my tools "I got here within the contracted two hours, I know it's hot outside so everyone wants a cool drink but you seemed to be extremely upset at the loss of your ice maker"

"I was" he replied "nothing to do with your timing, you've done a great job and I thank you"

"The problem was simple" he continued "We always fill our cups full of ice before we put in the drink. No ice means we had to dispense over three times as much coca-cola in each and every drink. Running low on drinks on such a hot day as this could have actually shut the restaurant"

———————————

Chapter 29

'Lost and Found'

In our highly technical and modern world we all take it for granted how to find an unknown location. We often ask people for their postcode and house number rather than their full address so we can easily google it. This information can be readily used in the map app on our mobile phones or maybe put directly into our Satellite Navigation device to find the desired location. No matter how you search or what device you use they will all very accurately find the same result. Even if there are several similar results we are often given a choice to ensure we select the correct location. I've sometimes been known to use an aerial view of the surrounding area to get a clearer picture of where the desired location actually is. Street view will even give you the experience of actually being there.

Modern technology is truly amazing!

In the early 1990's there was no such technology. Every service engineer out on the road had a mountain of map books. The road map books usually got updated once a year (if you were lucky) and the street A-Z books - well, I don't think I ever changed them. Today, electronic maps built into every sat nav device can get updated every few weeks and if you use maps directly from the internet, ie Google Maps etc., then you can be fairly sure that they are updated daily if not hourly.

Most places I went to with work were locations that I had been to before so I quickly got to know my way around. Some of the regular places I could drive to blind folded, No I didn't!!! but sometimes I was so tired from long hours that I felt I had been asleep for most of the journey. It was those one-off jobs or new contracts that caused me the most difficulty. I would always try to get as much information from the office before I set off and often then spend several minutes in my van studying the map books to ensure I knew exactly where I was going. Once I was on the road it was obviously difficult for me to look at the map again without stopping at the side of the road. My map books were always open at the right pages on the passenger seat and this enabled me to glance at them while I was still driving but I often found the place you were heading to was actually on the next page.

"Back to school for you today" said Barbara as I collected my jobs for the day.

"What!" I exclaimed "back to school? Which one?"

"A bit of travelling for you today I'm afraid" Barbara apologised "I have a little job in Bradford for you first before you head off to the seaside in Skegness"

"Oh! Thanks very much. How come it's me driving all over the place?" I queried

"Its because you're so popular!!" she said with a nonsensical smile.

I smiled back with a tilt of my head.

"If you can go to the Green Lane Primary School in Bradford first."she informed me "I don't think it's urgent as the message from them was simply 'a problem with their cold store'."

"Okey, dokey."I said as I took my list of jobs from Barbara "I've not been to that school before. Have you got the full address for me?"

"Well… as its called Green Lane Primary School I think you might find it on Green lane" came the sarcastic reply.

"Oh very funny!!"

As usual with any unknown destination, I sat in my van for several minutes outside the Wakefield depot offices studying my map books before I set off. I quickly found a Green lane in Bradford and calculated the best route for me to get there. Happy with the thought of a school run to start the day I set off to my first job.

Less than an hour later, I was gingerly driving up the Leeds Road in Bradford looking for Green Lane and my final destination. After a short while I spotted the road sign showing me that I was there. However, as I pulled my van off the main road into what I believed to be Green Lane I found myself on a footpath no wider than the van itself. With a puzzled expression, I looked again at the road sign now right next to me and sure enough, in black letters on a white background, it certainly did say Green Lane.

'This cannot be right' I said to myself looking around.

I turned my gaze forward looking out of the windscreen and persuaded myself that there must be another way into Green Lane and this must be a pedestrian shortcut from the main Leeds Road. I picked up my open map book from the passenger seat and studied my location. As predicted, the actual Green lane stopped short of joining the main road so I was going to have to reverse out of here and drive around the block.

Back on the main road I made several left turns until I found the other end of Green Lane.

'Ah, this looks a bit better' I assured myself.

As I drove down Green Lane I was aware it was a more narrow road that I would expect with a main public building like a school on it. Most of the properties on this street had gates into the backs of the houses rather than actually facing this so called road. There was every indication this was more of a Back Alley than a serious road. I got to the end where it turned a corner to the right and in front of me was the footpath that would lead me back to my original parking space (if I was on foot that is!). Still no sign of a school.

I followed the road to the right and the road started getting narrower.

'This doesn't look good' I thought 'I cannot imagine a school being down here!'

Then the tarmac finished and a two track gravel road continued.

'Definitely not down here' I thought 'Don't get yourself stuck Terry'

The gravel track took a bend to the left and I was then able to see a main road across the end of the track ahead.

'That looks more like it!'

The gravel track brought me out onto a busy main road. I looked both to the left and to the right right along the main road looking for the school. Then Deja Vu suddenly hit me and I realised I was back on the Leeds Road. I was nearly back where I had started!

Luckily for me at that very moment a passer-by was walking along the footpath past the front of my van. I quickly shouted out to him and asked if he knew of a school around here.

"There's no school around here mate" he replied

"I've been sent to Green Lane Primary school" I told him

"Well you've certainly found Green Lane" he said pointing to the road sign high on the building next to me.

"Yeah, thanks for that"

I pulled back out onto Leeds Road and I parked my van at the side while I decided what to do next. I intently studied my map book but eventually decided all I could do was to phone Barbara and check I did have the right address. She was obviously going to enjoy this.

 I dashed across the busy road to the phone box I had spotted and dialled the Wakefield office.

"Hello Gorgeous." I started

"Hello Terry" came the sarcastic reply "What's the problem? What do you want?"

"Green Lane in Bradford? I cannot find the school!"

"What do you mean you can't find it? Do you need glasses?" She laughed "Hang on, let me look at my map book....."

"….. Here we are" she said "yes, it looks like its not far off the football ground"

"What football ground" I exclaimed

"Bradford City football ground. Where else? You are in Bradford aren't you?"

"Of course I am" I said as I tried to balance my map book on the little shelf in the telephone box "Let me see if I can find that."

"Oh bugger!!! Yes I can see that now. Flipping heck, how many Green Lanes does Bradford have!!!!!!"

Barbara just laughed out loud. So loud in fact, I think I could still hear her as I replaced the receiver down on the telephone to end our call.

10 minutes later I was pulling up outside the kitchen entrance at Green Lane Primary School.

As I entered the kitchen area there was a fabulous smell of fresh baking. I took in the aroma just as one of the kitchen staff gave me their typical warm welcome in the form of a cup of tea.

"What a lovely smell" I complimented "What have you been baking?"

"Oh this." She said pointing to a large tray of cake "I've just took this Parkin out the oven"

"Park-what?" I exclaimed "It looks like gingerbread to me"

"No, no, no!!" she proclaimed "We don't do gingerbread! This is proper Yorkshire Parkin"

"Parkin?? So it's a Yorkshire thing is it?"

"What!!! You've never heard of Parkin!" said the cook "Oh my God - How Green are you?"

After my troubles with Green lane I struggled not to laugh. I did enjoy the cake with my tea though.

At the end of that day I was heading home from the Skegness area. I had successfully travelled north as far as Louth but a major accident further up the road closed it completely. A police car across the road stopped me travelling further along the A16 and a policeman in the middle of the road was directing me and all the other traffic off the main road onto the smaller country lanes.

It's not until the traffic from a main road is put onto the smaller country roads that you fully understand the volume of traffic our main roads usually accommodate. In front of me, and behind me, were an endless line of vehicles. Lorries, cars, vans, you name it they were there. Everyone ground to a slow crawl as everyone tried to decide which way to go now. I glanced at my map books but as I instinctively knew the usual way back home from Skegness I didn't have the right page open. It was difficult while watching the car in front to ensure I didn't run into the back of them.

A modern day sat nav would just reroute automatically but all I had in the 1990's was my set of map books.

'Never mind' I thought ' we are all in the same boat. I'll just follow all the cars in front of me until we get back onto the main road.'

I gave up with the map and placed the book back in its familiar location on the passenger seat.

I've always had a good sense of direction and I decided as long as we are travelling in a northerly direction I was sure to find civilisation or at least a recognisable main road again without much trouble. The day started with me getting lost in Bradford but it was now looking like I could get lost on the Lincolnshire Wolds too.

All of us turned left. We then turned right. We went straight on at some crossroads and some of the vehicles in this convoy turned off at junctions that, for me, looked to be going in the wrong direction. I kept following the vehicles that were still heading in a northerly direction. Although we had by now travelled several miles it all started to look very similar to roads we had just travelled along. I was sure we were not going round in circles as the car in front of me gave the impression he knew where he was going.

Eventually I realised the convoy had reduced in size to only a handful. There was now only one car in front of me but I got comfort at the 5 or 6 vehicles still following behind. The car in front seems to know where he was going with only slight hesitations at some turnings.

Then it happened. My worst nightmare. As we rolled into a small village of only a dozen houses, the car in front of me turns into his own drive!!!!!

I didn't follow him.

But now, I was the leader of the pack!

I suspected the half dozen cars behind me were as shocked as me. Something told them I didn't know where we were either as at the next crossroads we all parted company going in different directions.

After a short time on my own on one of Lincolnshires country roads I decided to stop and look at the map book. That didn't seem to help. I could see where I wanted to go but it's no good if you don't know where you are. I was completely lost. After a few minutes studying the map for clues as to where I was, I decided the best course of action was to just keep heading north at every opportunity. Surely I should eventually find some civilisation and maybe an indication as to where the main roads were. I set off along my now deserted road.

The first junction I came across was a T-junction. I stopped with the intention of turning right. As I looked for traffic from the left, to see if the road was clear before setting off, I noticed a van coming towards me. As it passed I laughed out loud. So did the driver of the van. That was the very same British Gas van that was behind me before the leader of the pack pulled into his drive.

Oh well, at least now I can follow him and I have someone else to be lost with!!!!

Chapter 30

'Don't eat yellow snow'

When working out on the road you sometimes have to have some ingenuity to adapt to certain problems and conditions. In those days when I was out on the road it was a lonely life as all service engineers worked on their own. Most of the time you didn't even have the luxury of being able to phone the office for any advice let alone pull out your mobile phone and google the answer.

One very cold and blustery day I was sent to a public house in a little village to the East of Lincoln called Cherry Willingham. 'The Cherry Tree at Cherry Willingham' seemed a mouth full when the office gave me the job but at least being in the centre of the country village it was an easy place to find.

As I pulled into the car park the snow was starting to fall with relatively large snowflakes. The snow was only just settling on the ground and so I was not concerned at the conditions on the road. Not yet anyway. This was my last job of the day and I warmed at the thought of home being within half an hour of leaving here.

I quickly dashed into the front entrance of the pub and found only a couple of locals sat on their regular bar stools at the bar. The landlord was in deep conversation with them and all three looked up at me as I shook the snow off my jacket in the entrance way.

"Hi there" I started "Kenyons refrigeration! You've got a problem with your beer cellar?"

The two locals expression changed to horror at there being a problem with their beloved beer and their gaze moved to the landlord for a reassuring reply.

"Yes, that's right" he replied "thanks for coming so quick. If you follow me its through this way"

He gave a reassuring glance that the beer was ok to the locals and led me behind the bar.

This was one of those relatively modern pubs where the beer cellar was not actually a cellar (i.e. under the pub). This was a purposely built room on the back of the building. We both entered the beer cellar and I was surprised to find it still relatively cool compared to the warmth of the public bar. Beer should ideally be store around the 10'C to 12'C and the landlord was quick to point out he couldn't get the cellar below 16'C as shown on his wall mounted thermometer. The locals were probably unaware their favourite tipple was slightly warmer than usual but the concern for the landlord is the shelf life of his stock.

The landlord showed me a doorway at the far end of the beer cellar which opened out into the rear car park. This allowed deliveries to be unloaded straight into the beer cellar. Opening the door outwards he showed me the condensing unit which was just outside nearly completely hidden behind a pile of empty beer barrels. I did wonder if any of these barrels had ever fallen onto the pipework etc. which would cause a problem but they all looked to be stacked quite neatly ready for collection. It was cold and snowy outside so I decided to start my investigation within the beer cellar. The landlord left me to it and returned to his 'busy!?!' pub.

The evaporative unit inside had two main fans blowing cool air out across the room. I moved one of the full beer barrels to below the unit, to stand on, and proceeded to take a small cover off the side as part of my investigations. Feeling the pipework within I could quickly determine, unfortunately, the problem with this system was not internally but externally with the condensing unit in the snow and cold.

I went out the back door and moved a couple of empty barrels to get a better look at the unit. The snow was coming down thick and fast now and although it was settling nicely into my hair making me look like Father Christmas the condensing unit was so hot the snow was melting in mid air before it even touched the hot surfaces.

'Surely this isn't just because of the empty barrels surrounding the unit' I thought. 'and its so cold out here this unit should easily be able to dispense its heat'

The problem became obvious when I cleared enough barrels away. The condensing unit fan was not rotating. It looked like the fan motor was faulty. In the warmer summer months this unit would have fully overheated just like a car radiator without a fan. Because it was winter time and it was cold and snowy the condensing unit had somehow managed to hobble along and not trip out. The whole unit was so hot you could fry an egg on it, even in these cold, snowy conditions.

I took shelter from the snow by going back into the beer cellar while I worked out what to do next. I knew I didn't have one of these motors in the back of my van, I was fairly sure we didn't even stock them in our workshop stores which was over 70 miles away anyway, and it was too late in the day for me to find a local trade counter to get a replacement. I wondered if I could leave the unit running like this? hoping it stays cold and snowy until I could obtain a new motor. I wasn't happy with that idea as I felt it couldn't carry on running for long before some serious damage was done.

Standing in the beer cellar looking up at the evaporative unit I eventually came up with an idea.

I often find when presented with a solution to a problem that is far from ideal it is best to offer the customer other choices that are even less desirable. I returned to the bar to discuss it with the landlord and after explaining the problem I set out his options.

"I have three options for you." I started "Leaving it running like this could cause more serious and costly problems, so I really cannot recommend that as a viable option."

"We could switch the whole system off until I can return with a new motor but that would be tomorrow at the earliest and you would be serving up warm beer until then."

The locals sat at the bar watching, both cringed at the thought of warm beer.

"You could always leave the back door open as it is actually colder outside than inside but then you have no control and run the risk of the beer being too cold"

"We are not doing that" he snapped and looked at the locals "I could loose all my stock!!"

The locals smiled at that comment.

"My final option is to try and use one of the fans from the evaporative unit to provide a temporary fan for the condensing unit. It may not work but I am willing to try it for you."

"That sounds like our best option" the landlord said as the locals nodded their heads in agreement.

'What had I done!!!' I thought as I battled my way back to my van in the snow 'I could have just switched it off and I would be heading home by now.'

I decided the only way to work on this condensing unit in the cold and snow was to get my van reversed up as close as possible to offer some shelter. After clearing all the empty barrels from around the unit I reversed my van up through the car park with the rear doors wide apart. A plastic sheet dropped over the open doors and down behind the condensing unit created a nice snug little tent keeping most of the falling snow out. Even though the whole system had been isolated for 20 minutes as I prepared my working area the heat from the unit soon warmed up my cosy little workshop.

"Can I offer you a hot cup of coffee" a voice penetrated my encasement and a hand with a steaming mug protruded through the plastic sheet.

"Oh brilliant" I replied with great appreciation while taking the mug from the landlord.

"I'm impressed with your inventiveness" he said "I was feeling sorry for you having to work in this weather."

"Thanks." I replied "However as Scott of the Antarctic would have said - 'I may be some time'."

"Just shout if you need anything" came the generous laughter as the landlord returned to the warmth of his bar.

This was one of those jobs which was not very easy. Not only were the conditions to work in exceptionally difficult (cold and cramped!!) but trying to get a totally different type of fan motor from the evaporative unit to fit securely and efficiently into the condensing unit demanded a great deal of ingenuity. Even after an hour of modifications to secure the motor and rewire it I spent some more time with cardboard and duct tape trying to make the modifications as efficient as I could.

After an hour and a half of working inside a cool beer cellar and a freezing cold makeshift workshop outside, I successfully completed my modifications. I sat in the bar next to the locals completing my paperwork with another of those lovely hot mugs of coffee. The landlord did offer me something stronger in appreciation for all my hard work but under the circumstances I declined. The snow outside was still falling very densely and a thick white blanket now covered everywhere including all the roads. I still needed to get home from Cherry Willingham and although it was only a 30 minute drive I knew the driving conditions would need my full attention. Alcohol was not going to help!

The snow on the ground was getting very thick as I set off and I could feel my van slipping and sliding about as I tried to get out of the virgin snowy car park. Once out on the village roads I realised it was not much better. The snow had come down so thick and fast that only suicidal drivers and service engineers were attempting to drive in these conditions. I could imagine the locals in the Cherry Tree pub with a big smile on their faces, hoping for a lock-in until spring.

Driving out of the village at a snails pace, due to the very restricted vision, I was hopeful the main roads would be better than the country roads. Usually the quantity of vehicles and especially heavy lorries often managed to keep the main roads relatively clear. The sun had gone down some time ago and so my vision of the road ahead was made even worse as my headlights seemed to light up every snowflake falling in front of me. The road ahead was just a spotty blur but I hoped it would get better once I reached the main A15 Roman road heading north, and home.

Looking back now at times like this I realise how worrying it must have been for my family, especially my wife. In the days before mobile phones there was no way Elaine could have known what time I would get home or even where in the country I was located. I could now imagine Elaine looking out at the atrocious weather and the ever increasing thickness of fluffy white snow on the ground, wondering if I was alright, wondering where and what I was doing, and wondering when I would finally get home.

In the 30 minutes it would normally have taken me to get home from Cherry Willingham I had only managed to get as far as the main road into Lincoln. I still had to get past Lincoln to pick up the A15 and so far the main roads were no better than the country roads. More traffic yes, but still the same thickness of snow and the same snails pace of speed.

Eventually I found the old Roman road leading due north and was very grateful in the knowledge that the Romans built their roads in very straight lines. If you look at the A15 on a map it looks like it was drawn with a ruler. The only bend in it from Lincoln to Scunthorpe is where the modern day Royal Air Force diverted it around the end of their runway at Scampton. Apart from that, on a clear day, you can see for miles. Today was not a clear day!

I got tucked in behind a large lorry going my way. I was very thankful for all the lights on the back of his trailer as it made a good marker for me to concentrate on. The snow, still falling in ever thicker clumps, restricted my vision through the windscreen and in fact any window I tried to look through. By now there was not much traffic on the roads and after leaving the street lighted roads around Lincoln I started to feeling a special bond with the truck driver in front of me. The darkness descended around us and I felt we were all alone in the world. The two of us probably made the smallest convoy ever seen in this world. We were still rolling along at a snails pace with the heavy snow falling around us and a thick blanket of snow beneath our wheels. I could see nothing but darkness in my rear view mirrors and only the shining beacon of the lorry's rear illuminated square of lights in front of me. I only hoped he was going all the way to Scunthorpe like me.

Over an hour since leaving The Cherry Tree in Cherry Willingham I had settled into driving at a steady pace. I had very little idea of exactly where we were, although I did know we were on the A15 and should eventually arrive in Scunthorpe. Sometimes I would sense I was too close to him, probably as he flattened some hazardous snow drifts, and I would slow down to keep a sensible distance from him. Sometimes the lights of the lorry would get further away and so I would try to speed up slightly to ensure I matched his speed. I had to concentrate hard to ensure he didn't disappear from my limited view as I really didn't want to be left alone out here. During all of this time, all I could see around me was the rear lights of the lorry shining out from the total blackness of the night.

We gently came to another halt and although I could not see around the lorry I imagined a large snow drift which I hoped the large lorry would eventually push through. This time however we stood still for a bit longer than usual. Instead of just a couple of seconds it had been maybe a full minute. I realised there was a problem and we were probably now stuck in the middle of nowhere.

Thinking I might be best to walk up to the cab of the truck to see what the obstruction was I opened my van door and stepped out into the deep blanket of snow.

'Maybe I could have a chat with my fellow convoy companion' I thought 'and we could maybe work out a solution.'

The headlights of my van, and the lights on the lorry, helped guide me through the falling snow and the darkness of the skies. I eventually battled my way towards the front of the lorry and I found the driver about to climb back up into his cab.

"IS EVERYTHING OK?" I shouted to him "IS IT CLEAR AHEAD?"

He turned his head in surprise to see me and shouted back…

"IT IS NOW…..   I WAS DESPERATE FOR A PEE !!!!!

———————————

Chapter 31

'Breakfast at Tiffany's'

An engineer on the road comes across some testing locations. From being in the deepest of quarries to being on the top of tall buildings. I'd been sent to prison and even to the mortuary, thankfully in a professional basis and not as a dead body! However the strangest of tests I ever came across was at none of the above.

I'm not sure if it still exists but the Lofthouse Abattoir was located just north of Wakefield opposite the large Coca Cola factory (which, at the time of writing, is still there).

We very rarely got call-outs to the abattoir as we had a resident engineer on that site who took care of all the maintenance and he was the first point of call if there was a problem out of hours. During one of the quieter, cooler months of the year I got my first taste of the abattoir. I had been assigned for the whole day to help our resident engineer get caught up on his regular maintenance. Not the sort of place I relished the thought of attending but like most new, unusual places I was intrigued at what went on in this place.

Mike gave me my morning instructions......

"They're expecting you but if you ask at security for the Kenyon cabin they'll point you in the right direction. You really cannot miss it as it is the only container on the right as you go in and Gerry is sure to be still sat in there!"

As predicted, the Kenyon cabin was a rusty old container not far from the entrance. I parked my van alongside the solitary Kenyon van expecting to see Gerry sat in his van. It was empty.

'Great' I thought 'now how do I find this guy!'

Then a head appeared around the side of the slightly ajar container door.

"Hi there, you must be Gerry" I stated getting out of my van "My name's Terry and you've got me for the whole day"

The head never spoke but just indicated for me to follow him into the container before disappearing.

I locked my van and followed the head into a surprisingly warm container. I was expecting it to just be a standard container probably full of spares and equipment but Gerry had obviously spent some time to make it as nice and cozy as he could. The first section nearest the door was a series of shelving containing a very jumbled stack of spares. There was no organisation to it at all, this was more like a jumble sale. Obviously spares had just been placed in whatever space was available at the time with no thought of how to find it when needed.

I walked through all the clutter and found the back of the container opened out into Gerry's office space. I am being kind calling it an office! Yes it had a desk with a chair but the rest of the space was more in tune with someones cozy little living room rather than an efficient office. Every item within this area looked like it had been acquired rather than bought. The table had a broken leg that had been strapped up with jubilee clips and a bit of pipe just like a splint on someones leg. The miss matched selection of chairs ranged from garden furniture to a ripped and torn armchair. There was even a bit of carpet under the scratched and very worn coffee table.

The 'head' which I had seen earlier sat on a plastic garden chair and continued drinking his hot beverage. Still not saying a word to me but looked from me to a newspaper in the armchair opposite him. The resident of the armchair lowered his newspaper.

"Hi there" he cheerfully said "you must be Terry!"

"Er, yes" I stumbled as I looked between the TWO occupants like I was at Wimbledon.

Gerry put his paper down on the coffee table preparing to introduced us properly. He then pointed to the guy in the plastic garden chair and declared...

"This is Tom and I'm Gerry"

Maybe it was the shock of the two people on site or just my comical sense of imagination but the lovable cartoon characters from the TV 'Tom & Jerry' came flooding to the foremost image in my mind.

"Welcome to our home" Gerry continued with a sweep of his open arms around the cozy little office.

Gerry could see the stifled smirk on my face and explained with a well practiced flurry that his name was with a 'G' like Gerry Rafferty and not like the mischievous little cartoon mouse.

"Now I would offer you a drink but its important we give you a full tour before the canteen closes for breakfast"

"Oh my god!! What time do we actually start any work?" I said in amazement at their laid back daily routine.

"Work!! Work!!! - is that what you think you're here for?" exclaimed Gerry "there will be plenty of time for that later"

Both Tom & Gerry stood up and I had to stifled more than just a smirk this time as I realised Tom was at least 6 inches taller than Gerry. This made the image of the loveable cartoon characters even stronger in my mind.

Tom, who I discovered was actually Gerrys apprentice, was a lot younger than he genuinely looked. He was a typical tall, skinny teenager who didn't say much and he mainly grunted or moaned about any work he was given. Gerry sent him off with a clipboard to collect some daily readings that they apparently need to do on a daily basis and Gerry took me on my guided tour.

Gerry was in his late 30's and was actually a very energetic person despite his initial appearance of being a couch potato. I discovered he loved football and although he was not part of any amateur team nowadays he was a qualified referee and would spend every weekend mediating between local under 16 teams. He said he used to play football for his local team but when once asked to referee he fell in love with the challenge.

We all exited the container together and Tom headed off to the right on his given task.

"WE'LL SEE YOU IN THE CANTEEN LATER" Gerry shouted after him

Tom simply acknowledged his acceptance of the instruction by raising his right hand in a thumbs up formation without even turning around.

"Right!" said Gerry rubbing his hands together "lets go see some pigs"

We set off at quite a pace and followed the edge of the road around to the left of the building that was in front of us. As we turned the corner of the building I could see several lorries queued up along the side of the road. The noise was atrocious. All the pigs in each and every lorry were squealing and jostling about making each lorry rock gently from side to side.

"People say they don't know where they are going" Gerry said to me "but as you can hear, I think they do!"

We arrived near the main entrance to the building and I could see a lorry was reversed up unloading its cargo. The pigs were being herded down the ramp on the back of the lorry and into a large doorway on the side of the building.

"I thought we would start at the very beginning" started Gerry "so this is the slaughter house where, as you can see, the pigs arrive by the truck load from farms from all over the place."

NOTE: the following few lines describe a slaughterhouse in some detail. If you feel unsettled or squeamish and would like to skip this section you can skip forward to the next pig.

Gerry led me though a side door where we stood watching the pigs that had been   jostling five or six thick though the main entrance. They were now being guided into a funnel arrangement of walls narrowing them down to a single file.

The walls seem to constrict the pigs more and more until it looked like some of the larger pigs would struggle to get through. The tapered walls eventually changed into two conveyor belts where the pigs were held quite firmly as the floor sloped away beneath them leaving their little legs kicking about.

After a very short trip on the conveyor belts the pigs looked like they had instantly fallen asleep. Their legs stopped kicking, their squealing was cut short and all movement ceased.

"That's where they are actually killed" Gerry informed me with a disrespectful cheeriness "High Voltage conveyor belts!"

The conveyor belts eventually opened out where it looked like the now dead pig would fall head first onto the floor, but somehow its hind legs had been gripped by a carrier and was being hoisted so the pig was now hung upside down on another conveyor system above our heads.

Gerry and I followed the production line along a dedicated walkway where we saw the cleansing section of the process. Here, the upside down pigs followed each other through a shower of water before passing through a strange blue ring of fire. It resembled one of those rings you see at a fete or festival where a daredevil rider on his motorbike flies through a ring of fire to great applause from the crowds. No one here was clapping but I was very curious to the purpose of the ring of fire and to why it was such a bright blue colour. Gerry explained that the blue flame removes all the hair from the pigs skin as well as drying it out before the next step.

I was amazed at the high tech, automated way the slaughterhouse processed these animals. However, from here on in it was very labour intensive.

The overhead conveyor transported the upside down pigs into the first of the clean rooms where a series of very skilled butchers slit each animal in two. From the top between the hind legs they would cut two halves of pork leaving the head always on the right hand side joint. The next butcher would scoop out all the guts that were not wanted in the finished product onto the floor.

"That's called the Offal" Gerry told me

"What happens to that? Is it just thrown away?"I queried

"Oh No! nothing is wasted. There is a use for everything and I will show you that later"

The 'Side of Pork' without the head looked nearly like the typical joint of meat we have all seen hanging in a proper butchers shop. I had almost forgotten that the side of pork was actually a living animal only a few minutes ago.

The next butcher in the room removed the head and threw it into a large square plastic tub on wheels. He also cut off all the trotters and threw them into a similar plastic tub next to the first. Obviously they had a use for those as well.

NOW it looked like a typical 'side of pork'!

All the sides of pork came to a rest as they lined up at the end of the room. They were all still suspended by a track system along the ceiling but were now free from the motorised conveyor and could be pushed around by hand. A butcher appeared through a plastic strip curtain which covered the doorway into the cold store. He grabbed three sides of pork and pushed them through the door curtain all together.

"And then this is our domain!!" declared Gerry as we followed the butcher into the cold store.

The ceiling was lower than the slaughterhouse meaning that each side of pork was now only inches from the ground. A series of tracks in the ceiling meant they could really pack them in here. The tracks were so close together you couldn't fit anything between each row. I was impressed how they had maximised the space by packing everything in.

"My god!" I exclaimed "they really pack them in tight don't they"

"Yes, this will hopefully be chock a block full by lunchtime" said Gerry "and we have two of these cold stores. Yesterdays and todays"

I looked at him questionably. "What do you mean?"

"When this is full the doors will be closed. They need to be in here for at least 16 hours, usually more like 18 hours, to get them all down to temperature before being processed along the production line out of the doors the other side. Yesterday's side of pork are now being processed out of yesterday's cold store.

"Come on I'll show you." Gerry said as he indicated with his head and hand motion for us to leave the way we came in.

We walked out of the cold store and then completely out of the slaughterhouse. We had to go outside to gain entrance to the main production line. The route the sides of pork take was not available to us. In the main production area there were two production lines that each consisted of several butchers with their own butchers blocks and a conveyor belt either side of them. Every butcher was facing the source of all the meat and they would pick up a large joint of pork from the conveyor belt on their left. They would then place it on their individual butchers block to carve it into smaller joints and place them onto the conveyor to their right.

Walking up the side of the production line we arrived at the source of all the meat which was the plastic curtained doorway from 'yesterdays' cold store. Here the sides of pork were chopped into the manageable sized joints before heading down the conveyors to the goring of butchers down the lines. All of these butchers were not only very skilled at how each joint needs cutting but they were very fast. I couldn't believe how quickly they were working.

"My god, look at how fast they can work" I blurted out

"They're all on piece-work!" Gerry explained "As soon as yesterday's cold store is emptied then it is the end of the day for them. The quicker they work the sooner they go home."

I looked around in astonishment at how quickly this labour intensive production line worked. The dozens of butchers around me looked at us without even glancing down at their dexterity with extremely sharp knives and cleavers. I wondered if they would even notice if they accidentally chopped off one of their own fingers.

"Right!" said Gerry as he broke my trance "I hope you've been paying attention as we now go off to the canteen for breakfast and give you a test"

As we entered the canteen I could easily spot Tom sat at a table at the far end as the canteen was relatively quiet.

"We are running a bit late but they are officially still open for another 20 minutes" declared Gerry as he got us both a tray each.

As we went down the line I hadn't at first notice Gerry tell each server that I was a rookie but was amazed at the quantity of choice that was available. Everything you could possibly think of on a big breakfast plate was there for the asking. I noticed Gerry was asked how much of each item he wanted but no matter what number I asked for I got three of everything. When we got to the till Gerry introduce me as a newcomer and I was left quite perplexed when Gerry's meagre breakfast plate actually cost more that my piled-high plate full of food. Maybe it's a custom where newcomers are given special discount I thought.

We sat down with Tom in an almost empty canteen and got tucked into one of the best breakfasts I had ever had. Obviously you cannot get much fresher than all the pork products they could get straight off the production line, and it showed in the taste. There really was too much for me but I did give it my best shot. Sausages, bacon, hash browns, beans etc I could handle all that, but three black puddings was the death of me. I finally lent back with a sigh as I placed my knife and fork on my almost clear plate with only one untouched black pudding left on it.

"Wow, that was delicious!" I declared "You guys are so lucky to be able to eat like that every day"

"So where's my test then?" I continued expecting it to be a jest from earlier.

"You've had it" said Gerry

I sat up to attention "What do you mean I've had it?"

Gerry points to my plate "The idea is that if you can eat all that after being shown the slaughterhouse then you will be ok here"

"THAT was your test!!!"

———————————

Chapter 32

The founder and top dog of Kenyon Refrigeration spent over 40 years building his business into a national company with offices all over the country. Eventually he looked at retirement and ideally wanted his two sons to take over the business. Unfortunately, they had taken different career paths and had no interest in taking over the reigns. Mr James Kenyon was put under more and more pressure from the company's own accountant to sell the company to him. Mr Kenyon didn't want to do that as he wanted to see the company continue to grow with the same passion and enthusiasm for refrigeration as he had had all his working life. He believed accountants only had pound signs in their eyes. They could destroy a company in their quest to make the quickest and most profitable financial gains.

Mr Kenyon was trying to take more and more of a backseat in the running of his company with the thought of easing himself into full time retirement. Mr Mitchell (the company accountant and next in command!) was taking more and more control of the running of the company but he still didn't hold the majority share. He knew Mr Kenyon really wanted to retire and was willing to try anything to get total control and ownership of the company.

For several years, in the early 1990's, the two high flyers battled with each other to control the future of Kenyon Refrigeration.

It was a time of shady business deals resulting in several companies around the country going bankrupt almost overnight. This was the era when billionaires like Robert Maxwell were being caught out on their dodgy working practices and there was a lot of money going missing, most of it into the fat cat's pockets! I believe this is what Mr Kenyon did not want to see happen with the company he had spent a lifetime building. I remember seeing some of the empty, run down buildings around the Kenyon Refrigeration headquarters on the Pontardawe industrial estate that used to house busy, vibrant and thriving businesses but never thought the same could happen to Kenyons.

At one stage Mr Kenyon tried to sell the company to a rival Refrigeration company but Mr Mitchell stopped the sale with legal action. Eventually, I think, Mr Kenyon gave up his fight and an undisclosed figure from Mr Mitchell saw the end of the road for the founder of Kenyon Refrigeration. Mr James Kenyon retired to his villa in Portugal and I am sure would have been very sad to see Mr Mitchell spend the next two years bleeding the company dry.

On taking full control, Mr Mitchell employed his wife and daughter into the company and gave them expensive company cars. We never knew what their jobs were or even saw them in the office but I believe they collected very good salaries. They were maybe what you call sleeping partners.

He started cutting everyones wages and when all the electricians in the main workshops walked out in protest at his changes he simply threatened them all with the sack if they didn't accept his deal and return to work. Mr Mitchell started closing offices around the country and aimed to streamline the business by cutting costs to the bone although the volume of work was still increasing.

The only expansion he did do was where he increased the size of the main headquarters by developing into the disused factory next door. This was seen as a completely unnecessary expansion by everyone in Kenyons and because Kenyon Refrigeration did not 'buy' the property the company ended up paying a very high rental charge to use the building. The private owner of the building had only bought the property a few years previously and was very happy to collect such a high rental from Kenyon Refrigeration. That landlord was of course Mr Mitchell himself!!!

Like Robert Maxwell, he even managed to walk off with most peoples pension money. Luckily for me I got out at the right time and I managed to get my pension pot moved to my next employer.

Life on the road was getting harder and harder. The hours were getting longer and longer. This was mainly because now we had fewer offices around the country and fewer engineers out on the road, but we still had the same (if not more!) amount of work. There just wasn't enough hours in the day to complete all the work. Now there were only three of us covering what felt like half the country and we would be expected to be on-call every third week. I had to be on-call for a full seven days from a Monday morning at 8am all the way round to the following Monday at 8am when one of the other engineers would take all the calls for his week on-call. Even on those weeks when we were NOT on-call it would be customary to work at least 12 hour days, with little rest at weekends, to support the volume of work coming into our office.

My average working week would be around 80 hours a week and occasionally I would work over 100 hours in a single week. To put that into context where nowadays a lot of employees would work around 35 hours a week, I was sometimes doing three times that amount of hours in one very busy week. Even with a pay cut the money was great.

One particular week, when I was on-call, I had actually managed to get some sleep on the Tuesday night before arriving as usual at the Wakefield office. It was 8am on the Wednesday morning and I was picking up my usual job list for the day.

"I'm sure these lists get longer every day" I said to Barbara as I studied both sides of the paper list she had just handed me.

"They are!!" She exclaimed "I'm sorry, I do try to split the work up evenly between you but there are not many of you left !!"

"Its not your fault, Barbara. I know it's that bloody Mitchell guy getting rid of people and shutting depots down. But I do worry where we are heading to and what the future holds. I hardly get to see my family nowadays!"

"I do feel sorry for you engineers" she said with great passion "at least I still go home at regular times"

"Never mind" I resolved "another day, another dollar! but I bet most of it is going in Mitchells pocket."

With that I set off from Wakefield on what would turn out to be the longest day of my life......

….. 45 hours later!!!!!!!

It was now 5am on the Friday morning but I was so tired I had no idea what day it was, where I was or even who I was. All I knew was that I had had no sleep since Tuesday night and I still had more breakdown calls coming in. I had a job list as long as your arm and now felt I could never get to them, let alone fix their problems. My brain was like mash potato, incapable of rational thought.

I had decided several hours and several jobs back that enough was enough. I needed to turn my pager off and go home to bed. Somehow I just seemed to keep going. Not sure why or how but I just did. I would fix someones problem, look at my list of outstanding jobs and think - well let me just get them sorted!

However, now at 5am, I could no longer do the work or even function as a human being. I believed I only had enough brain power and energy left to try and drive home relatively safely. I found a phone box and called the office.

"….our office is presently closed but please leave a message after the tone and we will get back to you as soon as possible" came the voice from the Wakefield answer machine.

"Hi Barbara, it's Terry here! I am absolutely exhausted and cannot do any more. I haven't slept for 2 days so I have now turned my pager off and I am heading home to bed. I just have to get some sleep before I can do anything else. I will try to call you when I have recovered."

With that I got back into my van and took a steady and gentle drive home. To this day I cannot remember the journey home. I have no idea how I got into bed and I would imagine I was in a deep sleep before my head even hit the pillow. I was totally zonked out and dead to the world for at least 12 hours. Nothing was going to wake me from my slumber.

Elaine told me later that Friday evening, when I awoke from my hibernation, that the office had tried to contact me. Even though we had a telephone right next to our bed it didn't manage to bring me back from slumberland. Elaine had quickly answered the call downstairs as soon as it rang hoping to prevent it disturbing me.

"Hi Elaine" started Mike our area manager "Is he awake yet?"

"No!" came the simple and stark reply from Elaine

"Oh! Well if you could wake him I've got some more work for him"

I'm not really sure how Elaine actually replied to Mike's request but I gather from her account to me later that it was not the sort of calm, civilised and polite reply you would expect from my wife. Whatever she did say to Mike did the trick because although I was still officially on-call until Monday morning I never received another call from work over the whole weekend.

That evening Elaine and I rationally and calmly discussed the escalating situation at work and we both agreed it was finally time for me to find another job. I had been at Kenyon Refrigeration for over 17 years and had learnt my trade with them from the age of 16. However any job had to be better than this! I needed to move on before the job actually killed me.

The long hours, all the driving and this particular 45 hour shift was…..

.… The Final Straw.

———————

Chapter 33

'A photo finish'

I was not the only one thinking of jumping off what looked like a sinking ship. Other engineers had also started looking for employment elsewhere. After my 45 hour shift I was desperate to get any work I could, as long as it was away from Kenyons. I was getting tired of driving hundreds of miles every week and being pushed and pulled from one angry customer to the next. It wasn't as if I had to put up with it for just 8 hours a day but averaging 80 hours a week meant I was working at least 12 hours a day every single day. Enough was enough!

I now felt like a complete change in career. Although I used to like the freedom of being out on the road and being (relatively speaking) my own boss I was now ready to get a job that was restricted to a 5 day week and meant I could get home to my family every day at a reasonable time.

Kimberly Clark had placed a full page advertisement in our local paper - The Scunthorpe Evening Telegraph. I'm sure they had adverts in most of the local papers within a 50 mile radius of their proposed development but we regularly bought the Evening Telegraph and so that was where I saw the advert. They intended to build a £100million factory which was to be a state of the art, high speed production line on the southern banks of the Humber estuary at Barton-upon-Humber.

They were offering very good salaries which, I found out later, was the way Kimberley Clark usually enticed the best employees to work for them. I'm not sure I was one of their top recruits but it certainly caused a lot of interest in the area.

In the first phase of their plans they were hoping to employ 300 people to start up the new factory and they apparently received over 15,000 applicants. That meant there was only a 2% chance of getting a job or to put it another way, I had a 1 in 50 possibility of securing employment with them. I was oblivious to the amount of interest they had created when I applied for a job but I believed it was my best chance of getting a Monday to Friday job with reasonable hours. The offer of a good salary was a bonus to me! especially as they were offering more than I usually earned, even with all the excessive overtime.

My application form was sent in after I had read and re-read it several times. In those days an application form was filled in by hand. I had carefully written all the details in each and every box with my best handwriting. I wanted to ensure everything was completed correctly and it was only then that I was confident of giving the best impression I could. I had tailor-made all the details to suit the job I was applying for and listed all the experience I had had in the world of refrigeration. I had no disillusion as to the possibility I would end up working on unfamiliar equipment on a high speed production line (if I got the job!), but surely in a futuristic factory like this, there would be some need for an experienced refrigeration engineer. In my mind I was going to try and portray myself as the best the area could offer and try to beat my fellow colleagues to secure that alternative employment.

Kimberly Clark's recruitment process was typical of other large corporations. They had four stages to their recruitment and the first stage was to be a series of tests. I had received my letter from Kimberly Clark telling me my application had successfully got me to stage one. I was asked to attend a testing session at a hotel in Hull, on the northern bank of the Humber estuary, and the session was to take approximately 4 hours to complete. I was to phone a number on the letter to book myself onto one of the many proposed sessions.

The mobile phone had not yet been invented (well at least it was not available to the masses like me) so calling Kimberly Clark to book my testing session wasn't the easiest of things to organise. Although I had a perfectly good telephone in my house to phone them I was never at home during normal office hours to be able to phone. So one day I departed the Wakefield office with my usual long list of jobs and immediately pulled up next to a telephone box just around the corner from the office.

"Hello, is that Kimberly Clark" I started

"Yes. You're through to recruitment. Are you wanting to book a testing session" came the reply.

Wow! I thought, as I confirmed my intensions, straight through to the right department! Very impressive.

"We have several dates available and we do a morning or afternoon session. When would you like to attend?"

I booked the date for my test and decided the next time I talked to Barbara in the office I would put in a request for that particular day off work.

About 25 of us sat in the hotel's small conference room. All the tables were set out across the room in rows all facing the examiner who stood at the front of the room. It reminded me of school days when we were taking our final exams. In front of us on the table was a pencil, a calculator and a testing paper that, to my surprise, had a simple question on the front cover.....

'If you spent £6 on four spark plugs -

- how much would each spark plug cost?'

"Now before we begin I want you to all to write your names on the booklet and look at the front question on your booklets" said the examiner "Do NOT open the booklet yet. This front question is just an example of the type of questions you will find inside."

I could mentally calculate the answer but the guy next to me had to pick up his calculator to work it out!!!

"On every test today I will tell you when to start and when to stop. At that moment you MUST put your pencil down whether you have finished or not. You have 30 minutes on this first test" Instructed the examiner as he studied his watch "and your time starts now."

The questions started easy enough just like the one on the front cover, but as you got further into the paper the questions got harder and harder. Eventually I needed the calculator like most others in the room. Although I did manage to get onto the last page I was several questions away from fully finishing when time was called. I was disappointed with myself as I laid down my pencil thinking I had to finish. Later, I found out that you were not actually expected to finish, as they were not just testing your speed but more importantly the accuracy you answered the questions under pressure.

The next test was a much larger paper and we were told there were two sides to this paper. The front section was for all those mechanically minded candidates and the back section was for all those electrically minded applicants. That was a big problem for me as my refrigeration trade is a multi skilled trade. I was adept in mechanical and electrical skills. At the start of the test I decided it would be best to read the first few question on each side and decide which skilled trade I would go for. The mechanical section looked the easier one and so that's the one I went for.

After a much needed tea break we all sat back down in our places to complete the last and final test.

"This final test' started the examiner "is the longest of all the tests but don't worry the questions are very simple to answer. There is no right or wrong answers, I just need you to answer honestly and to the best of your knowledge. Unlike the other tests there is no time limit but you must complete every question before handing the paper in to me at the front. Once completed you are free to leave and thank you all for attending."

I wasn't the first to finish, or even the last! I was surprised at how quickly some people completed the test. Maybe they had had enough of all the tests and wanted to get out of there but I was determined to do my best and so took my time. After a few pages of questions I realised some questions were the same as previous ones but just worded differently. One question I would answer 'most likely' whereas a later similar question would prompt me to answer 'highly unlikely'. This, I believed at the time, was probably to trick us into giving a more truthful answer. I just did as I was told and answered honestly.

Two weeks later I received a letter telling me I had successfully got through to stage two.

Stage two was an interview which would be held at the temporary Kimberly Clark offices in Hull. Kimberly Clark were renting some offices at The Maltings in the centre of Hull while the factory in Barton was being constructed. This was a large three story office block surrounding an inner courtyard with an ornate iron archway over the entrance. The magnificent archway indicated the building originally belonged to a large brewing company. Now I could understand the name 'The Maltings'. Kimberly Clark were obviously a very large international company as they had rented most of the offices in the Maltings and it must have cost them a fortune being in the middle of a large city like Hull.

I was shown into an open office area looking very modern with computers on every desk. A couple of individual glass walled offices were at the very end with a row of chairs placed directly outside them. I sat down next to a dozen other well dressed suited gentlemen who were obviously the other hopeful candidates.

I didn't have to wait long before a tall glamorous lady came out of one of the individual offices and called my name.

"Please take a seat" she said as she led me into the office.

She sat opposite me behind her desk and spent a couple of minutes in silence while she looked through my notes. All the time slightly shaking her head.

Suddenly she looked up at me and said "Well I don't know how you got this far!!"

I was left speechless and shocked.

"Er? Sorry. What do you mean?" I stuttered

"Well we had over 15,000 applications to sort through for the 300 jobs we have on offer. To sort through that volume of application forms we had a strict filter in place. Any application form that was incomplete would get thrown in the bin!!" she told me "but never mind, you're here now so we will still go through your test results."

I was perplexed by her answer and spent most of the interview wondering what I had missed off my application form. My mind was not concentrating on the actual interview but luckily the interviewer seemed more interested in my performance on the tests than asking me any of the usual job interview type questions. She eventually got to the long final test result and had a full A4 sheet and a half in her hand apparently describing my personality.

"I will simply read this out to you in its entirety." she said "and then I would like you to make any comments, on any aspects, you agree or disagree with."

I was still pondering over what was missing from my application form but acknowledged my understanding of her request with a nod of my head.

The interviewer read out my personality profile and I was blown away by how accurate the description was.

"Wow!" I said as she finished "that was amazing. I cannot disagree with anything you said and I'm truly amazed at how you can find all that out from just a list of questions. Wow!"

She smiled at me with a satisfactory smirk and concluded "Well that's the end of the interview. Have you got any questions for me?"

"Well, to be honest with you, you have been very thorough in all the information you've given me today but there is one burning question on my mind"

"And what's that" she queried

"What was wrong with my application form?" I said "I was certain I had completed everything and not only did I check it several times but I remember my wife also checked it before I sent it in."

"Oh that" she smiled "don't worry about it. You've made it through to the third stage anyway. The thing which was missing may even have become detached!!! On the front page of your application you needed to stick on ....

.... a profile photograph of yourself."

_____

Chapter 34

'Honest Cheat'

True to form, a week after my stage two interview I received a letter from Kimberly Clark telling me I had successfully got through to stage three.

Stage three was to be a series of tests that would check my skills and assess my suitability to work in a high speed production environment. According to the letter I needed to spend a whole afternoon at a training centre in Hull where I would be tested on my mechanical skills. If you remember, I had opted for the mechanical questions in the stage one exams as opposed to the electrical questions as they looked easier. Now I was worried that my multi skilled engineering trade would not stand up to the rigours of a serious testing regime.

The location of the tests was in an apprentice training workshop somewhere in Hull. I cannot remember exactly where the building was but I do remember it was a large industrial workshop run by some very clever engineering lecturers. When I arrived I was directed into a classroom where there were already 2 other candidates. Before one of the lecturers entered the classroom, to start his introductory speech, we had grown to a total of 6 stage three candidates.

"Welcome to our training centre Gentlemen" started the lecturer before he proceeded to tell us where the fire exits and all the facilities such as toilets and vending machines were located.

In those days it was very rare to see any females in the engineering world and so his introduction of 'Gentlemen' was the standard assumption. Thankfully since those days many more ladies have entered the world of engineering and discovered what a fantastically satisfying career it can be.

"This afternoon you will carry out a total of 6 tests." the lecturer continued "Each test will be no longer than 20 minutes in length. Some of the tests are to check your skills at problem solving and others are testing how quickly you can solve the problem. When your time is up the examiner will ask you to put down any tools you have in your hand and you will return to this classroom before being called through for your next test"

At this point I had noticed another 5 examiners had filed into the side of the classroom, each with a clipboard in their hands.

"Are there any questions?" concluded the lecturer at the front of the class.

We all shook our heads to confirm we fully understood what was expected of us and then each of the examiners read out a name from their list and led us into the main workshop area.

The workshop was a large shed with everything you could possibly need in the engineering world. A band of lathes and milling machines lined up along one side of the workshop. At the far end I could see several cubicles with thick black curtains across the entrances indicating where the welding bays were located. The main area of the workshop was taken up with lots of work benches neatly positioned in regimented lines like in a well organised classroom. My examiner led me to one of those benches where my first test of the day was laid out.

"Now on this test I am allowed to give you two minutes to familiarised yourself with what is laid out in front of you" said the examiner "and then I will tell you to start. It is up to you to find and fix the problem"

Fixed onto the bench in front of me was a shaft held between two pedestal bearings. On one end was a pulley wheel and a gearwheel was attached to the other end. To the side of the equipment were an array of various tools. Some of which I hadn't seen since I was at school. There were precision measuring tools such as a DTI gauge on a mag mount and Vernier callipers. Laid in a very neat line were a full set of combination spanners sat next to the more familiar adjustable spanners that we all tend to use in real life!! Hammers, pullers, allen keys and various screwdrivers, you name it and it was there. An amazing collection of engineering tools.

My heart finally slowed down to a more relaxed beat after recognising all the familiar tools and equipment of my trade.

"You can now start!" suddenly announced the examiner as he clicked on the stopwatch attached to his clipboard.

Unnervingly, every time I moved or touched anything the examiner noted something down onto his clipboard. I quickly deduced the shaft didn't turn smoothly and realised what was expected of me to fix it. Thankfully I kept my cool and only used the combination spanners to remove the shaft from the bearings. I never even touched the adjustable spanners that I knew could easily slip off or even damage the bolt you are using them on. I discovered later that I actually got extra marks for using the ring end of the spanner instead of the open ended part. That was how intense the testing was.

I confidently finished with time to spare and the examiner stopped the stopwatch after asking me if I was happy with my work. The time it took me was also entered onto the examination sheet. The examiner then asked me to return the bench to how I had found it placing the bent shaft back into the pedestal bearing housings before allowing me to go back to the classroom.

I grabbed a quick cup of tea from the vending machine and sat back into the classroom awaiting the others to return. I was quite smug at finishing my first test but was a little concerned that I had finished well within the time limit. I eventually convinced myself that the test was more concerned with my problem solving and repair skills rather than speed and pressure of working fast.

Each and every test started the same. Each examiner in the classroom read out a name and we followed them into the workshop to be shown a different scenario laid out on a bench in front of us. Most tests started the moment we arrived at the bench without any familiarisation time. All tests finished with us resetting the bench ready for the next candidate.

My final test of the day was a pneumatic problem solving exam. I was presented with a board on a wall with valves, switches and levers all attached to each other with pneumatic air lines. During my 2 minutes familiarisation the examiner showed me that when the green start button was pressed the pneumatic arm on the right, which should have raise slowly all the way to the top of the board, didn't move at all.

In my career as a refrigeration engineer I had never before come across any pneumatics and so it all looked alien to me. I had absolutely no idea of how to start diagnosing the problem. As the stopwatch started I stood back and looked at the board hoping some inspiration would hit me. Although I didn't recognise or even understand any of the equipment on the board, I did realise that all the connecting pipes looked like electrical cables. That's when I decided I should think of it as an electrical control board and simply follow the flow. In this case it was following the flow of air instead of electricity.

After only a couple of minutes of tracing pipes from one module to another across the board I ask the examiner, what I thought at the time was a stupid question but necessary to my electrical diagnosis.

"Is there a wiring diagram at all?"

The examiner hands me a circuit diagram from his clipboard with a smile on his face. Far from being stupid, that question earned me a tick on his clipboard! I examined the circuit diagram but a lot of the symbols were as alien to me as the board in front of me. I was determined to at least give the impression I knew what I was doing even if I was completely lost, like a fish out of water, so I carried on looking between the circuit diagram and the board.

Laid in a tray, that ran the full width along the bottom of the board, were several replacement modules that all looked very similar to each other to me. After some time looking around the board and examining the hieroglyphics on each module I decided I needed to just start randomly changing parts in the hope I get lucky! I picked up the first module I found on the tray which was directly below the first module on the board and swapped them over. I pressed the green start button to see what would happen and miraculously it all worked perfectly. A big smile appeared on my face as I turned to the examiner.

The examiner wrote something down and looked up from his clipboard in surprise.

"Well done" he said "Don't worry about resetting it as you're the last candidate on this board but could you tell me how you came to that decision to change that particular module?"

I was stuffed. He was not an idiot. I could tell he had deduced that I was struggling with this task and he was obviously surprised at how quickly I had fixed the problem. Without having an instant good lie in my head I decided to tell him the truth.

"I have never worked on pneumatics before but as I am primarily multi skilled I looked at it as an electrical control board."

"Very good" he said "but why that particular module?"

"It was the first one in the circuit and I just tried the spare module sat under it!"

He noted a few things on his clipboard and seeing my concern at whatever he had written he turned and told me not to worry. He told me that I had probably earned extra points because I had shown that....

Honesty is the best Policy.

————————

Chapter 35

'Mystery Man'

The fourth and final stage in the Kimberly Clark recruitment was a final interview to be held back at the Maltings in Hull. I was getting used to going to Hull and this time Elaine decided she would tag along for the ride and do some retail therapy around Hull city centre. Even my mum decided she would like to come along so it ended up being a whole family trip to Hull & back.

The mobile phone was still not available to the masses and so like previous times I gave Elaine my company pager so we could all meet up when I had finished. My pager was now one of the more modern sophisticated ones where it could display a number to call as well as making a sound. Just in case my office decided to try and call me on my day off, Elaine agreed to ignore any message unless it displayed our own home phone number. We would then all meet up in the Princess Quay food court in the centre of Hull. I didn't think I would be more than an hour or two as, in my mind, it should just be an interview like the last one. However this interview was aimed more at my technical skills.

Just like my stage two interview I found myself sat outside the glass fronted offices within Kimberly Clark's abode in the Maltings. Alongside me were half a dozen other candidates all holding thin A4 folders or envelopes on their knees.

"Oh dear!" I thought to myself "What have I forgotten to bring?"

I took the invitation letter out of my breast pocket and re-read it a few times hoping to find out what I had forgotten. It told me nothing. Not wanting to look stupid, I decided not to ask any of my fellow competitors what they had brought with them. We all sat there in silence. The odd glance at each other and a nervous smile to acknowledge that in fact we were all after the same thing. A job at Kimberly Clark!

I was eventually called into one of the offices and was confronted by an important looking but friendly man behind a desk. He asked me a series of standard interview type questions and then asked me to return to the waiting area outside.

"Oh good' I thought 'maybe they will tell me if I have the job or not today before I leave"

Twenty minutes later and I was called into another glass fronted office as one of the other candidates came out. Now I understood. This was not your usual type of interview but multiple interviews by several different interrogators. Other job interviews I had attended, the interrogators often sat behind one desk intimidating the applicant together in one interview. Kimberly Clark's way was much more friendly! even though it took longer to keep swapping candidates from room to room.

There was a total of three separate interviews with three difference interrogators. Each one asked questions about different aspects of engineering and not one of them asked me for any paperwork. By the end of my last interview I was getting more and more curious as to what everyone, but me, had brought to the interview. I never managed to muster enough nerve to ask any of the interviewers (in case it reflected badly on me) and no-one ever asked me for any documentation. My curiosity was killing me as I finally walked out of the offices. All the other candidates had departed and so there really was nobody left to ask.

What was in the mystery envelopes??

Leaving the Maltings I found a phone box and paged Elaine. When I finally arrived at the food court as arranged I found my family were already there. They were all sat looking out for me, eagerly anticipating my arrival. I put a sad look on my face and tried my best to give the impression of rejection. I was trying to indicate I had not got the job as today I was keen to play the family's traditional game of trying to misdirect each other. In reality, I really didn't know, so my misdirection caused total confusion, and a thump or two on the arm!!

A week later I received a large thick envelope which I instantly recognised as being from Kimberly Clark. I was very curious as to the thickness of this correspondence as I was expecting just a simple one page letter telling me if I had been successful or not.

Eagerly I opened the envelope to find a cover letter telling me the good news. Inside the envelope was also a comprehensive contract of employment and various other itinerary paperwork.

"I got it, I got it!!!" I excitedly shouted out loud.

"Oh well done" Elaine congratulated me "I knew you would"

I never thought I could be so excited at getting a new job, especially one that would be such a major change in my career path. I had been so used to being my own boss out on the road and travelling all over the country but this was going to be a job stuck in one place. The thought of being accepted by a large multi-national company made me feel quite humble. Especially considering the volume of people who eagerly applied for the relatively few jobs on offer in the first place.

Both Elaine and I spent the next few days reading all the literature that came with the job offer. I was very keen to get my acceptance letter returned to Kimberly Clark as soon as possible, before they changed their mind.

"It says here that I can start in November and after the initial induction week I will be flying off to America for 6 weeks of training" I read out to Elaine

"Wow!" She replied "Did you know the job involved foreign travel?"

"I had no idea" I exclaimed

"… and look at this" I continued "this is what they will pay me. That's more than I get now even with all the overtime I do!!"

Elaine's face suddenly dropped from a big happy smile to a more serious note as she read something on the front of the contract.

"Hang on a minute" she said pointing to the name at the top of the contract "Who the heck is this Lee guy?"

"What" I proclaimed as I took the contract out of Elaine's hands "That can't be right"

I looked at the contract and then frantically searched to find the original cover note to check my name was on the actual job offer. Relieved to see my name there, I let out a sigh realising I should still have a job to go to. All I thought of now was where was MY contract and who was this Mystery Man!

I contacted the Kimberly Clark offices in the Maltings and thankfully they assured me that it was a mistake on their behalf and they needed to send me another contract of employment before we could progress any further. Unfortunately, because of this slight delay, it meant that I missed the deadline for the November intake of employees.

As the next intake wouldn't be until the following February I was forced to work a few more months at Kenyons. At least now I could be happier at work in the knowledge that I was finally leaving the long hours, stressed working conditions and relatively low pay. I planned to hand my resignation in at the start of January giving the obligatory one months notice. In the meantime I needed to keep my excitement to myself as I didn't want my boss to find out I was leaving before then.

—————————

Chapter 36

'End of an Era'

Just before Christmas of 1992 I received a letter from Kimberly Clark asking me to attend a medical on Monday January 4th 1993. I was to report to a Chemical manufacturing factory on the Immingham docks where their own medical centre would perform a full medical examination on behalf of Kimberly Clark. As it was getting close to Christmas I was a little concerned at trying to book that particular day off, being the first day back after the Christmas break. I eventually decided there was nothing to loose and I just had to have that day off. Anyway, if I couldn't get permission for that day I would just phone in sick. Nothing was going to jeopardise my plans to leave Kenyons. I nervously phoned the office at Wakefield and Barbara approved my request without any problem.

The day after my medical, and the first day back to work after the long weekend, I pulled into the car park outside our Wakefield office and casually exited my van feeling quite pleased with myself.

"Ooo!! You're brave aren't you!" said Nigel as he exited the office with his list of jobs for that day in his hand.

"What do you mean?" I asked

"Mike is gunning for you. He is furious with you taking yesterday off"

"Why should he be cross?" I said "I told them before Christmas I wanted the day off so they had enough notice"

"Its not that" declared Nigel "He's not happy you've been looking for another job"

"Oh that" I casually replied as I entered the doorway, leaving Nigel in the car park stunned into silence with his mouth wide open.

As I entered the main office area Barbara was sat at her desk handing out job sheets to the other engineers and Mike was stood in front of her desk with his back to me sorting through his post. The room fell silent and they all turned to look at me.

Mike slowly turned to see what had created the sudden silence and then he instantly broke it.

"YOU. IN MY OFFICE NOW!!" He angrily pointed his finger toward his office door.

As I led the way into Mike's office he angrily instructed me to take a seat. Mike moved around to his side of the desk but made a point of not sitting in his executive leather chair. He stood tall behind his chair with his hands rested on the back.

I think it must be a standard management ploy! If you're sat down and they're stood up they can show their superiority to greater effect.

"So where were you yesterday?" Mike started

"I had a day off" I calmly replied

"I understand you went for a job interview" Mike declared

"No I didn't. You're wrong there" I answered

"I know where you were because you were spotted" Mike started to raise his voice

"It's none of your business what I do on my day off." I said keeping cool and calm.

"You were seen in Immingham docks going for an interview"

"Well you have been mis-informed" I told him

"So you deny going for a job interview!!" Mike bellowed at me

"I do indeed because it is not true" I announced "If you must know, I did NOT go for a job interview as I was actually given the job a couple of months ago. I was on Immingham docks yesterday for my medical."

I stood up and put my hand into my pocket to pull out an envelope.

"I am sick of the way you treat us all. So here is my resignation" I stated as I slammed the envelope onto his desk in front of him "I start my new job in 5 weeks time so there is more than enough notice there to help you find a replacement for me."

I slowly and calmly walked over to the door leaving it open as I returned to the main office. There was a dumfounded silence behind me. Barbara looked up at my smilingly happy face as I stood in front of her desk waiting for my list of jobs for the day.

"You look surprisingly happy after Mike's dressing down!" exclaimed Barbara.

"I am." I affirmed "I've just handed my notice in"

A big smile came across Barbara's face as she realised someone had finally managed to escape this madness. She tried to congratulate me but her voice was cut short by Mike storming back into the room.

"FREEMAN, GET YOURSELF OFF TO LOFTHOUSE! There's no job sheet for you here! You can spend the rest of your time at the abattoir."

He then turned back to his office and slammed the door behind him.

"Do you think I've upset him?" I calmly asked Barbara and we both laughed out loud.

Mike always saw the Lofthouse Abattoir as a punishment. Yes I agree it was not the most pleasant of places to work but the work was not difficult and it was very steady. Gerry, the resident site engineer, wasn't expecting me but he was very grateful for someone other than the grunting and groaning teenager Tom, to talk to. All three of us went straight to the canteen for a fat boys breakfast as I revealed the real reason why I was now permanently assigned to this site.

It was obvious I had managed to get the upper hand on Mike's attempt to give me a reprimand for looking for another job. This had then caused Mike to lash out with me ending up being banished to the abattoir. Although Mike saw this as a punishment I felt relieved that I could now look forward to regular hours and less stress in my final 5 weeks. Mike now had one less engineer with an ever increasing volume of work to organise.

My final day with Kenyons was very un-ceremonial. I had worked for them from leaving school at 16 and had had a varied 17 year career with them. I got no farewell card from anyone. Gerry did buy me my breakfast just like he had done on my first introduction to the slaughter house.

My final day was no different to any other day. I did leave the abattoir half an hour early but only to make sure I got to the Wakefield office before it closed for the weekend. I simply handed in my pager and the keys to my van, which still contained all the tools of my trade that Kenyons had supplied. A fellow engineer then drove me home to Scunthorpe. Barbara did wish me luck and she said a fond farewell but Mike was nowhere to be seen. In fact, after the day I handed in my resignation Mike never talked to me again, let alone saw me face to face. The last words he ever said to me was when he banished me to Lofthouse Abattoir. Thinking about it now I find that a little sad. I had known Mike for the whole 17 years I had worked at Kenyons and it feels like we parted on bad terms.

I finished working for Kenyons on a Friday and started working for Kimberly Clark on the following Monday. I may have started working for Kenyons 17 years earlier in white overalls on a dirty, dusty and smelly steelworks but due to changes in fashion and career path I was finishing with blue overalls in a clean, hygienic and smelly abattoir.

Whatever the future held it was definitely the .....

.... start of a new era.

Coming soon (well, when I've finished writing it!!!)

more shades of white

Book two in this series is starting

'A New Era'

in the life of our ever popular tradesman.

Printed in Great Britain
by Amazon